A VERY PRIVATE PLOT

The Blackford Oakes Novels

SAVING THE QUEEN

STAINED GLASS

WHO'S ON FIRST

MARCO POLO, IF YOU CAN

THE STORY OF HENRI TOD

SEE YOU LATER ALLIGATOR

HIGH JINX

MONGOOSE, R.I.P.

TUCKER'S LAST STAND

A VERY PRIVATE PLOT

LAST CALL FOR BLACKFORD OAKES

A VERY PRIVATE PLOT

A BLACKFORD OAKES NOVEL

William F. Buckley Jr.

CUMBERLAND HOUSE
NASHVILLE, TENNESSEE

A VERY PRIVATE PLOT
PUBLISHED BY CUMBERLAND HOUSE PUBLISHING, INC.
431 Harding Industrial Dr.
Nashville, Tennessee 37211

This is a work of fiction. Some of the figures who appear, however, do so under their own names.

Cover design by Gore Studio, Inc., Nashville, Tennessee

Library of Congress Cataloging-in-Publication Data

Buckley, William F. (William Frank), 1925–
  A very private plot : a Blackford Oakes mystery / William F. Buckley, Jr.
    p. cm.
  ISBN-13: 978-1-58182-477-3
  ISBN-10: 1-58182-477-7 (alk. paper)
  1. Oakes, Blackford (Fictitious character) Fiction. 2. United States. Central Intelligence Agency—Fiction. 3. Intelligence service—United States—Fiction. I. Title.
  [PS3552.U344V47 1998]
  813'.54—dc21   97-47692
                                                    CIP

Printed in Canada
1 2 3 4 5 6 7 8 — 09 08 07 06 05

FOR ALISTAIR HORNE

A VERY PRIVATE PLOT

CHAPTER 1

● APRIL 1995

Senator Hugh Blanton addressed the problem as an Old Testament prophet might have done. It was a few minutes after ten when the chairman tapped his index finger on the wooden desk. Tapped it ever so lightly. That was all that Senator Blanton needed to do, in the spring of 1995, to make his wishes known. His wishes at this moment were, one, to stop the chatter and, two, to get on with the business of the day. The business of the week, of the month, *the business of the legislative session,* as far as Hugh Blanton was concerned. Covert activity was the screen for indefensible, inexcusable government activity. Lying, cheating, seduction, poison, threats, violence, war-risking—*sinfulness.* He did not use the word "sin." In the first place, he didn't want to get mixed up with the evangelical right. In the second place, he never could understand how anybody over twelve years old, not counting old ladies, could countenance the very idea of God. And sin was a God word. If ever you use it, he told his wife, Alice, one night at dinner—just the two of them, in the candlelight, he wearing black tie, she a long, sleeveless dress—it must be made clear that you are using a metaphor. He did not mind classifying the covert activity of the

CIA, when speaking to Alice or to close friends, as "sinful." To make up for using such a biblical word and to remind the listener that Hugh Blanton was a man of the world, he would as often as not denounce covert activity as "sinful *tout court.*" There! A simple use of the French intensifier as a substitute for "sinful—pure and simple" had the effect of reminding Alice and his friends that they were dealing with a cosmopolitan man.

So his objective now was to frame a bill that would forbid the exercise of covert activity by the Central Intelligence Agency or by any other government agency except when there was a state of national emergency, declared by the President, confirmed by Congress.

Dr. Blanton had given the Godkin Lecture at Harvard the year before and later in the spring had accepted a half-dozen honorary degrees from universities, some of them distinguished. His citations were much alike. They spoke of "the scholar," of the scion of old New England virtue, of a sometime Rhodes scholar, a Ph.D. in political science, an adjunct professor at Berkeley, the author of *The Evolution of the Protestant Ethic* and *The Maladministration of Justice—1981–1993.* And it was in an address to the American Association of University Professors that he revealed, on the tenth anniversary of his appointment to the Senate by Governor Little of Illinois, that he would sponsor a resolution in Congress to bare all the records of the Cold War. "That war is over. Why should we not know what we did in pursuit of our objectives?"

"Did he then say, 'Ye shall know the truth, and the truth shall make you free'?" Anthony Trust had asked Blackford Oakes when told, the day before, about Blanton's speech, the whole of which Oakes had watched on C-SPAN.

"No, no, Anthony. It's important to size this guy up. He can quote Saint John, but he does not use clichés. He is not in the least the demagogue. He would rather lose the next election than split an infinitive. But he knows his own mind and what he wants to do better than anybody in the history of certitudes. Compared to Blanton, Hitler was an ambiguist. He's glad to get the honorary degrees not so much because he covets them but because he calculates that they add to his authority. And they do. Look, he was appointed to the Senate only nine or ten years ago and already he's chairman of the one committee he wanted to be chairman of, parlayed himself into that position with the help of Al Gore—the Honorable Vice President is terrified of Blanton. And Blanton has this fastidious distaste for covert action."

"Does he fuck in public?"

Blackford smiled, stood up in the roomy study of his house in rural Virginia, and leaned back on the bookshelves. "Anthony, you'll never change."

"Is there any particular reason why I should? I mean, Black, how long have we known each other? We went to boarding school together in England—an experience you're happy to forget. I was one year ahead of you at Yale—an experience you correctly cherish, if only because that's where you met Sally. I recruited you into the Agency in which we have engaged together in what . . . a dozen enterprises over the years? You never *asked* me to change."

The expression on the face of the lean six-footer who would be seventy on his next birthday and might well celebrate it by running in the Boston marathon was one of mock surprise, disappointment, desolation.

Blackford didn't pursue the charade. He returned to the subject. "Obviously Blanton is, on this matter, on this one matter, a fanatic. But some fanatics get their way. There is this about him, though. He is willing to debate his position. On C-SPAN yesterday there was a pretty bright dissenter, a girl. I didn't get what college she's associated with. Hillsdale, I think. Maybe Grove City . . . is there a third right-wing college in America? She really lit into him, but she's the exception."

"You're right, Black, Blanton has solid support from the academic class.

—Oh my God, Blackford!" Anthony suddenly looked up at the ceiling, his mouth wide open.

"What's the matter?" Blackford asked him sharply.

"Can you *imagine* what Blanton would say if ever he found out some of the things we actually did do—for our country?"

Blackford smiled. "Yes, there is that. I'm not sure I could tell a priest everything I've done—for God and country. Though in most cases—not every case—I'd probably do it again."

"I can think of at least one thing I know you wouldn't hesitate to do again."

Blackford paused. "Anthony, did you ever read *Stalky and Co.?*"

"By who?"

"Kipling."

"I forget. What's your point?"

"There's a line there, the headmaster I think it was, addressing a couple of sixth-formers. He wonders at their 'precocious flow of fetid imagery.' Wonders whether they will ever grow up."

"In my case, the answer is clearly No. Though I wonder that at my age anything about me can be said to be precocious. . . . But to get to the business at hand, are you going to try the same thing on Blanton that you did on Rockefeller?"

"I haven't decided."

"You may as well think about it, Black, since tomorrow is pretty soon. Ten a.m., I suppose. The usual hour. You have tonight and the early morning to perform your ablutions. In this case, your *toilette des condamnés.*" Anthony sat up and went to the bar, carefully measuring the bourbon he poured into his glass. Without looking up he asked, "The usual?" Blackford grunted Yes. Anthony prepared a second glass and said solemnly, "You know I'm here to help you, buddy. Any way I can. You know and I know what Blanton really wants, which is to put you in jail. And maybe me too, when he gets around to the second echelon."

"Yes," Blackford said, twirling the ice in his drink with his index finger.

"And who could we get to rescue you, if that law against covert operations is passed?"

"GENTLEMEN, ROBERTA, did you have an opportunity to read the minutes I sent over to you of the Rockefeller Commission's session with Mr. Blackford Oakes back in 1975?"

The honorable senators buckled down to the business at hand. No one spoke up.

Until: "To tell the truth, Hugh, I just simply didn't have time." Senator Roberta Albright, alert, composed, mildly defiant, confessed her delinquency, something she would not have done in an open hearing, not if the press had been present.

"It would not have taken much time." Senator Blanton's voice was that of the headmaster.

His fellow panelists looked up at the chairman, waiting for an explanation.

"Because the passage I called to your attention, the exchange between Mr. Oakes and Chairman Rockefeller, consumed all of three paragraphs of printed matter."

"Took the Fifth?"—the senior senator from Florida contributed the likely explanation for so brief a section on the testimony of Blackford Oakes.

"No. He refused to take the oath. He refused to be sworn in." There was consternation, curiosity. "Here exactly," Senator Blanton opened his folder to the page, "is what the record reads:

"'*Why do you decline to swear to tell the truth?*' Rockefeller asked.

"'Because, Mr. Vice President, I am involved in a conflict of interest.'

"'Will you elaborate on this, Mr. Oakes?' the Vice President asked him.

"Oakes answered: 'To the extent I can, sir. If I swear to tell the truth, I am bound to answer truthfully questions you might put to me which, if I answered them truthfully, would jeopardize those interests of the United States which I have been trained to concern myself with as primary.'"

"Sounds like a prefect at Culver Academy," the senator from South Carolina interrupted.

Blanton continued: "Rockefeller came back with this:

"'I appreciate very much your devotion to duty, Mr. Oakes. But the fact of the matter is that this panel was appointed by the President of the United States precisely to inquire into questions raised publicly about the Central Intelligence Agency. For instance, Is it always engaged in matters that enhance the national interest, and, if so, by the use of methods that are compatible with American ethics? Now, it ought to be clear to you that the authority of the President of the United States exceeds the authority of the Director of the Central Intelligence Agency, let alone any of his subordinates. So that by telling us the truth you are in fact upholding the integrity of the democratic chain of command.'"

"Good old Rocky"—Florida was heard from again. "*That* certainly should have taken care of the little p . . . prefect."

"Here was Oakes's answer," Blanton went on. "Something we may have to cope with this morning.

"'Mr. Vice President, I understand your theoretical arguments. I reach different conclusions on concrete questions. I would most willingly give you the reasons why I reach these conclusions if you desire me to do so. But if you feel that merely to listen to me give my reasoning is somehow a waste of your valuable time, and that of your distinguished colleagues, then it would save time—all the way around—for me to say nothing at all, beyond what I have already said. I am of course aware of the penalties you are in a position to impose on me for failing to cooperate, by your definition of cooperation.'"

Blanton stopped, and the ensuing silence was general. Finally Roberta Albright asked, "What happened?"

"Minutes were not taken of the discussion of the panel—whose members, you may remember, included a future President of the United States, Mr. Reagan; a sometime Cabinet officer, Douglas Dillon; and Solicitor General Mr. Erwin Griswold. The record shows only that forty-five minutes later, the clerk was sent out to tell the witness he was dismissed."

"Shee-yit," the senator from South Carolina muttered. "Excuse me, Roberta. Shee-yit, Hugh, he got away with it? I don't remember anything in the press about it."

"It was one meeting of the Rockefeller panel not leaked to the press."

"So what do we do if he treats us the same way?"

"I recommend, with your permission"—Blanton usually knew when the score called for a caesura of courtesy—"that we face that problem if we need to. If you are ready, we will call in the witness."

He turned to his junior aide. "Bring in Mr. Oakes."

CHAPTER 2

ALREADY THERE WAS TALK that Hugh Blanton might be a presidential candidate in the year 2000. It was characteristic of him that although he dismissed his nomination as all but impossible ("By the year two thousand," he commented to his wife, "most Americans will either hate me or fear me—but my reforms will be law"), he had only one thing to say when asked by reporters for a reaction: "No comment." It did not injure him at all, he reasoned, to be thought of as a presidential possibility, and he knew that as long as he continued with the formulaic "No comment," he was thought to be a candidate. He had very much enjoyed his exchange with William Buckley on *Firing Line*. It had gone, "Senator Blanton, your anxiety to press your position on covert action seems to me as at odds with your personal predilection for clandestine political activity. Are you against the public knowing whether you want to be President?"

To this, Senator Blanton had responded, "My concerns become public when I decide to make them public. My point is as

16

easy to understand as that you journalists have no right to spy on me or feed me truth drugs or torture me, which is the kind of thing the CIA has engaged in."

And anyway, why shouldn't he think in terms of the possibility of going on to the White House? Just exactly, why not? In the first place, by the highest criteria, such criteria as would have commended themselves to Aristotle (*had* commended themselves to Aristotle), he was supremely well qualified to be President.

But he acknowledged two strikes against him. The first was that he lacked that distinguishing touch of vulgarity necessary to bring in the voters in huge numbers. Adlai Stevenson, he knew from his reading and from seeing old film clips in the library, had had a little of that same problem, though given the popularity of General Eisenhower, Adlai hadn't done all that badly in 1952. But he, Hugh Blanton, would have trouble emulating even Stevenson's come-on-into-my-tent moments.

"I am more like George Kennan," he said now to Alice, after the guests had left the little fifteenth wedding anniversary party she had given him. It had featured her husband's diet food—his beloved Maine lobster, crepes suzette, and Moët champagne. He was stretched out on a chaise longue, she beside him, stroking the back of his head. He seldom, almost never, spoke about himself, and Alice was alert and excited when he did. She pressed her luck.

"You are every bit as bright as George Kennan." She thought this a measured compliment—he would not have liked it if it were hyperbolic, if she had likened him, say, to Aristotle.

"Probably. Kennan had special strengths, of course, and his knowledge of diplomatic history was greater than mine. And he was capable of aphoristic thought. He greatly moved me by that one sentence—I think you remember, Alice, which one I am talking about?"

"Tell me again, darling."

"He said in the eighties that if covert action could be kept secret, we might countenance it, but inasmuch as it can't be kept secret, it should be abolished."

"Do you really think, dear, that all our covert actions are no longer secret?"

"No. But all of them will eventually be exposed and much of it will be nationally embarrassing. You do remember, Alice, that in an attempt to murder Castro, the CIA devised a cigar that was supposed to explode and a diving costume that would poison him? I say: The sooner we get it all out the better; and, meanwhile, put an end to any more of it."

Alice did not reply.

"You agree, of course."

"Not entirely, Hugh."

"Why not?"

"If somebody was planning to assassinate you, I'd hope that some FBI agent posing as, oh, a member of the Mafia, or whoever the killer was associated with—I'd hope the FBI agent would be allowed to, well, pretend he's a friend of the killer in time to keep him from killing you."

Hugh Blanton's impatience showed, ever so slightly—he was very careful with Alice, whose health was frail. He was much more careful with her than with Rodney, their fourteen-year-old son, or Minerva, their daughter, now ten. When they were denser than at their age they had any right to be, he would tell them so in as many words, and occasionally he would whip Rodney, if he thought him insolent, or lazy.

"The kind of covert activity I am seeking to eliminate is done against foreign governments with which we have diplomatic relations. At home, we do not have diplomatic relations with potential assassins, and the FBI is encouraged to penetrate their designs."

"Well, that is very good to hear, dear Hugh. And it is nice that, on our anniversary, the *Washington Post* devoted that lovely editorial to your work. Who wrote it?"

"I don't know. There are a lot of bright, well-informed people on the *Post*."

Alice continued to stroke him on the back of his head, and Hugh Blanton allowed himself to nod gradually, and then to allow sleepiness to overtake him. Alice pinched him lightly on the back of the neck, rousing him. "It's been a long day. A wonderful day. Let's get some sleep."

ON THE same evening, in their country house in Virginia, Blackford Oakes was celebrating the thirtieth anniversary of his wedding to Sally Partridge Morales. Sally's son, Anthony, was not there. Anthony Morales de Guzmán was himself married. With his wedding certificate came formally the title to the ancestral mansion in Coyoacán, the old colonial section in the heart of Mexico City where his mother had brought him up during his early boyhood.

Anthony had never coexisted with his father, who was shot down by a Castro agent months before Anthony was born. Blackford Oakes, his stepfather, brought him up, and although from time to time his Mexican relatives formally reminded him that he, Anthony—Antonio—Morales was not an Oakes, Anthony thought of Blackford as his father, while acknowledging the biological point. He could not remember when he had begun referring to Blackford as Papabile. (Could he have been witty enough, at age six, to take the measure of his stepfather and decide that he was fit to be his father?) Anthony could dimly remember the great domestic disruption in 1968 when his Papabile left Mexico to perform a special assignment for what in due course he knew to be the Central Intelligence Agency. And then, after what was to have been only a single mission, the father remained absent from home in Mexico. Anthony had learned that his father was back in Washington, so to speak working full-time for his old employer. Even so, his mother stayed doggedly on in Coyoacán. Papabile visited Mexico four or five times every year, staying sometimes as long as a month, but then sometimes his absences were for as long as four or five months. His mother told the boy that these absences were the result of the secret profession in which his father was involved, that he did very important work, but that she wished he would leave that work and settle down permanently in Mexico.

It was she, measuring the need of her eight-year-old boy to be with his father, who finally relented. She and Anthony left the handsome old estate in Coyoacán, letting go or retiring one half the staff, and went to Washington. In Virginia, Sally bought a large and comfortable farmhouse. (*"Tu mamá es muy rica,"* Anthony was startled to be advised by a Mexican schoolmate when he was seven. His mother's wealth was exaggerated, Anthony would eventually discover, but not greatly: The Morales trust had left her wealthy.)

In rural Virginia, in what Mexicans would call an hacienda, Blackford, Sally, and Anthony were surrounded by six hundred acres of redolent Kentucky bluegrass. Sally superintended the raising of cattle and the maintenance of a stable of five horses. Anthony and his mother and his Papabile rode together on their saddle horses when they could. When Blackford was away, his mother went out several times every week with Anthony, who breathed with pleasure the scents of the seasons: the hot humid summers, the little tang of autumn, the blustery chill of mid-winter, the sensual budding of spring. If Sally was unavailable, Anthony was accompanied by the groom until he was ten, after which he would ride on his own. Sometimes he rode with a companion from school who was himself an accomplished young horseman. When he was twelve his mother built an outside course with six varieties of hurdles winding in and out over the area where the junior hunt now convened. And there Anthony learned to jump and competed regularly in the horse shows in Virginia and Maryland.

Anthony loved his life, his mother, his Papabile, and Ed Turpin, the groom. But in his senior year at St. Albans he made his solemn decision. It was to go to college and law school, as his father and grandfather had done, at the University of Mexico, with the view eventually to occupying the spot that had been held for him ever since his father's death, in the ancestral firm of Morales y Morales.

There were just six guests at the anniversary party, one of them the sister of Sally's late husband, who came with the Mexican ambassador, her husband. "Do you know something, Sally," Blackford said in the presence of the one remaining guest, his old friend and professional colleague Singer Callaway, "I hate to say it, but Consuela has become rather pompous. You think?"

Sally looked up at him with a half smile, in answer. She dissolved in Blackford's eyes to the serious young graduate student who on that crowded afternoon at the fraternity when they first bumped into each other had an effect on Blackford he was forced to think of as hypnotic, delirious, because nothing else at Yale mattered to him after that, other than Sally, for ever so long, until she herself brought him down to earth. He neglected his studies in engineering, twice forgot a rendezvous to take the controls of the newest jet fighter his disorganized father was trying to sell to foreign governments. . . . How strikingly beautiful she still was, forty-five years after they first met. He could not believe that he had allowed fifteen years to go by before marrying her.

But the happy day had finally come. It was after his disillusionment with his role in Vietnam, thirty years ago, at the little chapel on the family property in Coyoacán. Sally had now been widowed for a year, and had done the traditional one year of mourning, mourning a husband she had deeply loved. In Blackford's imagination she now flashed forward from college girl to the thirty-five-year-old woman he had married—an adjunct professor of English literature at the University of Mexico, a scholar of standing, and the dueña of her late husband's large home, a woman of bearing and refinement, whom he had seduced (actually, there was a trace of a smile in his memory, *she* had seduced *him*) ten nights after that fraternity party. There would always be a strain of independence in her, as there was in him: that was what had kept them apart and, very possibly, what kept them so devotedly together.

The separations would no longer need to happen, he thought, sipping the end of the wine, now that he, Blackford

Oakes, was discharged from his post at the CIA, along with most of his friends, including Anthony Trust and Singer Callaway. Granted they were all in their late sixties; but age had never really mattered, not within the CIA. "Mr. Dulles," as Blackford always thought of him, had been in his seventies. And Rufus, the master spy, had still been coaxed into delicate missions at eighty.

Rufus! Blackford had heard, just two years ago—it was on the day of President Clinton's inauguration—of the heart attack. He was grateful that it had done its work decisively; flabbergasted to learn, on his return from Beirut, that Rufus, a widower without children or relatives, had left his entire, but not entirely immodest, estate to him, Blackford—with a testamentary note that burst the seams of Rufus's legendary self-restraint: *After the death of Muriel, you became a son, and so it is to my son that I leave what I have, in gratitude. Rufus.*

Rufus knew the whole story of Nikolai Trimov. *Reagan* knew it. No other American alive, Blackford kept reminding himself, knew it. Sally nudged him back into the conversation.

"My point"—Singer Callaway, made aware that Blackford's mind was elsewhere, repeated what he had just said—"is that we've got a good chance to stop Blanton. The President isn't really on his side—no President wants to be without a covert arm. But he's being cautious on how to handle Blanton. And there are more and more people around who think the congressional investigating committees are going too far. Professor Glasser, granted, is devotedly attached to lost causes, but his paper in *The Harvard Law Review* has had a big impact, and it's only a matter of time, maybe even next week, before we get a cert from the Supreme Court, probably in the Wohlenberg case—"

"What is the Wohlenberg case?" Sally wanted to know.

"Carl Wohlenberg was indicted after the Blanton Committee referred his case to the Justice Department, charging that he had violated Section 1001 of Title 18. That's the law that says that if you don't tell a committee something you have good reason to suppose the committee wants to hear, you are somehow guilty of perjury. There's a countermovement coming up here, Black. Say, Bush was great last week, you agree?"

Blackford said Yes, he agreed. Former President Bush had been invited to appear as a witness before the Blanton Committee, both because he had served as President and because he had served, in the 1970s, as Director of the Central Intelligence Agency. Bush had answered Blanton with a polite letter, leaked politely to the *Washington Times,* saying he would be glad to make his views on executive authority and clandestine activity known to the committee, but that he declined to testify in a closed session: his views were for all the American people to hear. Senator Blanton concluded that he did not want George Bush solemnly affirming on nationwide television his devout belief in the continuing necessity of covert activity.

"What I'm wondering is what exactly Reagan is going to say." Blackford had his own reasons for worrying about the only other American alive who knew about Trimov and the Narodniki testifying to the Blanton Committee. "I can't believe they invited Bush without inviting Reagan."

"Reagan is an . . . old man," Sally said.

"He was an old man when he was elected President."

"I hate to remind you of it, Black," Singer Callaway interjected, "but when he was elected President, he was your age—and mine."

Blackford appeared quite surprised to hear this. He took the bottle of champagne and poured what was left in it into Sally's glass. She looked at him: a bit annoyed, a bit exasperated, very, very protective.

"No rest for the weary," she said, affecting a tone of voice far gone in weariness.

Blackford tipped his empty glass to her. "No rest for the weary." He would not contest this. Even Sally didn't know the full story of Nikolai Trimov.

CHAPTER 3

● APRIL 1995

BLACKFORD OAKES ENTERED the room. He blinked when, the door opened, he was hit by the scene. He had simply forgotten. This was the identical chamber in which the Rockefeller Commission had officiated, before which, twenty years earlier, he had appeared. The faces floated by his memory. Great political figures of 1975. Vice President Rockefeller, affable, well coordinated, tough-minded. Ronald Reagan, until the year before Governor of California—nobody took him seriously as a presidential candidate. John Connor, Secretary of Commerce under Lyndon Johnson. Douglas Dillon, smooth, aristocratic Secretary of the Treasury for John F. Kennedy and Lyndon Johnson. Erwin Griswold, Solicitor General for Kennedy and Johnson. Lane Kirkland, number-two man at the AFL-CIO, a backbone of the anti-Communist movement. General Lyman Lemnitzer, Chairman of the Joint Chiefs under JFK. Edgar Shannon, former president of the University of Virginia. A formidable array.

Today the velvet curtains seemed newer, but the windows were still glazed, and the daylight that entered the room did so with manifest reluctance. Four senators were present—he recognized them all. Between the table where he would sit and the raised table at the center at which Senator Hugh Blanton sat, the stenotypist squatted, poised to make lapidary the proceedings. He was a middle-aged man who sneezed self-effacingly twice while Blackford was walking toward the seat to which the clerk-escort pointed him.

On reaching it, he remained standing.

The chairman spoke. "Mr. Oakes, you will be sworn."

A second clerk intoned the usual words. Blackford looked directly at Senator Blanton. He saw the glimmer of light in the eyes of the well-known face, the angular chin, the hair parted directly in the middle, the steel-rimmed glasses smaller than was stylish. He wore a dark gray suit and a regimental tie, and his long fingers were spread out over the documents in front of him.

"Well?"

The chairman was asking why Blackford had not taken the oath. He raised his chin and stared hard at Blackford, whose right hand was poised upright, in the oath-taking position.

Blackford lowered his hand and said, "Senator, may I raise a matter with you and your colleagues before I reach a decision on the matter of the oath?"

"Mr. Oakes, you are here under a subpoena. You are obliged to take the oath and cooperate with the committee. You do not have the alternative of refusing to take the oath. To do so would be to act in contempt of congressional authority to investigate."

"That, Senator, is the question I would like a minute or two to talk with you and your colleagues about."

Chief counsel Arthur Blaustein, seated just behind the chairman, leaned forward and whispered in his ear. The chairman whispered back. The colloquy took up a full two minutes.

"I am inclined," said the chairman, "to grant you the courtesy you request. You have worked for an arm of the government for many years, and I have been told, though I do not have the details—it may indeed be the business of this committee to discover what are those details—that you have engaged in numerous enterprises which in your judgment were in the interests of your country. So you may be seated, and tell us what are your reservations. Be so kind as to be brief."

Blackford sat and said, "Thank you." He looked up at the senator from South Carolina, and then at the senator from Florida, gave with a slight nod of his head a gesture of thanks for not raising any objections to the unorthodox procedure.

But then Blackford leaned back, and for a brief but intense moment the blood rushed to his head. He saw the face of Rufus. Of Trust. Of Michael. Of Tucker Montana. Of Peregrine Kirk, heading his jet fighter down to the earth at the speed of sound in order to shelter the reputation of the Queen he had betrayed. All this in a short moment generated a near-explosive wrath, which he labored to subdue. He was left with a concentrated indignation that framed the way in which he spoke.

"Senator Blanton, you are engaged in an effort which you have spoken about before several forums, which were it to succeed would make a mockery of the forty-five years I have given to the Central Intelligence Agency. It would be to tell me and my colleagues that many of the enterprises in which we engaged were morally wrong, and if you have your way they would in the future be legally wrong.

"Now I don't question your authority to build your case as best you can—I respect the sincerity of your concerns. But I do very much question your right to build your case on words from me which I have promised not to utter. And I don't wish to help you contrive a law that would leave my country, Senator—my country every bit as much as it is your country—powerless to execute certain maneuvers judged by the Chief Executive to be in the best interests of the United States—"

Senator Blanton didn't need to bang down his gavel so explosively, given that Blackford Oakes was seated only eight feet from him.

Blanton quickly decided that he had overreacted. Better to be patronizing.

"Mr. Oakes, my colleagues and I are too busy to be lectured by you on a matter to which we are giving grave attention. If you wish to write me a letter, or write an article for the *National Review,* you may do so. I promise to read the former, and might even read the latter, though that would depend on alternative opportunities. Kindly take the oath."

"Mr. Chairman," said Blackford, "I cannot take the oath unless you agree to permit me to decline to answer questions I deem out of order. I have taken formal pledges not to reveal the nature of certain activities I've engaged in and others have engaged in at my direction or with my knowledge, and to reveal all this could endanger the reputations and even the lives of people I pledged *our*—"

Senator Blanton banged the gavel again. "You have one minute in which to take the oath."

Blackford looked now at Hugh Blanton almost absentmindedly, as though he had given pending matters all the time he had for them, all the time they deserved, his mind turning to other matters.

Arthur Blaustein rose and whispered to the chairman. Senator Blanton spoke: "I shall recommend to the committee a vote to be called immediately to the attention of the president of the Senate, citing you for contempt and recommending your incarceration until you elect to comply with the law of the land, which requires of its citizens that they give such testimony as the duly appointed committees of Congress feel they need in order to perform their duties. The clerk will escort you to the office of the sergeant at arms, where you will be fingerprinted and photographed."

Blackford rose, turned, and walked toward the door. The clerk walking behind him whispered, "Sir, if I may, I'll lead the way."

Blackford followed him out.

CHAPTER 4

I DON'T LIKE IT, Boss. Don't like it at all. Don't like it for two reasons. One of them is Blackford Oakes can become the next Ollie North, only he's got a lot working for him that North didn't have—"

"Like brains?"

"Yes—though North isn't dumb, but he chose to play a kind of I'm-the-American-flag role. Oakes wouldn't do that. He'd be more like General MacArthur when he was fired. He accepts the consequences of what he's done, but he doesn't abandon his own principles. North had a problem: he was meddling with policies Congress hadn't authorized and the President said he knew nothing about. Nobody is saying Blackford Oakes did anything he wasn't told to do. By the way, did you ever run into Oakes before you canned him?"

"No. But I know something about his reputation. Brainy, self-confident, impressive record, admired by just about all my predecessors, very close to JFK and to Reagan, I've been told."

"Well, I gave you the first reason we should be careful. But the other reason is I know you don't want that legislation that Blanton is so goddamn fired up about."

"Damned right we don't want his law. On the other hand, we don't exactly want to come out *against* it. Don't want to sound like a cold warrior. It's not easy." He stretched out his feet, put them on his desk, and loosened his tie.

"I know, I know that. On the other hand, if we let Blanton's law just slide in, it hits a lot of people like a part of our whole disestablishment package. Down with military activity, down with paramilitary activity, down with official state secrets, down with dirty tactics, down with the kind of thing your predecessors went in for. The whole academic parade is behind Blanton on this, you know, and they would not—"

"—like it one bit if I scuttled the Blanton holy crusade. Meanwhile we're sitting looking at two covert operations recommended by the CIA and the NSC which could make a hell of a difference in the problems we got in Libya and Iran."

He smiled. *"Of course,* the way these problems are usually settled, Mack, is—is a matter of *nomenclature.* What the Blanton bill would forbid as a 'covert act' we could probably do by simply calling it something else, like a capital investment." He giggled.

"You forget the kind of language Blanton is likely to come up with in his bill. It's likely to be specific enough to forbid any American agent from slipping a ten-dollar bill into the hands of a Swiss Guard to find out what time the Pope is going to preach."

"Yes." The President pursed his lips.

He seldom put an end to conversational exchanges. He operated on the assumption that the greater the quantity of words said, the likelier it was that a truth would crystallize or an agreement suggest itself. But now he was silent, and in deference to that silence Mack was quiet, but he did not leave the Oval Office. He knew exactly with which gesture the President gave *that* particular signal. He simply sat. Eventually the President spoke: "Before we fasten in on the language of the bill, let's talk about this business of Oakes going off to jail. How is that situation sitting?"

"Not good. He's got to go, looks like. The civil liberties people don't like it, but the pride of Congress is on the line. I can give you the hot poop, got it from you-know-who, who was there when old Bob Dole had Oakes in. Dole *begged* Oakes to go back to the committee and just *bug out,* plead the Fifth. Oakes said he could only plead the Fifth to guard against self-incrimination, and he hadn't done anything illegal, not that anybody knew about—"

"What do you mean, *'that anybody knew about'?*"

"Those are the words he used—they stopped Dole too, who asked what *did* he mean, and Oakes just said something about how he was using a common expression. I don't know what he's referring to. We all know a lot of those black activities Oakes engaged in were pretty hairy, but they were legal under U.S. law as long as they were okayed by the Director, and the Director checked with the President, and the President within the stated period took select members of the House and Senate into his confidence—"

"And blah blah blah"—the President wasn't in the mood to be told what he already knew. It wasn't as if he were campaigning and had to stroke some junior high school student. "Yeah, I know you know all that. What did Dole say to answer Oakes?"

"What do you think the old coot came up with? Leave it to Bob Dole. He said, 'Look, Oakes, you can cite prosecutions in the past under Section 1001—'"

"What's Section 1001?"

"That's the 'false testimony' statute the Special Prosecutor—Walsh—used against North and threatened to use against Elliott Abrams. You remember? 1991? Abrams had been Assistant Secretary of State for Inter-American Affairs? He tried to conceal that he had got some sultan or sheik or somebody to help out the Contras. The old law says that nobody can, well, sort of *hold out* on Congress—not tell Congress things the witness really should have known Congress would have been interested in, but wasn't aware of. It's a hell of a provision, very old, early this century, but wasn't ever used except against people who were hiding out on money questions. Dole's point is that the committee could turn Oakes over to Justice and ask for an indictment not on the grounds of what Oakes told them, but on the grounds of what Oakes *didn't* tell them—things they found out about from somebody else, and Oakes's failure to tell them in the first place is 'false testimony' under 1001."

"In other words, Oakes could take the Fifth . . . Hey, that's good! 'I plead the Fifth on the grounds that I might forget to tell you something you might think relevant to whatever it is you decide later is relevant . . . ' Have the courts passed on Section 1001 used like that?"

"There's pressure on the Court to clamp down on the Walsh use of it. Get the AG to tell you about the Wohlenberg case, if you want particulars."

"Did Oakes cave?"

"He told Dole he would think about it."

"Think about it in jail, or before he goes to jail?"

"Oakes is tough enough to accept jail. But he doesn't go in for melodrama, at least so far as we can figure. He thinks the position he's taken is the correct position for somebody in his shoes, and he doesn't want to give the impression that he is willing to abandon his position in order to spare himself a month or two in jail."

"But how in hell would he be sacrificing his position if he appeared and then didn't give out his secrets—by taking the Fifth? He would simply have outwitted Blanton, no?"

"Dole stressed just that. But Dole couldn't deny the public perception: Oakes would be seen as hiding behind the same Fifth Amendment that sheltered the Commies for a couple of generations and is mostly used by criminals. On the other hand, Oakes says he doesn't want to go to jail for the purpose of becoming a martyr."

"So what's he going to do?"

"He's going to think about it."

"How long's he got?"

"I imagine the Senate will act within a week."

"If the Senate acts on anything within a week, it will make history. Thanks, Mack."

That was the signal. The chief of staff got up and left the Oval Office. The President had already started talking over the telephone before he reached the door. Mack shook his head slightly. The President had, in his presence just a moment ago, gone *a full three minutes* without talking or being talked to. Time spent thinking. Grave stuff. Heady stuff.

CHAPTER 5

● AUGUST 1975

NIKOLAI TRIMOV WAS RAISED by an aunt whose job it was to cook eighteen meals every week for the kolkhoz—collective farm—in Brovary, a half day's journey from Kiev on bicycle, over mostly flat farm country, lumpy only here and there with groups of glistening birch trees. His aunt was responsible for feeding 112 farmers, and they breakfasted at 6:45. This meant that she had leisure time with Nikolai only on her day off, which was Wednesday; but Nikolai was at school for most of Wednesday, so that it was only late in the afternoon and early in the evening that Nikolai really had time with his aunt.

He looked forward eagerly to those Wednesday afternoons, when Titka would read to him and talk to him and play chess. She owned only a dozen books, so she went regularly to the library. Nikolai couldn't remember ever being without reading material. Titka would always ask, when she was still reading out loud to him—he took to reading for himself when he reached six—"What would you like me to read to you about?" His answer was always the same, and Titka loved to hear it from him: "Anything." That meant, for a year or two, stories about animals or knights or high adventures on sea and on land.

But one day Titka thought to play a little trick on him. She had brought home from the farmers' refectory a discarded copy of *Pravda,* which she privately considered the most boring text in the Soviet Union, in particular the editor's page.

"Anything?" she asked teasingly.

"Yes, Titka. Anything."

So Titka opened the paper to the editorial for the day before, August 27, 1968. She read in her usual monotone, but moving along at a good clip, and the words were clearly enunciated. "'The developments in Chicago yesterday at the Democratic National Convention resulted in a clear collision between the progressives, who were represented by Senator George McGovern, and the warmongering forces represented by Vice President Hubert Humphrey. Mr. Humphrey emphasized the need to bring more armed pressure to bear against the revolutionaries in Vietnam in order to frustrate them from achieving socialist liberty. President Lyndon Johnson, who remained in Washington because he is clearly afraid to expose himself even to his own Party, has thrown his considerable weight in favor of Mr. Humphrey as presidential candidate, in arrant opposition to the popular will. The fascist police of Chicago, who are creatures at the disposal of the Mayor, one Daley, whose public career has consisted in imprisoning and torturing any progressive voice in Chicago, in particular among the oppressed Negro people . . .'"

Titka stopped. She had expected to be interrupted after the second or third sentence. She turned to Nikolai, who sat on the floor next to her, his bare legs crossed, his coarse shirt open at the collar—it was warm in August in the Ukraine—and said, "Are you . . . enjoying this, Nikolai?"

"Yes," he had replied. "I do hope that the progressives in Chicago will prevail."

Titka blinked. She laid the paper down on her lap. "What do you know about the progressives in Chicago?"

"Only what you just said, Titka. They are being opposed by the fascist police of one Daley."

Titka was flustered, but continued to read through the one-thousand-word-long editorial, right to the end. Then she picked up the volume of Grimm's Fairy Tales and read to Nikolai the tale about "Iron John." His expression did not change.

But the following Wednesday, after he had returned from school and done his chores in the little patch of vegetable garden, when they sat down he said to her, "Did they win? The progressives in Chicago?"

Titka said that she did not have that day's edition of the newspaper but she had scanned it at the collective and in fact they had not won; Mr. Humphrey had been nominated and would pursue his warlike course in Vietnam. Nikolai said that that was truly a pity, and he hoped someday Mr. Humphrey would come to Kiev, and maybe even to Brovary, so that he could see how progressives can live peaceful and orderly and productive lives. Titka turned her head away, her heart pounding, so he would not see the flush she knew betrayed her feelings. She thought fleetingly that perhaps now was the time to tell Nikolai about his grandparents in the winter of 1933, or about his parents, one month after he was born. No, she stopped herself. Not yet. . . .

Now, seven years later, she still had not told him. Titka was prudent, because she had been under regular surveillance by the local KGB ever since . . . Grigori and The Episode, as the farmers in the village continued to refer to it.

It had all begun when Nikolai's father had taken the lead in organizing a protest. With twenty dirt farmers grouped about him, he approached the Chief of Section to request slightly higher hourly pay and shorter hours—a work week of sixty hours instead of sixty-six. The Chief of Section said he would refer the request to a higher authority. At the end of the day, four uniformed officials came to the small cabin—the same cabin in which Titka and Nikolai now lived—and informed Grigori that he was under arrest. He was taken off to spend the night at the collective's little detention center. The following day, after a half-hour trial before the Chief of Section and two magistrates brought in from the neighboring collective, Grigori was sentenced. He was taken off to ten years of hard labor for counterrevolutionary activity, under Article 70 of the criminal code.

The following day, Lidya went with her month-old baby to her sister Titka at the collective center and asked her to look after him.

"I will be back before the end of the day" were her last words as she bent over and lingeringly kissed her baby.

Lidya then went to the detention center, her husband's army rifle in her arms, cocked. She walked to the desk, pointed the gun at the startled sergeant, and demanded the release of her husband. The sergeant, wide-eyed, rose and told Lidya to follow him to the cell. While pretending to cope with the key to open the cell, he brushed his holster, pulled out a pistol and shot Lidya, whose finger closed simultaneously on the trigger of the rifle, firing a shot that killed her husband.

There was wide resentment over the treatment of Grigori and much grief over the fate of Lidya and her husband. The Chief of Section felt a near-mutinous resentment and made a public gesture designed to appease: Instead of sending Nikolai off to an orphanage, he turned the little family cabin over to Titka and the baby. But even now, ten years later, The Episode was memorialized. Every year, on September 11, the 112 farmers in the collective departed after lunch to their living quarters. A half holiday, so to speak.

Titka knew it was inevitable that the details of The Episode would reach Nikolai before too long. But it would be better coming from one of his schoolmates than from her, because Titka could not trust herself to keep her emotions under control. It wasn't only Lidya and Grigori, but the memory of her father, Nikolai's grandfather.

Titka remembered it all vividly. She had been seven, after all, and many details of her life at that age stayed in the memory. But as she grew older she learned from her reading, and from a cousin who studied psychology, that ugly memories of youth tend to fade away, and sometimes at night she would dream that this memory would fade away, but it never did.

Central to it was the Red Army's long log building, squatting a mere thirty meters from where she, her sister, and her mother and father lived, or rather tried to live, through the famine. What was special about the building in which the Soviet officers met when completing their rounds was the smells that came from it. She spent many hours, along with Lidya, just staring at it, and watching officers drive in in their cars and little trucks. It seemed to serve them (there were about sixty, she counted) as a recreation building, a meeting room for staff planning, but above all as a place in which they had their meals, special meals she had supposed, though now she knew that from the perspective of the famine, any meal was special. The smells of soup and chicken and cabbage and pork and turnips seemed to aim at the little cabin in which she and Lidya shared a bedroom with their parents, the second room serving for all other purposes, including the tool shed from which, every day, her father brought out his equipment to wrestle with the planting, which, when it yielded crops, yielded them to the Soviet monitor pacing alongside. He would seize them—barley, wheat, vegetables—roughly and stack them in the truck nearby. She and Lidya shared a single piece of bread in the morning, on which a kind of gruel was poured, something boiled from what seemed like leaves stripped off a neighboring tree. Her mother ate nothing, waiting until the afternoon for hot water and tea leaves, and the dried wheat soaked in water on which she and their father gnawed at sundown.

It was the day when her mother could not lift her head even to take the cup of tea that her father acted. It was the habit of orderlies from the army detachment in the officers' recreation room across the road to bring out the leftovers from the midday meal and pour them into a barrel right by the barbed wire that protected the enclosure from the surrounding farmers' cottages. From their little window, Titka's father, Fyodor, could see poured into the barrel in a single deposit, as garbage, enough food to keep his family healthy for a month. He looked back at his wife, lying motionless on the cot. He grabbed the pitchfork in the corner, opened the door, and moved with determination toward the barbed wire. He asked the orderlies please to pass him the refuse they were throwing into the barrel. They answered with laughter and taunts. Using his pitchfork as a kind of rough shield, Fyodor threw himself against the barbed wire, seeking to reach a hand into the barrel.

The rifle sound came from back at the officers' quarters. A single shot fired by a lieutenant sitting on a bench outside. He had been fondling the rifle, and found now something quite unexpected, something practical to do with it.

He was a good marksman. Fyodor was dead, straddling the barbed wire. His widow did not have the strength to rise to help pull him away—she did not leave the cot until she was placed in the rude coffin. Titka and Lidya did their best, finally recapturing their dead father with the help of a neighbor who labored with the corpse at half strength because he was weak from starvation.

. . . Titka would not be the one to tell Nikolai about the death of his grandparents, though someone in the community of course eventually would. Everyone knew about those terrible days and months in 1933. The grandparents of a half-dozen boys and girls in Nikolai's class had been victims of the great kulak purge.

All in good time, Titka reflected, looking over at young Nikolai, buried, as ever, in his books. What, after all, was the hurry?

NIKOLAI ADVANCED quickly in school, so much so that when he was fifteen the principal reported to her superiors in Kiev that the boy was two, perhaps three years advanced beyond his fellow students and that she had nothing more to teach him. Either, at age fifteen, he would join the farm work force, or else he would go to Kiev and attend the university.

He was summoned to an interview. The rector, peering over his eyeglasses, studied him carefully. The boy sat respectfully on the bench at the far end of the office while the rector attended to random paperwork. Nikolai Trimov, like so many Ukrainians, was blond, but his features were not those of the typical peasant. The fine nose and chin were more Mediterranean. His lips were thin, his expression sober. He looked more nearly seventeen or eighteen than fifteen, the rector thought as he lowered his eyes and turned his attention to the folder supplied by the Chief of Section at Brovary.

It told the story of Nikolai's parents, of the dramatic events of September 11, 1965. But there had been no adverse notation on the boy's own record. Nikolai had been elected president of his class, he was skilled in chess—in fact he no longer had a challenger of any age in the village—and the physical education director had written that Nikolai would certainly qualify for special training, should Kiev wish to aim him for Olympic qualification in figure skating.

The rector summoned the boy to approach, pointed to a chair at the side of his desk, and told him to sit down. Wool cap in hand, Nikolai did so, furtively tightening his tie, though his Adam's apple protruded through a shirt clearly too small for a boy already grown to five feet ten inches. The rector was an academician by training, not a bureaucrat. While administering the affairs of the 15,000 students on his campus he also taught one course in the philosophy department. It was called the Philosophy of the Working Class, taught to the top-rated one hundred students, who were summoned to take that course in their senior year.

The rector faced a problem he had faced only once before—a fifteen-year-old academically qualified for university training. The time before, it had been a disaster, because the girl could not adjust to the company of young men and women three, four, five years older than she. He had sent her away after two months, back to her village. It would not be easy to predict whether young Nikolai would get along with the older students.

The rector decided to begin by probing the boy's mind and his capacity to handle himself.

"Is it so, Nikolai, that you have read all the books in the library at Brovary?"

"I think so, Comrade Rector. At least I cannot find any book I have not read. Of course, I haven't read every word in the Soviet Encyclopedia, although I consult it often."

The rector reflected that a student bent on reading any edition of the entire Soviet Encyclopedia would have to rush to do so before a revised Soviet Encyclopedia came in, according as this revisionist in Moscow prevailed over that one. "Have you read Marx?"

"Oh yes, Comrade Rector. Although I cannot say that I fully understand him. But of course that must be the reason why Marx is taught all the way up"—Nikolai gestured with his hand pointing to the ceiling—"through graduate school."

"Do you have any difficulty in understanding the central thrust of Marx-Lenin historical imperatives?" Perhaps that would slow the boy down, the rector thought.

"Oh no, Comrade Rector. None at all. Marx and Lenin divined the secrets of history, and we need now only to wait until historical evolution validates, as it must, their thought."

The rector eyed Nikolai Trimov. The rector was on guard. Nikolai's responses might have been written for a student prepared to be exhibited to visiting ideologues. But there was no trace in Nikolai's face of disingenuousness, let alone cynicism.

"You realize that the Soviet state is being asked to bear the very considerable burden of sending you to a university where all your expenses are paid, and where you are provided with free room and board?"

"Yes, Comrade Rector."

"What is it you wish most to study?"

"Anything, Comrade Rector. I am interested in every subject, and will be glad to specialize in any field you recommend."

This boy is . . . the rector was inclined to smile, but he was accustomed to suppressing such temptations. There was clearly no point in questioning Nikolai Trimov's capacity to mix with older students. If anything, he would find them childish.

The rector dispatched Nikolai home to Brovary. Three weeks later, Nikolai was back in Kiev, moved into a dormitory with twenty other students, each with his own cubicle. Nikolai had his own desk and a small locker, a bed and a lamp, and this room he occupied for five years. At first he was the object of much raillery from lusty eighteen-year-olds who thought him a quaint biological anomaly, a fifteen-year-old with the manners of a confident but self-effacing young man. He accepted their taunts, but his behavior was altogether conventional. In two respects he dissimulated. When he played chess, he would often contrive to lose to his competitors. And when, at the end of the first semester, the time came for posting grades, Nikolai requested an audience with the rector. His plea was straightforward, and modestly put. Might it be contrived to reduce his grades by one or two levels? The rector's astonishment Nikolai had anticipated. He gave his reasoning before being asked to do so. He said that at his age it was difficult as it was to be in competition with young men and women who were older. If his grades were dramatically in the first rank, this would make social adjustments even more difficult. The rector smiled inwardly—he almost never smiled on the outside.

He said quite simply that he would confer with the relevant faculty and see what could be done. This meant, when spoken by the rector, that what would be done was what the rector ordained would be done. When the grades were posted, Nikolai Trimov got straight B's. In fact he led his classmates in every subject. In his third year, the rector summoned Trimov and told him that as a practical matter, he needed to decide in which subject he would acquire professional accreditation. Nikolai replied that he would do as counseled: In which field of studies did the rector think he might be most useful to the Soviet state, which was treating him so generously? The rector responded that students should never forget the apothegm so firmly grounded in

Soviet legend, Lenin's doctrine that communism was Soviet power plus the electrification of the whole country.

It followed that Nikolai should become, by training, an electrical engineer. He would not be discouraged from developing his other affinities, most especially the study of foreign languages, in which he was singularly gifted.

The years went by, and Nikolai not only was accepted by his classmates but became a favorite. He was nominated for president of his class when he was a junior but declined, pleading that he did not feel that at his age he was equipped to assume any position of leadership in dealing with his elders. His withdrawal from candidacy as president was accepted as another token of the young man's modesty. But when time came to begin the military training in which all the students participated, he was not able to shrink from the responsibilities that attached to someone of his standing: He was required to accept officer training. He did his work as an officer candidate with characteristic calm and proficiency.

What seemed a mere season went by quickly: five years, at the end of which he received two certificates on the same day. He was now an electrical engineer and a second lieutenant. He could not know when he would be put to work as a professional, but it was instantly clear that no time would be lost in dispatching him to duty as a soldier. The need for platoon leaders on the Afghanistan front was acute. After a two-week leave spent with Titka in Brovary, he reported for duty. He found himself, with the soldiers assigned to him, on a troop train headed for Kabul.

It had been a tortuous journey of very nearly 4,200 kilometers, even though the distance as the crow flies was only 3,500 kilometers. Kiev, Nikolai calculated, was closer to London than to Kabul.

The trip had begun on March 2. On March 11, 1985, Lieutenant Nikolai Trimov and his relief company of infantrymen reported for duty, and Mikhail Gorbachev, a junior official in the Kremlin, was named General Secretary of the Communist Party.

CHAPTER 6

NIKOLAI HAD READ REPORTS about Soviet wounded in Afghanistan in the great military offensive under the leadership of Leonid Brezhnev that dismayed those who believed Soviet expansionism had finally ended with Moscow's consolidation of its hold over Eastern Europe. But the reports that reached Soviet citizens were oblique and muted. At Kiev, Nikolai had seen at first hand a dozen disabled veterans. One he saw struggling across the cobbled pavement of Lenkomsomol Square, trying to get used to artificial legs. Another, a startlingly young-looking boy, blind, being led by a young woman through the market while he maneuvered his long, slender white cane, feeling out, tentatively, the contours of the ground.

And there had been all those whispers at the university. He had enrolled in January of 1980, only one month after Brezhnev began the military operation, after solemnly announcing that the Afghan government had petitioned for help against fascist elements. It was everywhere assumed that the war would quickly be over, given the preponderance of Soviet arms. But by the third year, at the end of which Andropov succeeded Brezhnev, fighting was still going on and triumphant reports in the

Soviet press about front-line activity were increasingly rare, supplanted more and more by rumors of extraordinary Afghan resistance. The students drew the obvious inferences.

In Nikolai's fifth year at college, Andropov died and the doddering Chernenko became General Secretary. The dominant rumors were to the effect that the old man would find a means to acknowledge that the Afghan venture was no longer, well, required, even under the Brezhnev Doctrine, which held that any land once governed by Soviet socialism would forever be socialist. But there was no sign of decreased military activity or of official irresolution, and the war went on and on, and relief units like the unit Nikolai was now attached to were sent down regularly to the front.

As the capital city of Kabul came finally into view after the long journey from Kiev, Nikolai sensed that he might come upon discouraging sights. Carrying his full field pack, leading his platoon toward the assigned barracks, he found himself marching parallel to the hospital unit. He had been prepared for the wounded, but he now got a sensation of the scale of the suffering. The army "hospital" was one barracks building after another, converted from their use as shelters for able-bodied soldiers into shelters for soldiers who were casualties. Nikolai counted thirty-two such buildings in a row, and at that, he could not tell whether the parallel lines of barracks were also being used for the wounded. His platoon followed him, in loose formation. As they walked along the length of the barracks, Lieutenant Trimov attempted to mute the sounds they heard from within the hospital by gradually widening the distance between his unit and the hospital complex. But he had to follow the jeep with the guide from headquarters, which was showing him the way to his platoon's quarters. He could hardly ask the driver and warrant officer kindly to move out of earshot of the moaning and screaming they now heard even through the husky wooden barracks walls, designed to shield soldiers from the fabled Kabul winter.

They arrived at last. After seeing that his platoon was housed and that arrangements were made to feed his men,

Nikolai walked to the bachelor officers' quarters, into the room he had been assigned. He opened the door and saw a very large figure entirely naked, straining, before a small mirror fastened to the wall, to trim his mustache. The man turned his head slightly, seeming to keep one eye on the mirror, and said, "You Trimov?"

"Yes," Trimov said, tossing his heavy pack on the unoccupied bed.

"They told me I'd be sharing a room. If you don't mind my saying so, Trimov, I rather wish you were a girl." He laughed as he snipped the final hair on his mustache and put down his scissors. "Belinkov. First Lieutenant Andrei Belinkov, when I have my uniform on." He extended his hand, and Nikolai took it.

"I suppose," Belinkov continued while dressing, "that at some point we can become acquainted. But my suggestion is that we go now to the field club and have a vodka before supper. It is quite necessary, Trimov—your first name?"

"Nikolai."

"It is quite necessary, Nikolai, to have some vodka before you eat. Otherwise you will not ingest, to say nothing of *digest*, the food they serve here. In fact, it would be quite useful if you brought a blindfold into the mess hall. The food tastes better if you do not view it."

Nikolai said he would be glad to accompany Belinkov. "But I shan't join you with the vodka. I have never taken vodka."

Belinkov, struggling to put on his trousers, stopped in midmotion, unbelieving. "*You have never taken vodka?* Eighteen weeks of basic training and no vodka?" He paused. "What did you do before basic?"

Nikolai explained that he was a university student, that his monthly allowance had been barely sufficient to buy him an occasional foreign book—

"You know a foreign language?"

Nikolai said that in fact yes, he had studied foreign languages.

"Foreign *languages*? What languages have you studied?"

Nikolai had once or twice before run into this problem. Either he would tell the truth or, for fear of being thought a braggart, he would dissimulate. The fatiguing experiences of the three hours since getting off the transport bus at Kabul impelled him to recklessness. "I have studied English and German. Also French and Italian."

Belinkov completed pulling up his pants, reached for a shirt, and, finally, spoke softly. *"Can you understand English when it is spoken?"*

"Yes. Provided it is not too rapid." The hell with it, Nikolai thought. He would tell the whole truth. "But even if it *is* rapid, I can understand quite well."

Belinkov leaned over to his locker, dug his large hand deep within it, and came up with what was discernibly a portable radio. "The Russian-language channels from England and America are blocked. But at ten-thirty at night and six-thirty in the morning there is a news broadcast in English. It will tell us what is going on. Or at least, that is what old Foxov told me he heard from one of the doctors who was English; the poor dumb bastard, why didn't he stay English?"

"Who, Foxov?"

"No!" Belinkov exploded with frustration over such a gross misunderstanding. "The *doctor* who heard the broadcasts and who told Foxov—*he* was raised in England. Foxov is dead. Maybe the doctor is dead also. But the English broadcasts continue, they are not dead. Every now and then I tune in, just to check that they are still there." Belinkov was dressed now, and while he talked, Nikolai had prepared himself—he threw off his bulky jacket and put on a lighter parka—to go to the club and the mess hall.

At the club they occupied a small corner of the crowded room. Belinkov had a half pint of vodka, Nikolai a bottle of ginger beer. Andrei Belinkov was beginning his second year of duty, he revealed, and would serve as company commander of the unit, one platoon of which would be led by Nikolai. "I will not tell you about conditions out in the field, because what you are drinking is not enough to anesthetize you to what I would describe. You will of course get the regular indoctrination from General Zaitsev—you will be interested to know that officers who have been in combat not only aren't invited to be present at indoctrinations of new officers, they are not permitted. Such . . . *manure* as they will give you. Much good it does, since it will be only a matter of weeks—who knows, maybe days—before they move us all out; and then you will see for yourself." He stared into his glass. "But sometimes I wish to scream because the same human beings, flesh and blood, who fill those festooned uniforms know exactly what is going on, and what use is it for them to think they can hide it from such as you, when you will see it yourself, taste it yourself, in no time at all? What did you study at the university? I mean, besides Dutch, Urdu, and Romansch?"

Nikolai laughed, and told Andrei he was now a licensed electrical engineer, and that he had done twenty-two hours of history.

"Russian history? Or Soviet history?"

Nikolai replied cautiously. "Both."

"I should have known. They do run into each other a bit, ho ho, but let's get off that. Me, I did not go to college, I went right to the army. I was commissioned an officer in the field three months after I got here. Promoted in January. I could use the extra pay. Ah!"—Andrei wavered: Should he order another tumbler of vodka?—"*Money,* it is so important! If I did not have a little money, including"—his eyes widened, his hand slipped under his trousers, moving quickly from one side of his stomach to the other, a zipper unzipped—"including *this!* One, two, three, four, five, six, seven, eight, nine, ten, eleven, twelve! Twelve U.S. dollar bills, oh my what they will get for you! While you lie down in the room and dream of it, I will be"—he got up, closing his eyes in rapture—"experiencing it. She costs ten—ten!—rubles, or one—*one*—American dollar, my little dark-skinned beautiful slut, my Akta! Come along, or the mess will close down and the horse manure they serve us will poison the pigs."

Nikolai Trimov followed Andrei out into the dark, into the cold, past yet two more barracks-type quarters to the squat compound that served as the officers' mess hall. Nikolai knew that his grandfather would have killed to have whatever they would be given to eat at the mess hall.

For the thousandth time in the six years since in his teens he had pieced together his family history he felt those pulsations of fury against the system for which he was now being asked to fight, if necessary to death.

CHAPTER 7

● MARCH 1985

COLONEL STEPAN DOMBROVSKY ADDRESSED the assembly of regimental, battalion, and company commanders. Dombrovsky had taught at the War College. He was too young to have seen action in the Great Patriotic War against Hitler, so that when he arrived at the front he was received with some skepticism by the veteran soldiers. That skepticism went quickly, after he was observed in command of the front regiments, which he directed with bravery, assurance, and sophistication. He was promoted now to operations officer. He was entirely comfortable back at a lectern, as in the old days at the War College in Leningrad.

The plan, he disclosed, was to drive the mujahedin resisters up to the high peak of Mountain "A"—the colonel pointed to the enlarged section of the map. "Behind it is the high range, this side of the Pakistani border. We will"—he described a semicircle with his baton—"use small arms, artillery, and mortar right along this line. The rebels will need to seek shelter in the mountain crevices. From there they have no alternative, as we

keep up the fire, than to head for the range, along this line"—
again he used his baton.

"Beginning on the third day, the whole regiment is bound to
seek relief. It is the toughest of the resistance units, seven to ten
thousand men. But they are armed only with rifles. *Then,*" said
Colonel Dombrovsky, who spoke with something of a lisp because two teeth were missing, as also a section of the adjacent
lip, "when they begin to go for the range, our fighter planes will
go to work and our bombers will drop big payloads. They will
be bottled up"—he pointed to the map—"in this ravine here.
There is no way to avoid traversing it when seeking the shelter
of the range. With luck"—the colonel tapped his baton playfully
on the head of Battalion Commander Major Lapin—"we will
put the Zeta mujahedin regiment completely out of business before the end of the week."

Were there any questions?

There were. But it was only the question asked by Lieutenant Andrei Belinkov that rattled the colonel. "Will there be
Stingers?" Andrei asked.

"How in Hades would *I* know, Lieutenant Belinkov, if there
will be any Stingers? In the engagement last Thursday there
were no Stingers and our fighters managed to do plenty of damage to the enemy, would you not agree, Lieutenant Belinkov?"

Belinkov said yes, he certainly agreed that there had been
plenty of damage done to the enemy on Thursday. He had no
problem recalling the events of the day. Soviet fighter planes had
ripped into a column of mujahedin, killing and wounding over
sixty rebels. The survivors of the Afghan unit, surrounded, had
dropped their rifles. You could hear the clatter of steel barrels
landing on the rocky soil. The cold mountain air, working on
the warm exhalations, gave the impression that the rebels were
all smoking cigarettes. They were led, their hands behind their
necks, to the edge of the neighboring forest. At a signal from
Major Lapin, a Soviet machine gunner stationed just inside the
forest that gave him camouflage began firing. He mowed them
all down, investing at least five bullets in each of the resisters.

The major had then walked nonchalantly along the row of scattered bodies, firing his pistol into the heads of the half-dozen soldiers that showed any sign of life.

"The Stingers are the responsibility of the air force," the colonel explained, "with which of course our own operation is completely coordinated."

There being no other questions, the company commanders were told to give the appropriate instructions for the next day's operation to their platoon leaders.

INSIDE THE combat zone, ten days later, Andrei Belinkov, along with Nikolai, faced the problem of the evening meal. It was necessary to eat early—in the daylight hours cooking fires didn't attract sniper fire. Andrei took his ration of beans and rice and that evening's fishy gruel, wrapped himself in his great coat, and sat, his back against the side of a tank, alongside Nikolai, who had not fully mastered the technique of handling his army fork while wearing the heavy gloves without which his hands would freeze in the bitter cold at 7,500 feet.

"Great sport, eh, Nikolai?" Andrei began. "It will not be so easy tomorrow, you will see. Well, but then tomorrow will not be so difficult, because our artillery is very heavy, and there will not be much counter fire. We will drive them up to shelters in the mountain, yes, and probably, yes, Muhammad Ezi will seek the greater refuge of the range, perhaps even the shelter of Pakistan. But the success of the operation will depend entirely on the air offensive, the fighters especially. We will not be able to use our artillery effectively into the ravine—"

"Why not?"

"Why not? My dear Nikolai . . . because the same artillery we will be using to assault Mountain 'A' will require four, five hours, maybe more, to transport around the mountain to get within firing range of the ravine. We rifle soldiers will be able to ascend and take our positions and begin firing into the ravine quickly, in less than an hour. So the heavy barrage will need to be from the airplanes. Without American-made interference— You have seen the American Stingers? . . . Of course not. We have been in the field only ten days, and on Thursday there were no Stingers, I do not know why." The pitch of Andrei's voice was interrogatory: "It is very surprising.

"Oh my God what I would do for some vodka, it is two days since I ran out. Do you know, Nikolai, I have absolutely *no* idea what you think of this madness we are engaged in. *You are the most reserved man* I have ever associated with! As a matter of fact, Nikolai, I do not really know why I continue to seek your company. We have slept in the same two-man shelter now for ten days. You listen to me, and sometimes you laugh, and you answer my questions. But I do not know what is on your mind, and surely you are the only officer in the army who does not complain of Moscow's policy in this accursed war."

Andrei put down his aluminum plate. He spoke now gruffly. "Say *something,* for the love of God, Nikolai, *say something! You may not be able to say something two days from now, because you may be dead!*" Andrei stared into the eyes of Nikolai and, grabbing his collar with one hand, shook him hard, though suddenly his voice modulated, as it traveled from exhortation to entreaty. Andrei Belinkov wanted desperately to hear Nikolai condemn the mad vicious bloody venture in which the Soviet Union was engaged *"for no purpose except a meaningless enlargement of empire and the sweet smell of nearby Iranian oil.* That's the *only* purpose of it," he half muttered. His hand loosened its grip on Nikolai's collar and a tear came to his eye. He dropped his hand. "It is a quite dreadful way to die, is it not, Nikolai?"

Nikolai spoke now. His voice had acquired a new timbre, one Belinkov had not heard before.

"It is a terrible way to die, yes, Andrei. The death of the mujahedin who surrendered to us two weeks ago, that too was a terrible way to die."

Belinkov turned away. "What are we *supposed* to do with the prisoners?"

Nikolai did not answer.

Belinkov relented. "You are right, it was a terrible way to die. I have not got used to it."

OPERATION BOTTLENECK worked according to schedule for the first two days. Early on the third day, a Soviet surveillance plane flying at 50,000 feet reported that the mujahedin appeared to be consolidating on the southern base of Mountain "A" preparatory to crossing the ravine to the safety of the high range, two miles across. Colonel Dombrovsky was elated and ordered two battalions of light infantry to begin the forced march to the east side of the mountain, proceed to deploy, and fire at the enemy. Orders went out to the artillery to begin their arduous trek to both sides of the mountain. The radio from the surveillance plane alerted the Soviet fighters and bombers on standby 75 kilometers to the north.

One hour later, several hundred mujahedin began to cross the ravine. At 8:35 a.m. the Soviet air force could be spotted on the western horizon—as heavy a concentration of Su-17s and Su-25s, thought Nikolai, as one might expect to see flying over Moscow on May Day! He continued to lead his men, at quick-time, to the eastern side of the mountain, where they would squat down and contribute their own firepower to the slaughter. The bombers, he guessed, would come in at about 5,000 feet, the fighter planes at 1,000 feet. And now the explosive sounds of falling bombs began, synchronizing with the deadly rat-tat-tat of the fighters' machine guns.

And then—Nikolai stared in disbelief. Six fighter planes, almost as if exercising a joint maneuver, abruptly left their offensive configuration. Three exploded before hitting the ground. The ten surviving planes in the squadron, executing the Soviet plan, consummated their 180-degree turn at the south end of the ten-mile-long ravine and whizzed back to strafe again the mujahedin, whose numbers, designed to swell as Muhammad Ezi's regiment made their way to the range, were however rapidly diminishing. Suddenly, four more fighters were struck, three going down directly in flames; one, with a smoky contrail as if gasping for air, lost its altitude slowly, crashing, finally, an eternal twenty seconds later, into the west face of the range. The surviving six fighters abandoned the cauldron, and suddenly the bombing fleet dematerialized into the horizon.

It was then that the rebels' rifle fire concentrated on the Soviet battalion that had been poised to fire into the ravine, by now almost empty of targets as the mujahedin completed their ambush. Nikolai shouted at his men to take cover. It seemed only seconds before Nikolai heard a bullet's thud a few yards ahead of him. And it was only minutes later that he discerned that the heavy rifle fire was coming not only from ahead of him, from the southern flank of the mountain, but from behind. The mujahedin had descended from their mountain crevices, taking positions to the rear of the Soviet regiment, which now was taking concentrated fire from ahead and behind. Belinkov's voice came in over the radio to Nikolai. *"The bastards are everywhere. Dig in. I am radioing to the artillery to head back and give us cover."*

Soon after midday, Soviet artillery began to pepper the northern flank. The withering fire from the rear gradually decreased and the order came to the Soviet commanders to turn about and make their way back to where they had come from. Nikolai shouted out the order for his platoon to retreat. Platoon B provided cover from the front. At this moment, standing to shout out his commands, Nikolai felt the bullet in his thigh. He dived down and began to crawl. He could no longer run, though he'd have felt no safer doing so.

It was midafternoon before there was anything like a reassembly at the regimental station from which the offensive had begun. Thirty-five men in Nikolai's platoon were checked in, ten of them wounded. Twenty-five were not accounted for. The casualties in the other platoons were comparable.

Colonel Dombrovsky did not appear, and no one came forward to testify to what had happened to him. It was not until nightfall that the military radio from Kandahãr brought them the news: a radio intercept of the enemy revealed that Dombrovsky had been taken prisoner.

Andrei Belinkov made it back with a dozen survivors of his own platoon. He went to the field hospital and found Nikolai. Only penlight flashlights were permitted and it was with a penlight trained on his thigh that Nikolai saw the scalpel dig into his flesh to bare the cavity in which the bullet lay. He did not remember the yank that dislodged it, feeling only the intense pain and hearing the voice of Andrei ("Easy, Nikolai Grigorovich, the worst is almost over . . ."), who held a second flashlight for the pharmacist's mate officiating. He remembered hearing the voice of another officer saying hoarsely to Belinkov, "A bloody ambush. The whole thing. Including two weeks ago—no Stingers—whole thing—bloody ambush."

Nikolai woke the next day in a truck in which he and a half-dozen—a dozen?—other soldiers lay, some of them moaning, all of them freezing in the cold as they made their bumpy way back to the division headquarters fifty kilometers away. Every day for four days Andrei would come and exchange a few words with him. They spoke about every subject except the war, except the killing. Nikolai spoke of his childhood, ascribing his orphan status to a local plague, and then about his college years. Andrei spent relaxing moments describing the sports he had so much enjoyed, the karate lessons he had mastered, and the friends in boyhood who joined him in attempting to eke some pleasures from their drab lives. Where-were-you-when-Stalin-died did not work for them, since neither had been alive in 1953, but they did recall the great Olympic triumphs of the gymnast Nikolai Andrianov in Montreal in 1976. Neither of them brought up the American boycott of the Moscow Olympics in 1980. That had been a reaction to the Soviet Afghan offensive that had brought them here, an engagement they would not willingly evoke.

On the fourth day, using crutches, Nikolai made his way to the canvas-covered army theater, where movies and documentaries were shown. Three hundred men and officers were assembled there, under regimental orders, to view a documentary flown in from Moscow. Andrei Sakharov had denounced the Afghanistan war from his exile in Gorky, the announcer reported. The camera then focused on Sergei Chervonopisky, a thirty-two-year-old former major in the Soviet airborne troops who had lost both legs in the war. He was one of 120 Afghan war veterans in the Congress. Chervonopisky lashed out at Sakharov for telling the reporter from a Canadian newspaper, the *Ottawa Citizen,* that Soviet pilots sometimes fired on Soviet soldiers to prevent them from being taken alive by Afghan rebels.

"To the depths of our souls we are indignant over this irresponsible, provocative trick by a well-known scientist," Chervonopisky declared. He accused Sakharov of trying to discredit the Soviet armed forces and attempting "to breach the sacred unity of the army, the Party, and the people." The camera turned then to General Secretary Gorbachev. He was joined by the entire Politburo in a standing ovation for Chervonopisky's censure motion. Chervonopisky had shouted out, *"The three words for which I feel we must all fight are state, motherland, and communism."* Speaker after speaker heaped opprobrium on Sakharov. "Who gave him the right to insult our children?" a middle-aged farm worker had declared indignantly.

Nikolai Trimov closed his eyes and formulated a sacred pledge. Something that had been gestating deep within him since he first absorbed the details of The Episode from the lips of a schoolmate six years before, and fused them with what he had learned about the death of his grandparents.

Nikolai resolved to assassinate the leader of the Soviet enterprise. That meant, to kill the General Secretary, Mikhail Gorbachev.

CHAPTER 8

WEARING LIGHT CORDUROYS AND a crew-necked gray
sweater, Blackford opened the door of his house in Virginia to Arthur Blaustein, chief counsel to the Senate Committee
on Intelligence. Blackford had read several months ago—and this
morning had got from Nexis a copy, to refresh his memory—the
profile of Blaustein published in the *Washington Post* the day his
appointment was announced by Senator Blanton.

Arthur Blaustein was born in 1960, the son of a federal
judge in Milwaukee. At the University of Wisconsin he majored
in Russian studies and served as editor of *The Daily Cardinal,*
the student newspaper. In a widely discussed editorial published
a week before the 1980 election, the student newspaper, at the
direction of editor Blaustein, endorsed the candidacy of Barry
Commoner and LaDonna Harris, who were running for President and Vice President on the American equivalent of a Green
ticket, calling for environmentalist totalism and unilateral disarmament. From there to the law school at Harvard, after which
Blaustein clerked for Justice Thurgood Marshall. From there he
went to work for independent counsel Lawrence Walsh, who
was investigating Iran-Contra, the gravamen of which was that

the Reagan administration had illegally supported the Contra movement in Nicaragua, using funds illicitly obtained for that purpose. Blaustein was prominently associated with the trials of John Poindexter, Oliver North, and Richard Secord. He was highly visible in the prosecution of Elliott Abrams and Caspar Weinberger, whose prosecutions were aborted by the controversial pardons handed down by President Bush in the last days of his presidency.

One week ago, the Senate had voted a contempt citation against Blackford Oakes. The sergeant at arms to whom the matter was assigned had yesterday announced that the malefactor, Blackford Oakes, should report to Room S321 in the Capitol at noon, April 19. This was a most unusual procedure, reactivating congressional punitive dramas associated for the most part with the nineteenth century.

The news story describing the Senate vote and the order given to the sergeant at arms explained the procedure in some detail. Any failure by Mr. Oakes to report as ordered would result in his arrest. The debate in the Senate had featured the spirited opposition of senators from the right and from the left. The conservatives were antagonized by what they viewed as recriminatory persecution of a Cold War hero. The civil liberties left railed against the resurrection of a congressional power so long unused, a power that permitted the legislature to transgress against the doctrine of habeas corpus: What the detention of Blackford Oakes amounted to was punishing a citizen without trial, in flat violation of due process. Senator Simon argued that the Fourteenth Amendment had de facto anachronized this ancient and arbitrary power of the Senate and of the House to incarcerate intransigent witnesses, and that to revive the power now would set civil liberties back "by a century." Senator Blanton countered with the argument that to fail to exert the authority of the Senate was in effect to fail to exercise the responsibility of the Senate adequately to inform itself before proposing legislation. Senator Hatch stressed that Blackford Oakes, although practically nothing had been published about his career, was known within the intelligence community to have risked his life more than once to further U.S. interests; that Presidents Kennedy and Johnson had availed themselves of his special skills, entrusting him with special responsibilities; and that to punish him now, "using Tower-of-London sanctions," would be to punish someone whose valiant conduct in the past was entirely consistent with his reluctance now to give out information that might endanger the lives and careers of men and women who had helped the United States during the dangerous days of the Cold War. Senator Hatch's speech was the grist for one hundred editorials the next day.

Senator Nunn said that he would vote against the contempt citation. He delivered a speech on the need for covert action to defend American interests, and nominated Blackford Oakes as an "unsung hero" of the Cold War. The *Washington Times* quoted a paragraph from the senator's speech: "Consider the moral dilemma in which the Blanton Committee and its energetic counsel, Mr. Blaustein, have put the 69-year-old American, legendary in the shadowy world in which so many enemies of America have lived and worked. That much of their work was frustrated is owing to the efforts of such as Mr. Oakes. And now we wish to put him in jail for the crime of respecting pledges he made in pursuit of his country's objectives." Several opponents of the Blanton Committee's war on covert activities spoke up, declaring the objective of the Blanton Committee to be dangerous. The majority leader reminded the honorable gentlemen that they were not here to debate CIA policy but to reaffirm the division of powers under the Constitution. It was then that Senator Albright announced that she felt she had no alternative but to vote to punish someone who disdained, in effect, a Senate subpoena. "We cannot leave it to individual consciences whether to cooperate or not with congressional committees charged with gathering information on the basis of which laws are made," Senator Albright kept stressing the point.

The vote was 65–30 to punish Blackford Oakes.

IT WAS one hour after the vote was taken that Blackford got the telephone call. Blaustein sought a private session with Blackford, "any time today after 4 p.m."

"I told him," said Bob Lounsbury, his spectacles as always at the end of his nose, his ballpoint pen, as always, doodling on his yellow pad, "that of course I would need to be present at such a meeting. He asked me to ask you, on his behalf, to meet without me. I told him I would relay the request and advise against granting it." Lounsbury was known in the legal community as the most unambiguous naysayer since the hanging judges of frontier days.

"Oh hell, Bob. I know that's the way lawyers act. And there are good reasons for it. But look. I come out of a different tradition from you guys. I've met with maybe a hundred people in the last forty years to discuss critical matters, including my own safety, more hazardous than any problems I have with the U.S. Senate. Which simply wants to send me to the joint until Senate pride is assuaged. I've told too many people too many times *I have to see you alone* to say No to Blaustein, when he says the same thing to me. If he yaks on about legal questions I can easily shut up. Or call you up. Or tell him unless he goes away I'll . . . *have him assassinated!* Tell him to come to the house at six."

Lounsbury knew he wasn't going to get anywhere with his old friend, client, and classmate.

"But you can tell me this, Bob," Blackford went on. "Is there a typical maneuver done by congressional counsel before actually dispatching somebody to jail? And by the way I forgot to ask you, but when I was at school I think I remember that in the early days of the republic, recalcitrants were jailed—is my memory correct on this?—within the walls of Congress? Have they now got themselves a Lubyanka somewhere nearby?"

"I knew you'd ask that, and I've done the research. The best treatment has been missed by the press. It's in"—Lounsbury shuffled some papers—"it's in the 'Public Officials Integrity Act of 1977,' a 'Report of the Committee on Governmental Affairs,

United States Senate,' page ninety-six. And what it says is, 'Subsection (g) expressly provides that the enactment by Congress of a mechanism for the civil enforcement of a subpoena does not affect the power and authority and absolute discretion of Congress, or an appropriate House of Congress, to choose to enforce a subpoena by either of the two existing methods rather than by initiating a civil enforcement action.' Now this, a civil action, is what they haven't done to you—yet. 'The first of these two existing methods is certification by the President Pro Tempore of the Senate or the Speaker of the House of Representatives to the United States Attorney for the District of Columbia of a matter pursuant to section 104 of the revised statutes (2 U.S.C. 194). This procedure provides for a criminal prosecution brought by the United States Attorney to punish an individual or entity for refusing to comply with a congressional subpoena or order.'

"And here is what they *have* done to you: 'The second existing method of enforcement is for either House of Congress to hold an individual or entity in contempt of such House of Congress. This method is commonly referred to as trial before the bar of Congress. While historically this method has been used numerous times, it is generally considered to be time-consuming and not very effective. No one has been tried for contempt of Congress before the bar of Congress since 1945.'

"So what will they do to you like, tomorrow?" Bob went on, drawing a jailhouse with bars on his pad. "The report then says, 'In exercising its discretion with respect to enforcing a subpoena or order, Congress may decide that it is important to secure production of the subpoenaed documents or compliance with the order and that a civil action is quicker and more effective in achieving these purposes. In other cases'—and this seems to me to apply to you, since you aren't going to yield those 'documents,' ever—'In other cases, Congress may decide that it is more important to punish the individual or entity who has refused to comply with a congressional demand and thereby to deter violations by others. In that case the contempt should be

certified to the United States Attorney for the District of Columbia for criminal prosecution.'"

"So I'm supposed to cool it somewhere until the Senate de-
cides whether to press for federal criminal action?"

"Correct. That is my reading of it. And, of course, smart
people avoid your problem by the simple act of pleading the
Fifth. Which I, your former colleagues, your wife, your stepson,
the army, the navy, and the marines have been urging you to do
for thirty fucking days. But no, you are too accustomed to the
great days of brinkmanship—"

"Bob? Bob, do you hear me, buddy? You are becoming—
noisy! You remind me of that wonderful ruckus you generated
when, stark naked, you ran up Church Street followed by half the
New Haven police force, the night you were initiated into Deke.
And who, dear Bob, *who,* filing out of the Fence Club, saw you,
took off his overcoat in the freezing cold, threw it over your manly
torso, spirited you into the club, tucked you into the big fireplace,
and got our faithful John Huggins to tell the police (a) you weren't
there, and (b) if they wanted to search for you, they'd need to get a
court order? Did I leave you in the middle of the street, and say,
'Wait here, Bob! I'll call Wiggin and Dana and get a lawyer'?"

Lounsbury, whose detailed memory of the event had been
blissfully erased that same night by the bottle of gin he had been
forced by the initiating club to chugalug, remembered only his
gradual recovery of consciousness sometime after midnight.
Blackford alternately squirting cold water on his face and pressing him to drink more black coffee. He muttered now, "You
bring that old chestnut up about every ten years, and it's becoming tiresome."

"I bring it up only when provoked."

"Okay. Now listen, Black. Blaustein will come at six. I'll be
in my office—you have the private number—till seven-thirty,
and you can reach me at home after that. And you'd better
damned well tell me *exactly* what he said. And don't make any
deals with him without first checking with me."

Blackford replied with something soothing.

ARTHUR BLAUSTEIN was carrying what Blackford assumed was the heaviest briefcase ever manufactured. He was dressed as if headed for a funeral, where he would deliver the—was there such a word as "dyslogy," Blackford wondered. Surely Arthur Blaustein would never mourn the passing of anybody, except maybe Ralph Nader. Framed against the light blue sky and the setting sun in pastoral Virginia, the scene might have made a picture for Andrew Wyeth, it occurred to Blackford, opening the door to the bulky six-footer. He asked his guest if he might help him with the briefcase—"I'm surprised any one man can lift it."

Blaustein smiled perfunctorily, shook hands, and peered into the hallway, awaiting instructions.

"Just follow me. We'll go to my study." Leading the way, Blackford took Blaustein through the comfortable living room, decorated in discreet ranch style, with here and there a touch of Mexico, as in the blue tiles that framed the fireplace. They went into the book-lined study, dotted with the paraphernalia of a complete computer life. Blackford pointed to a sofa and sat opposite Blaustein in an easy chair. Blaustein put down his briefcase and removed a folder and the standard yellow legal pad.

His first question was, "Are you by any chance, Mr. Oakes, recording our conversation?"

"If I were, Mr. Blaustein, I wouldn't feel obliged to tell you."

Blaustein's expression did not change. He spoke in a deep bass-baritone. "I am here, as you will have supposed, to explore the possibility of keeping you from having to go to jail tomorrow. You should know that Senator Blanton has considerable professional respect for you but that he is genuinely concerned, especially now that the Cold War is over, to put an end to covert activity. And he feels that he can best persuade his colleagues on the Hill to join him in approving an end to such activity by apprising them of the dangers we ran in concrete situations in recent history."

He paused. His design was clearly dramatic. He cleared his throat. "Of course, we know about many covert activities, for instance those that were exposed by the Church and Rockefeller

Committees in 1975. But they were, for the most part, idiosyn-
cratic in character, like the business of poisoned cigars for Fidel
Castro. We know that you have engaged in many covert operations, and we have an idea what some of these were. Indeed we
know that you were discharged from the CIA in"—Blaustein
consulted a folder—"in 1957 for failure to give the Agency notice that a high-tech satellite unit was being shipped across to the
Soviet Union—"

"I don't know where you are headed on this matter, Mr.
Blaustein. But the reason I did as I did in 1957 is complicated,
and had to do with sparing the lives of two Soviet scientists who
had defected. What is your point in bringing the matter up?"

"My point is that we have information about some of your
activity, but we don't have the information we most want—
information which, in the opinion of Senator Blanton, would
conclusively establish the need for an end to this kind of thing."

"May I make a diplomatic point?"

"Why of course, Mr. Oakes."

"It really isn't very . . . *endearing* of you to refer to what I
have devoted my life to as 'this kind of thing.'"

"I apologize. I have no training as a diplomat. I should have
said, 'the kind of thing to which you have devoted your quite
extraordinary skills.'"

"You could say that about Goebbels."

"Why don't we then, as they say in court, just strike that
phrase?"

"You will not succeed in erasing from my memory your
having used it. And anyway, I am not a juror, for you to instruct
what to remember, and to forget."

Blaustein reddened, paused. And then began again. "I have
been authorized by Senator Blanton to say that he is prepared,
in his capacity as chairman of the committee before which your
contempt was executed, to call the U.S. Attorney and ask him to
suspend the arrest order for thirty days, during which he will
advise the Senate that the contempt has been purged."

"So what is expected of me, in exchange for my liberty?"

"The full story of Cyclops."

Blackford was genuinely astonished.

Who? How? Where? When?

He said, as matter-of-factly as he could manage, "What brings you to use that name?"

"Such knowledge as we have been able to assemble about . . . Cyclops."

"You will need to catch me up on the matter."

"It is precisely we who need to be caught up on the matter. Who was he? What was the nature of the CIA's dealings with him? And what was the disposition of the Cyclops operation?" He leaned forward. "We know this much: That you were the officer in charge of dealing with him. And that the late William Casey left no notes, nothing whatever, that so much as mentioned the Cyclops operation. Nor have we come upon any officer in the Agency now, or active in it ten years ago, who admits to knowing anything about Cyclops."

"What causes you to believe that I have a link to this . . . this Cyclops?"

"That much the committee has established. That and more, but not enough."

Blackford shrugged his shoulders. "Why is it so important to you, Mr. Blaustein?"

"Because—because, Mr. Oakes, we intend to demonstrate to the Congress that the Cyclops operation might have resulted in . . . a nuclear war."

Blackford touched his lips with his tongue. He knew that a lifetime's practice in the histrionic arts was quite sufficient to handle Blaustein in any way Blackford chose, intending any effect. It was therefore a careful calculation that led him to respond as he did. Tomorrow at this time, he said to himself, I will be behind bars thanks to the manipulations of this bastard and his team. So what the hell, why not let him feel what I think of him?

"Mr. Blaustein, permit me to say that while you were an undergraduate screaming and yelling about our defense expenditures, some of us were doing what we could to avoid the need to *use* the American military. As you know, I was one of those . . . 'soldiers,' if the term does not offend you. And I will advise you, and you may repeat what I say to Senator Blanton, that there is no reason to suppose that I'd have enjoyed a nuclear war any more than you'd have done. I speak here, while I am at it, in behalf of my wife and stepson. I remind you, and Mr. Blanton, that the kind of people who have offended you since you were at college are the people who won the Cold War and, at least for a while, gave the whole world immunity from a nuclear exchange. How this was done and how credit for it should be apportioned is something historians will decide. Meanwhile, my judgment of it is that the country will not be helped by the immobilization of the CIA. The story of Cyclops the Soviets were not able to get from me. It is unlikely that you will succeed in doing so. Do you feel like going home? Because I very much feel like your going home."

Arthur Blaustein reached for his briefcase and inserted in it the folder and the legal pad. Blackford led him to the front door. Blaustein hesitantly proffered his hand. Blackford took it, quietly closed the door, and went to the telephone.

"Bob? Black."

"I've been pacing the floor. What did the mortician want?"

"He thought it might be patriotic for me to commit suicide."

"Come on. It's late."

"He said Blanton would get the jail order vacated if I spilled my beans to Blaustein about a certain Agency operation in the past. He was willing to spare me the humiliation of spilling the beans to the whole committee."

"And you said?"

"I guess the only way to put it is that I spilled my . . . thoughts on him."

"Told him off?"

"Told him off. But you know something, Bob? I don't feel particularly good about it. It left me feeling sanctimonious, and I try to avoid that—maybe you've noticed; I hope so. I guess I

just couldn't help it. No. That's not right. I could have con-
trolled myself. I elected not to."

"Has he got anything on you?"

Blackford paused. "No. Just wants information on My Secret Life, and I'm saving that for a higher bidder. Know anybody
at the *National Enquirer*, Bob? . . . Bob. Bob? Still there?"

"Yes. I just finished letting out a sigh. They don't register,
most sighs don't, over the phone. I'm surprised mine didn't,
though. It was a whopper. . . .

"Well, Black, I guess there's nothing more to it than tomorrow. I'll come by and pick you up."

"Bob, I've been thinking about that. I appreciate it, of
course, but you know, I don't see any reason for me to go with
my lawyer at hand to the sergeant at arms en route to whatever
detention center they're going to plop me into. I mean, there's
nothing you can do. And if I go with a lawyer, somehow, it
seems to me, there's an aroma of guilty-not guilty, and I'm not
eager to pitch my problem to the press in those terms. Do you
see what I mean?"

Bob Lounsbury was silent for a while. And then said, "I understand. You make your own way. If you need me, I'll be there
in a flash."

"Yes, Bob. I appreciate that. But don't be in such a hurry
you forget to put on your clothes."

"Fuck you, Blackford."

"Thank you, Bob. I'm doing my best."

Blackford hung up and went then to Sally in her own study.
She was waiting for him.

He caught her up. And requested that they drop the subject
for the rest of the evening.

"All right, darling." She played with her pearls after they sat
down, and Blackford remembered when he had first seen her do
this, the night before she had to defend her dissertation at Yale.
He could never imagine her without her pearls. But then he
couldn't imagine anything without Sally.

CHAPTER 9

NIKOLAI TOOK THE METRO, got off at Kievskaya, and set out on foot to number 2 Kutuzovsky Prospekt. He wondered idly if anywhere in the entire world there was a larger apartment building. Certainly there could not anywhere exist a building of this size in which more apartments were crammed. To get to the single room he shared with Andrei Belinkov he needed to go through the main archway and across the large courtyard, often bulging with old furniture and bags, lamps and mattresses and ancient trunks—people from number 2 Kutuzovsky moving out, others moving in. To reach his entrance he needed to walk across the courtyard at an angle of five degrees. He would climb six flights of stairs to apartment 6K. Yes, there was an elevator designed to serve his apartment section and the adjacent section, but it hadn't worked during the two months Nikolai had lived at number 2 Kutuzovsky.

A few minutes later Andrei said to him, huffing from the six flights up which he lugged the week's provisions, which included three bottles of his precious vodka, "Nikolai, you goat, it suddenly occurs to me that you are *an electrical engineer.* So, you were not able to find a job in Moscow as an electrical engineer, and you do not wish to move from Moscow. I understand that. I know the reasons for that. What I do not understand is why you do not practice your profession *right here at number 2,* and fix that accursed elevator."

Nikolai helped Andrei store the rations. "I did go down and have a look, four, five weeks ago. The generator is dead. I asked the superintendent when the new generator would come in."

"What did he say?"

"He said, 'Comrade, maybe before Christmas. But if you wish to quit your apartment, I know someone who would be happy to take it off your hands, and pay you a nice bonus in addition.'"

Andrei sprawled his large frame on the couch opposite the single bed. "Yes," he muttered. "Incredible as it may seem, there are people who envy our palazzo. Is that the right word for it in Italian? The fancy word for palace?"

"That is the word you are searching for, Andrei. But listen. I have something very important to read to you. But let's wait until after supper."

It was Nikolai's day to cook. He fiddled with the electric hotplate and began to boil water. "We can have one of our eggs, hard-boiled, with your vodka and my tea. And *my sugar*"—he reached up into the cupboard and picked out two cubes of sugar. He drew water from the same basin in which they washed dishes, brushed their teeth, drew water to sponge their bodies, and urinated. The single toilet and shower room for their floor was at the end of the hallway, shared by the twelve occupants of that landing. The pot in place on the electric hotplate, Nikolai sat down in the upright chair, waiting for the water to boil. "Yes, Andrei, we are lucky."

"*I* am lucky. *You* were given the apartment as a disabled veteran with the proviso that it had to be shared. And you share it with me. I will toast to you, Nikolai." Andrei lifted his glass of vodka and breathed a grateful sigh. "Ah, Nikolai, this fucking country."

Nikolai turned on him. He spoke in a hoarse whisper. "Andrei! You have violated a covenant between us. *Never never never ever criticize anything relating to the government!*" The other part of his reprimand went unspoken but was clearly understood: You could jeopardize our mission.

Andrei had recognized the violation even as he blurted out the word. He was genuinely contrite. He had made the pact with Nikolai on that frozen night at the military base outside Kandahār after Nikolai spoke out his intentions. Andrei had no inclination to deviate from his commitment, but he had made it, he knew, without fully understanding its solemnity and the derivative self-disciplinary requirements.

"I'm sorry, Nikolai"—he reduced his own voice to a whisper, casting a ritual gaze about him as if he could sweep the room of imaginary KGB listening devices with the penetrating force of his eyes.

It was unlikely that the KGB would bug the one-room apartment of two discharged veterans, one of them occupied as a teacher, the second as a physical education instructor in the Moscow Police Academy. It was the principle of the thing. Besides, one could never *absolutely* know that there were no listening devices about. You cannot take anything for granted, he reflected. Meanwhile, Andrei was thinking to himself: There is in fact *no human being* in Russia I absolutely trust, other than Nikolai. My parents are dead, my only brother is an ardent party functionary in Sverdlovsk, and I certainly do not trust Nina. I love her, especially to sleep with, but I know very well that if some porky commissar came about and offered to get her a better apartment, she'd migrate there and then.

Yes—he looked up at Nikolai, who was now lifting the egg from the pot—yes, he is the only one I absolutely trust.

He took another draft from his glass.

A HALF-HOUR later they had finished their meal. Cooking by Nikolai, dishwashing by Andrei. They sat now, both of them, on the couch. It was here that Andrei would sleep until Sunday night, after which the bed would be his for a week, the couch Nikolai's. It was here that they pooled their thinking, here that Nikolai stoked their commitment to their purpose.

Most afternoons, before taking the metro to come to number 2, Nikolai would go to a library, frequently the great library at the University of Moscow, which was said to contain twenty-five million volumes. He had gone there the day before to search out a volume by the American, Whittaker Chambers.

Chambers had been a Soviet spy but he had broken with communism, after which break he testified against former colleagues, most spectacularly sometime U.S. State Department official Alger Hiss. At college in Kiev, Nikolai had read and reread *Witness,* Chambers's autobiography, and he had narrated its story in some detail to Andrei. He was left in awe of its author, of his singular poetic grasp of the evil Nikolai was now pledged to combat.

He had learned a few days earlier about a second volume by Chambers, told of it by a colleague at the Pitkin People's School, a young historian who taught while pursuing graduate studies in Russian history at the university. Viktor Pletnev had last Monday startled Nikolai by mentioning, in connection with his studies of pre-revolutionary Russia, the "Narodniki." He had heard it said, Pletnev told Nikolai, that Lenin had once singled out the Narodniki for special praise. But search though he had in the Lenin division of the library, Viktor had been unable to find any such citation; then a fellow Muscovite who was studying at the University of California in Berkeley had written and related that he had come upon substantial paragraphs on the Narodniki in a book by Whittaker Chambers, a book of letters written to an editorial colleague during the few years preceding Chambers's death in 1961. Viktor Pletnev hoped that Nikolai would look up the book and translate the passage, inasmuch as Pletnev's knowledge of English was insecure. A favor, scholar to scholar.

Viktor Pletnev could not have known that in mentioning the Narodniki he had set down a word that electrified Nikolai Trimov. It was the vision of the Narodniki, stumbled upon in his discursive reading in Kiev, that he had attempted to communicate to Andrei, but to come upon an adequate encapsulation of their historical and spiritual meaning had proved all but impossible; they were a legend, a legend known to only a very few. But in Kiev he had come upon one such, and that old scholar's brief description of the mission of the Narodniki had been for Nikolai an epiphany.

So that it was with great eagerness that Nikolai set out that Sunday morning, when freed from school duties, to the great library, to do his friend's bidding. He was elated to find a library card establishing that, indeed, the Chambers volume was there. He ordered up the book and sat down to read it. Well into the second hour he reached his goal. The passage began on page seventy-six.

No schoolboy searching out a book detailing the mechanics of sexual union had ever been more excited. Nikolai read the substantial passage through twice. Then he removed his large notebook from the canvas tote bag he had walked away with when discharged from the army. He filled four pages of his notepad, translating the text line by line. The book was Restricted, which meant that only university faculty could take it away from the premises. Nikolai would tell Viktor the next day that he had established that the book was there as part of the library's collection, but that a faculty member had removed it. He would promise to try again the following Sunday.

"Then you did not finish reading the book?" Andrei asked.

"No. It is important that I read it all before I alert Viktor to the passage on the Narodniki. I don't want to run the risk of Viktor telling other people about it, and maybe I'd have to wait months to get the book again to finish reading it. I will finish it next week. It required a good two hours just to translate the passage on the Narodniki."

Nikolai leaned down and took his pad from the canvas bag. His hand was trembling.

"Now listen, Andrei. Chambers is writing to his young friend about the forces that brought him to the Party in the early thirties. Here is the passage. Listen:

"'I came to Communism under the influence of the anarchists: Kropotkin, Tolstoi, and Edelstadt. But, above all, I came under the influence of the Narodniki—'"

Nikolai paused, an excited smile on his face as he looked up at Andrei. "Again, listen:

"'It has been deliberately forgotten, but in those days, Lenin urged us to revere the Narodniki—"those who went with bomb or revolver against this or that individual monster."'"

"Andrei, those are *Lenin's own words!* They no longer exist in the established libraries! *'Who went with bomb or revolver against this or that individual monster'!*"

"Go on, go on, Nikolai." Andrei was caught up with the meaning of the words he had heard. Lenin! Sanctioning individual acts of what would now be denounced as terrorism.

"'Unlike most Western Communists, who became Communists under the influence of Social Democracy, I remained under the spiritual influence of the Narodniki long after I became a Marxist. In fact, I never threw it off. I never have. It has simply blended with that strain in the Christian tradition to which it is akin.'"

Again Nikolai paused. "Do you recognize the importance of that, Andrei! ' . . . *to which it is akin.*' The spirit of the Narodniki and the spirit of Christianity!" He bent his young head again to his notepad, the picture of a student entranced by his notes:

"'It shaped the particular quality of my revolutionary character that made me specially beloved (of course, it is wrong to say such things, but it is true) even among many of the crude, trifling American Communists. To the Russians it made me seem a freak of nature—an American who was almost a Russian; a fact that endeared me to them while it perplexed and troubled them. And, of course, it was the revolutionary quality that bemused Alger—*mea culpa, mea maxima culpa.*'"

"What is that?"

"It is Latin, meaning 'my fault, my most grievous fault.' It is a line from the Christian contritional liturgy. I'll go on.

"'I remember how Ulrich, my first commander in the Fourth Section, once mentioned Vera Zasulitch and added: "I suppose you never heard that name." I said: "Zasulitch shot General Tropov for flogging the student, Bogomolsky, in the Paviak prison." And I remember the excited smile with which he answered, "That is true. But how do *you* know that?" For the spirit of the Narodniki, all that was soldierly and saintly in the revolution, found its last haven, O irony!, in the Fourth Section (one purpose of the Great Purge was to kill it out once for all).'"

Andrei interrupted. "But the Great Purge was—"

"Wait, wait, Andrei. Listen . . .

"'Like Ulrich, I may presume in supposing that the name of Ragozinikova is unknown to you. But the facts are these. In 1907, the Russian government instituted a policy of systematically beating its political prisoners. One night, a fashionably dressed young woman called at the Central Prison in Petersburg and asked to speak with the commandant, Maximovsky. This was Ragozinikova, who had come to protest the government's policy. Inside the bodice of her dress were sewed thirteen pounds of dynamite and a detonator. When Maximovsky appeared, she shot him with her revolver and killed him. The dynamite was for another purpose. After the murder of Maximovsky, Ragozinikova asked the police to interrogate her at the headquarters of the Okhrana. She meant to blow it up together with herself; she had not known any other way to penetrate it. But she was searched and the dynamite discovered. She was sentenced to be hanged. Awaiting execution, she wrote her family: "Death itself is nothing. Frightful only is the thought of dying without having achieved what I could have done. How good it is to love people. How much strength one gains from such love." When she was hanged, Ragozinikova was twenty years old.'"

Nikolai stopped, laying down the notepad on his lap as though it were the Sacred Host.

He looked up at Andrei and saw, for the second time, a tear in his eyes.

Neither of them spoke. Until Andrei said, "Twenty years old. Your age, Nikolai."

"Yes," said Nikolai. "My age. We, you and I, are Narodniki."

CHAPTER 10

IT WAS EARLY IN September and the weather in Moscow was, as Tatyana had put it in English, "strutting its very stuff." Tatyana taught the second-level classes in English and French. The more advanced students attended Nikolai's English classes in the adjacent room.

Tatyana was fiercely ambitious. Two weeks after they began their duties she confided to Nikolai—he an injured veteran from the Ukraine, with a slight but distinct limp, she a spirited Muscovite, the daughter of civil servants—that her intention was to work very hard for five years. If, at that point, she achieved the school's gold medal, and if she passed the advanced examinations, she would apply to spend one year studying English in Great Britain or in America. She would continue to work on her French, but, she explained, the demand for civil servants fluent in English greatly exceeded the demand for French-speaking Russians, so she would put special emphasis on the one language. She conveyed all of this as naturally as she might have answered the question of what she had taken for breakfast.

"Five years is a very long time to wait, is it not, Tatyana?" Nikolai asked.

"In five years I'll be twenty-five. That's not so old. How old are you?"

"I am—the same age, twenty."

"You look older than twenty."

"You look younger than twenty."

She smiled, and agreed, when asked, to lunch with Nikolai the following day. "There is a great deal I need to talk to you about," she said. "I want to know especially how you learned to speak English. I heard you lecturing to your students. The door to your classroom was slightly open yesterday and my class had let out. I just stood there in the hall and listened. It is quite extraordinary." Nikolai acknowledged the compliment, and changed the subject.

—Tried to change the subject, as he discovered the next day at lunch. To do that, he ascertained after a half-dozen lunches shared together, would not be easy.

Tatyana . . ."*Tatyana with the light brown hair,*" she quietly hummed the words. "Have you heard the tune?"

No, Nikolai said, he had not.

"I have a collection of English and American records, and I listen to them all the time and try to imitate the words. I know most of the words of 'Jeanie with the Light Brown Hair.'"

Tatyana was single-minded in her pursuit of English. One day Nikolai found her waiting outside his classroom for the hour to end. She was tapping her foot in anxiety. "Nikolai, I need to know. What exactly is the difference between the English '*alternative*' and the English '*alternate?*'"

Nikolai smiled, but he was careful not to appear condescending. He furrowed his brow.

"I wouldn't know exactly how to *define* the difference, but here are two sentences in which the words are properly used. One, '*Viktor and Lev are alternates at the factory. One works in the morning, the other in the afternoon.*' Two, '*Viktor asked Lev if he could think of an alternative to working at the factory.*' . . . Does that help?"

Tatyana breathed more easily.

He marveled at her absorption with the language, an absorption that appeared to exclude any other interest. Her dress was unvaried, not all that different when arriving at the classroom, after changing into the neat blue cotton school uniform that reached down below her knees, from what she had worn in. But Nikolai had noticed from the very beginning a scent; not perfume—schoolteachers could not afford to wear perfume every day. It reminded Nikolai of the moment in Brovary when spring came. It came in Brovary suddenly, decisively. There was never any mistaking it. One morning Nikolai would wake and think, Spring is here! It was that scent, a freshness that went with Tatyana's wholesome absorption in life and language, a suggestion that growth and blooms were in the offing.

They began to stay on at the cafeteria after school hours with their tea—at the Pitkin School, as it came to be known, there was always tea in the faculty lounge. Nothing else, but always tea. No sugar, unless the teachers brought their own, except for one lump per day provided by the school, which was handed out to the teachers as they walked by with their trays for the noon meal. After that one lump there would be no more, not until the next day. When Nikolai commented on the scarcity, Tatyana replied that she would explain her own curiosity on the subject, but she would like to do so speaking in English, and he was to correct any mistake she made. "Are you ready?"

"I am ready."

Tatyana looked up with excitement and then closed her eyes in concentration. "It iss most bizarre because we have so very much sugar which Fidel Castro makes in hiss country and transports it to us because we transport to him in . . . in ex-change . . . our oil. So it iss most bizarre that we have not so much sugar ass the people would wish to have sugar." She opened her eyes. Her smile was triumphant, the expression beatific.

She paused. "Was that pretty . . . okay?"

Nikolai told her that it was very, very good, that he had absolutely no doubt whatever that in five years she would be as fluent as Yevtushenko. True, the English and the Americans had certain . . . idiomatic ways of saying things, as she of course knew, but these would soon come to her automatically, he had no doubt, and before too long he would feel absolutely confident, if one day he were sick or whatever, turning his advanced class in English over to her to coach.

She looked at him adoringly. She closed her eyes again just slightly, this time to reach over—the only mark of reticence he had ever spotted in her—and place her right hand in his. He felt the pressure, and returned it. And felt suddenly a wave of feeling he had experienced only in a few isolated moments in his busy young life, years during which he nursed only the one abiding passion, unrelated to what he felt now. They both recognized at this moment that they were heading, inevitably, toward the consummation of a passion new to both of them. It would have to happen—when it could not be denied.

He allowed himself to analyze it. Nikolai Trimov, he did not mind admitting to himself, was as self-disciplined a young man as anyone he had ever known: self-disciplined at Brovary, at Kiev, in the army. Nothing was allowed to distract him from the evolution of his mandate, one whose meaning he had spent his young lifetime struggling fully to discern. All those years spent in internalizing a compulsion seeded when he was fourteen years old, a compulsion he had fondled so diligently, if speculatively, through the fairy-tale, magic-dragon phase (I will wave my magic wand and the bad men will crumble to ashes!), on to the David and Goliath phase on which he was now embarked. A passion that had crystallized into high resolution on the evening—March 24, 1985—when he saw the news documentary depicting the head of the Soviet state declare his wholehearted commitment to fight on in the holy war against the people of Afghanistan in the name of *communism* . . .

She sensed his distraction and reverted to English: "Is Nikolai unhappiest?"

He woke quickly from the trance. "'Is Nikolai *unhappy?*' Tatyana. That is all you need to say. 'Unhappiest,'" he explained in Russian, "is the superlative form."

She put on the facial contortion she had trained herself to exhibit when one of her students flagrantly misspoke an English passage. "Iss Nikolai on-heppee with Tatyana?"

He renewed the pressure on her hand and said in English, "No, Nikolai is not unhappy with Tatyana. Nikolai loves Tatyana very much. Do you think you can remember that phrase in English? It will take us very far."

Yes, she said, she would commit the words to memory.

CHAPTER 11

● SEPTEMBER 1985

THE SCHOOL CLOCK RANG at three, signaling the end of the class hour. The bell was especially welcome when fall was moving in, with its exhilarating cool, and only just a hint of the winter ahead. Viktor Pletnev, short, slender, direct, his eyes light blue and reflective, hurriedly told the students to read the next two chapters in the text in preparation for class on Wednesday. He then sped down to the faculty room to pick up his fortnightly paycheck and any reading matter placed in his open wooden mailbox.

There was a message for him. Professor Shalamov, the chairman of the history department at the university, had called. Pletnev was to report to him as soon as possible.

As he embarked on the long metro ride carrying him to the opposite end of Moscow from where he lived with his parents, Pletnev wondered what Shalamov, the grand martinet, wanted to see him about. It was not grossly inconvenient to go to him now—Viktor would have traveled to the university in any event for his regular night classes, but not until 7 p.m. Now he would have to while away the time between his meeting with the department chairman and the start of his own classes. It did mean that he would need to pay for his own supper instead of taking it at his mother's table. Well, he had his fresh paycheck.

He did not look forward to his session with the department chairman. Shalamov was a bloated, baby-faced zealot given to ideological pettifoggery. From time to time he would descend on one of the dozen professors who served under him and catechize him on historical rectitude, as defined the day before by the official press of the Union of Soviet Socialist Republics. He was drawn to do this by random reading in the papers of the graduate students, whom he would also chastise.

And yes, it transpired that Viktor was today's aberrant. Chairman Shalamov had asked to see papers done for the history class devoted to the events of 1917, beginning with the abdication of the Czar and going to the arrival of Lenin at the Finland Station in what was then Petrograd. Shalamov was clutching Pletnev's paper, and his disfavor was choleric. Pletnev had written that Trotsky's surreptitious help had been indispensable in arranging safe passage for Lenin through Germany. Now Shalamov was screaming that Trotsky had only *pretended* to be cooperative, that in fact he had all along been secretly scheming to take power from Lenin for himself, resulting—as of course everybody now knew—in his exposure and subsequent exile, and, ultimately, in his assassination, in Mexico, by a valiant Bolshevik who, to be sure, was operating on his own initiative.

When Shalamov engaged in such exorcisms there was nothing for the errant student to do except to wait, standing, until dismissed. Shalamov did not pause to ask where Pletnev had got his historical misimpression. He disdained to acknowledge that a perverted version of history, contradicting the correct version, was anywhere extant. It was manifestly a parthenogenic creation of the diseased imagination of the delinquent student.

After a half hour or so, it was over. Pletnev was told to go back to work.

He walked across the campus listlessly, moving inertially in the direction of the library, where he might use an hour or two before dinner. He seethed with contempt for Shalamov, in fact for the whole wretched university. He'd have loved to rise from his chair and tell the chairman that he, Shalamov, was a disgrace to the historical discipline, a contemptible courtier to the whims of Kremlin intrigue—Viktor stopped in mid-campus and added aloud to his platonic tirade, *"And on top of everything else, Shalamov, you are a corpulent visual mess and I would be ever so grateful, as would everyone you encounter, if from now on you would wear a face mask."* Viktor broke out in the special laughter of retributive satisfaction, and suddenly felt much better.

Needless to say, he would suppress his feelings, as he had so many times done against the entire communist fraternity, of which Shalamov was only one, noisome example. What mattered most, he knew, was to get his advanced degree. And then.

And then! Perhaps and then, one glorious day, to travel. If ever he found himself outside the borders of the Soviet Union, Viktor knew he would never come back.

He passed through the main entrance to the library, intending to spend an hour in the periodical room, when suddenly he thought to pause to see whether the Chambers book Trimov had called for had been returned by the faculty member who had taken it out. He went to the card catalogue in the foreign books section and presented the request card to the clerk at the desk.

In a few minutes he was handed the volume. He took it to a desk and opened it at the back to trace its recent movements. The card attached to the back cover listed the dates on which the book had been consulted by a student and the dates on which faculty had withdrawn the book from the library. To his surprise there was no notation of the book's recent withdrawal by faculty from the premises. And it had been called down for examination in the library only once during the month of September. He read the librarian's notation: "Sept 21 '85, N. Trimov."

Pletnev was perplexed. Nikolai had told him the book had been absent from the library and for that reason he hadn't been able to examine it. Pletnev had been lied to. What could have been Nikolai's motive?

THE NEXT day, at the tea break in midmorning, he accosted Nikolai. "You are going to look again next Sunday for the book by Chambers?"

"Yes, yes, Viktor."

"It was not at the library when you went there last Sunday?"

"I already told you, Viktor. No, it wasn't there. A faculty member had removed it."

Viktor Pletnev sipped his tea. After a moment he said to Nikolai, "It is very kind of you to take the trouble."

"I am glad to do so. I am told Chambers was an interesting man."

"Yes," Viktor said. "He was very interesting. He wrote a book which prompted many people to anti-Communist thinking."

Nikolai was silent.

"His book, *Witness,* is very moving."

"Is he still alive?" Nikolai thought it tactically wise to feign ignorance.

"Alive! He died"—Viktor quickly calculated it—"twenty-four years ago. In 1961."

"If he was so ardent an anti-Communist, how is it that we have such easy access to his book?"

Viktor opened his mouth wide, thought better of it, and asked Nikolai to lunch with him after the late morning classes, which now impended.

Two hours later, seated with their vegetables, potatoes, and soup, Viktor started in. "Nikolai, on the matter you raised this morning, your surprise that critical books are to be found in the library. You must know that, with very few exceptions, a student could always get such books. Periodicals, no. But it's also true that things are a little bit different now, you know. The glasnost of Gorbachev is not entirely meaningless."

"I saw what he did to Sakharov when Sakharov protested the war in Afghanistan."

"Well, yes, I am hardly suggesting that Gorbachev is about to change the policies of the Soviet Union. But it is no longer simple suicide to ask a question or two, or to read more widely than we were permitted to do even a year ago. Sure, you have to follow the official line very strictly—you should have heard my department chairman chew me out just yesterday afternoon. But you have not been in Moscow very long, and perhaps in Kiev it is different, but we *can* talk, if we want to—to be sure, using sound judgment—about the war, about how misdirected it is."

Nikolai found himself uncomfortable even listening to such heresy. "As you may know, Viktor, my interests are exclusively in engineering and in languages. I have never—interested myself in political discussion."

"Well, I don't say that that isn't the safest course. It probably is. But at least you should know that, here and there, there are people like me, interested for instance in the historical role of the Narodniki. They were, in case you are unaware of it, the true purists of the revolution. They wished to protest against tyranny, not to be catalysts of a fresh tyranny."

Nikolai rose. "I'm sorry, Viktor. I don't want to continue this discussion. My thoughts and concerns are on other matters."

Viktor, flushed, looked up at him. "Well, go ahead and concern yourself with whatever you like. But let me tell you this, Nikolai. The line Gorbachev is taking, in speech after speech—in connection with the disarmament talks, in connection with the summit conference with Reagan coming up—is simple, simple, simple. He wishes to arrest the American pursuit of a strategic defense, what they call 'Star Wars' in America. That is his line. *Don't involve the Soviet Union in another arms race.* We are bleeding in Russia, Nikolai, and the greatest lesion is in Afghanistan. I hardly need to tell *you* that we are losing the war in Afghanistan. And my bet is that Gorbachev will recognize this before too long for one simple reason. He has no alternative."

"Viktor!" Nikolai shot up his hand, palm upstretched. "*You must not go on!*" He was breathing heavily, his complexion pale. "And I certainly won't repeat what you have said!" He walked away, leaving his lunch half eaten.

Viktor Pletnev, his spoon playing with his unconsumed soup, was deep in thought. His eyes followed his colleague. Nikolai's stride toward the entrance door was interrupted by Tatyana, seated with a companion woman teacher. Nikolai resisted, but was constrained to sit down with them.

Pletnev resolved to attempt to probe deeply into the character of his colleague, the slim young man with the arresting face and the reputation as a scholarly polymath. Nikolai did not know that Whittaker Chambers was dead? But the book Nikolai had withdrawn from the library last Sunday carried the date of Chambers's death on the first page.

CHAPTER 12

● SEPTEMBER 1985

O N THE FOLLOWING MONDAY, Nikolai approached Viktor at the morning break, told him that he had got hold of the Chambers book, had found the passage on the Narodniki, and translated it. He handed him the sheets.

"That is most awfully kind of you, Nikolai. I shall look for an opportunity to return the favor. Did you find the passage interesting? I am anxious to read it."

"Yes," Nikolai said noncommittally. "It was very interesting. As you will see, it provides a very . . . passionate view of the Narodniki."

Viktor stretched out his arm and touched Nikolai's shoulder, a gesture of thanks, and sat down at one of the tables to read. Nikolai left the room.

At three, after classes were finished, Nikolai walked hand in hand with Tatyana, speaking to her in English. They would have time to promenade only once around the block because she had an appointment. There was the nip of autumn in the air and, coatless, Nikolai was glad to reach the shelter of the metro. He would go directly home. He did not need to pause at the library for more books—he had three in his apartment, including a little-used book on the structural work done on the Kremlin when the decision was made in 1901 to electrify the palace. He would devote himself to further study on the morphology of the Kremlin and then share his findings with Andrei when he came in at six from his police work. He took out his key, opened the door to apartment 6K, turned the tap for some water to boil, and was startled to hear a knock on the door. He looked rapidly about him to make sure there was nothing sitting in the room that should be concealed. Of course there wasn't. He opened the door to Viktor Pletnev.

Viktor did not give Nikolai an opportunity to be inhospitable. He walked in directly, his tattered briefcase in one hand, a paper parcel in the other. He closed the door behind himself. "I need to talk to you."

"Very well, Viktor. Sit down. A cup of tea?"

"Yes. And," he struggled with the package, "I have something for you, a little gift to thank you for the trouble you took." He took from the bag six bananas and a box of dried figs.

"You didn't have to do that, Viktor, but thank you. Sit down."

"Nikolai, I discovered quite by accident that you . . . deceived me. You had already seen the book last week. Your name was on the card." Viktor continued talking without pause. He did not want to prolong the humiliation. "My purpose is to tell you that I was enormously moved by the information you brought me about the Narodniki. And to tell you something more, Nikolai, which is that I flatly disbelieve what you say, that you are not interested in the political cauldron we live in. I know you are some sort of an academic star, that you have mastered several languages and electrical engineering, and that you fought bravely in Afghanistan. But I know also that our country needs help and I believe that in your heart you know that it needs help and that in reading the book by Chambers you were reaching to feel the purity of the experience of a liberated man.

"I could *feel* it in the paragraphs you gave me, the way you set down the words, not the translation of an engineer unmoved by what the words said. Even with my poor English, I shall now return to the library and read more in that book, even as I read all of *Witness,* although it took me almost one month. I am here, Nikolai, to plead with you to join me and two other young people devoted to a freer Russia, a man and a woman, brother and sister. Our goal is the liberation of our motherland—I say it dramatically, and although I know that you are very circumspect, I know also that you know I am not an agent, attempting to snare you. I know that you trust me."

Nikolai was rescued by the hissing teapot. He needed desperately to think. To talk with Andrei. To his surprise, he was not in the least frightened. He absolutely believed in the sincerity of Viktor, who sat there, his brown hair falling over one of his eyes, both of which were half closed, staring at the moldy carpet on the floor, waiting for a reaction.

He was not scared but neither was he prepared to induct Viktor on the spot into the New Narodniki, in which only he and Andrei were members, sworn to give their lives to advance liberty. He poured the tea. He had to say something. What he said was, "What do you propose to do?"

Viktor was enormously heartened. With that simple statement, Nikolai had dropped his pose. He had jettisoned the unbecoming masquerade that he was indifferent to the atrocities of the world they lived in and unwilling to speak of them. Viktor felt that he needed to reward Nikolai's act of faith in him. He would do so by communicating his most sacred, most incriminating secret.

"You should know," he said, "I am in touch with American intelligence."

Nikolai responded quickly: "I am not sure it is wise for you to give me the details."

"I won't. Those are the basic rules of my business. But what I am telling you is that any information I—we—wish to pass on to Washington, to the CIA—I can do that. In fact I have already tested it out."

"What on earth could you know, teaching history and studying at the graduate school, that Washington would want to know?"

"There are always, *always*, opportunities. I will be concrete. On March 8th, Aaron Sablin—you know Sablin? He teaches physics at Pitkin, and attends, like us, the graduate school—he invited me to his house for dinner. I went and the food was very good. His father lives well. He is a widower and a medical doctor. He had several vodkas, and I had several. The subject came up of the health of Chernenko. All of Moscow was talking about the health of Chernenko after his public appearance in January, you remember. No, you were away, in the army.

"Anyway, I said, quite matter-of-factly, that from all appearances one would not suppose that Chernenko would last out the year—this was early in March. Dr. Sablin turned to me and said, 'Viktor, he will not last out the month.' Aaron looked in my direction and, when his father was not noticing, gave me a wink. Later we went to a bar and he confided to me that his father was a specialist who had been called in to the Kremlin and regularly treated Chernenko."

"What did you do with that information?"

"I gave it the very next day to my contact."

"You know that it got to Washington?"

"I know the ma—person I deal with. If he had been an agent he'd have turned me in long ago."

"How many people do you suppose your contact has reporting to him?"

"I haven't the least idea. And maybe the information about Chernenko is entirely trivial compared to the information he comes up with himself, or gets from other sources. He is very well placed. And he has been secure for many years. In the post-Beria purge he was sent to Gulag, but after a few months he was released and given back his old job. A few years before that he was sent on a six-month mission to Indonesia. When he returned he could find no trace of his brother or of his aged mother."

"Stalin—"

"Yes, it was in the last days of Stalin. Perhaps one million—no, more—disappeared in the same way. Just no trace of them."

"Does your friend have any . . . more ambitious plans?"

"If he does, he wouldn't tell me. He wants to live to see our country free."

"I fear he will have to live a very long time."

"My friend is already old, but he is healthy."

Nikolai stood up and walked the two or three paces one could move in the room without having to turn around. "What, other than to communicate anything to your contact that would be useful to the other side, do you plan to do?"

"I don't know. I must do something. And it is less fruitful to work alone. I told you, there are three of us who meet with great caution. Again, you do not need to know who they are. But they trust me, and I trust them. Consider just a little thing: I shall make out of the passages you just finished giving me— Chambers on the Narodniki—a *samizdat,* and in less than one month those few paragraphs on the Narodniki will have had an impact on hundreds, maybe thousands of students. Imagine how the next issue of a newspaper would sell if it carried *just those three paragraphs!*"

Nikolai looked down at his army-issue watch. "Viktor, I need to think. And you need to think. And we must take every precaution. We must not, while at Pitkin, be seen together more than casually. And Viktor . . ."

"Yes?"

"When I next approach you, I will have proposals for regular meetings, and you can make your own proposals to me. It will be a very long time before we can—well, act decisively. We must be patient, but also inventive."

Nikolai felt the special intensity of the grip of Viktor's handshake.

CHAPTER 13

● SEPTEMBER 1985

Blackford Oakes reached CIA headquarters in Langley, Virginia, just after eight. At the same time, Director William Casey drove in, secure in his secure limousine, an armed guard sitting in the front seat beside the driver, the windows bulletproof, the route taken from his dwelling circuitous. It infuriated the Director to submit to the same disciplines he rigidly enforced on others, such were his carefree ways.

He had been around a long time; his associates were used to him, they liked and respected him, and they knew that his intimacy with the President guaranteed his tenure as Director. As Deputy Director for Operations, Blackford was indispensable to Casey, in big ways and little ways. There was, for instance, the Director's incapacity to handle any mechanical object invented after the wheelbarrow. He had mastered the use of the telephone, and it was rumored that while at college he typed his own papers, but no one alive, as far as Blackford knew, had seen Casey handle any mechanical or electronic gadget more complicated than a radio, and sometimes he wrestled with the doorknob, having forgotten that it needed to be turned clockwise in order to function. Blackford regularly opened the Director's safe for him.

It amused Blackford to think of Casey's wrestling with a computer and doing such things as inserting codes and commands and chasing the cursor this way and that. Casey communicated in writing, done by dictation to his secretary, or else orally, imposing a major strain on the listener—Casey spoke indistinctly, requiring of the addressee a kind of onomatopoetic facility to understand what it was the Director was saying. President Reagan's wise-crack about Casey, that Casey actually contrived his unintelligi-bility—"That way, whoever he is talking to simply agrees from sheer fatigue with whatever he has said"—was widely circulated.

Blackford got on well with the Director, and vice versa. Casey respected the field experience of his chief of covert opera-tions, who had been (to be sure, with not uninteresting interrup-tions) with the Agency ever since graduating from college in 1951. There were many rumors about Blackford's first tour of duty in England, the details of which were known to only one man, the Director learned on coming into office, the legendary Rufus. And Casey knew that around Blackford Oakes a quiet cult, mostly made up of retired agents, thrived. Oakes never en-couraged it, never spoke about his background or his work.

Stepping out of his car, Casey greeted Blackford. "Black, you got any input for the session on Soviet investment in their strategic defense operation?"

"I'm up on it," Blackford replied. "If the figures you get from our analysts are way off, I'll tell you."

"That's what the President most wants to shove at Gor-bachev in Geneva."

"Yes. I'd have guessed that." The two men walked into the main entrance and went separately to their offices before con-vening for the 9 a.m. senior staff session, which focused prima-rily on arming the President with arguments to use in defense of his Star Wars program.

The Deputy Director reported the Agency's estimate that the Soviets were currently spending "over twenty-five billion dollars" in developing their own strategic defense, hardly consistent with their disparagement of the U.S. effort. Casey looked over at Black-ford, who nodded his head slightly: the figure was right. "Okay," Casey said, "and that's a nice round figure. The President will like that much of it." He got up. "See you around," he said to his five primary assistants. He signaled Blackford to stay on.

"How is it going with the Stingers?"

The Pakistanis had received a threat from Gorbachev, delivered through his ambassador in Karachi: If Pakistan's General Zia didn't stop conveying U.S. Stingers to the Afghan rebels, the Soviet government would devise a "suitable means of retaliation."

"We've set up an alternative delivery route, in case Zia gets cold feet, which I doubt he'll get."

Casey nodded. "He told State he wanted indemnifications."

"He's had those."

"*Arhhreuh!*"

Blackford had got used to the emunctory sounds distinctive to the Director. The consensus was that the sound he had just now emitted meant: "You're-goddamn-right."

Blackford said, "I think the last time around we promised to give Zia Detroit. Or was it Illinois?"

"He can have New York, far as I'm concerned," Casey nodded. Blackford left the room and went to his own office.

He then undertook his Monday morning ritual. He went to the computer and wrote into it his personal code. He painstakingly tapped in a second code he had committed to memory five years ago. The technician who had written it into the telecomputer had kept no record of the operation. The key to opening the line of communication rested exclusively in Blackford's memory.

It was still gripping to recall, even after almost five years, the corner of the little café in Paris where the startling arrangements had been made. The Soviet's terms were explicit. Blackford Oakes, and only Blackford, would cue in to receive information. He would do this unfailingly once every week. The communications link, to fortify security, would be only one-way: Cyclops could relay information to Oakes. Oakes could not communicate with Cyclops, except through an emergency procedure in Moscow, which, if used, might jeopardize the continuation of the contact. It was not, for that reason, an ideal arrangement.

But during the fifty-eight months that had gone by, much vital information had come in. And none of it had proved deceptive.

Cyclops was a laconic communicator. He did not use more words than he needed to use. But, experienced as he was, Cyclops knew how many words Blackford would need in order to put the information to use. Blackford was never shortchanged.

Sometimes two weeks would go by with the screen entirely blank. But Cyclops would never let a third week go by. To do so might give the impression that he had been detected. If there was nothing on week number three to report, the screen would ring in merely the one word: "Okay." Blackford had had an Okay the preceding week. It had been three weeks since Cyclops reported that an extra one hundred Soviet scientists had been diverted to Krasnoyarsk, to augment the force at work on a defense shield.

Blackford completed the coding and stared now at the screen. He could feel his heart beating. He reached over to the desk and grabbed a legal pad. He wrote down the exact message from Cyclops. Word for word. He then closed the circuit, electronically blocking it, and went to his desk chair. He tore off the top sheet of paper, brought out his scissors from the desk drawer, cut the sheet of paper in half, discarded the blank bottom, then folded and refolded the top half. He pulled out his wallet and stuck the paper between the bills. He thought deeply for a full half hour, and then dialed dear, reliable Kathy in the White House. Fifteen minutes later his private line rang. Kathy. The meeting was set: 5:45, and yes, the President agreed that no one else would be in the Oval Office, just the two of them.

RONALD REAGAN had worked closely with Blackford, most recently on the Grenada operation. He liked Blackford's directness, and his capacity to laugh, spontaneously and easily. He knew that Blackford had himself engaged over the years in covert activities, some of high importance. And he knew that several of his commissions had been directly supervised by John F. Kennedy and, later, by Lyndon Johnson.

He had been told that Oakes quit the Agency in 1964, protesting Executive ambivalence over the Vietnam war. This identification mark greatly appealed to Reagan, who during the Vietnam years had assailed the Democratic administration for failure to define a coherent policy. "It would have made a very bad movie script," he once said to Blackford as they waited in the Situation Room for news that the marines had landed in Grenada. "You can't do what we did. LBJ managed to betray both our allies in Vietnam and our soldiers in the field."

Reagan had paused. "Well, 'betray' is a pretty tough word. Managed to let them down. That sounds more presidential, doesn't it, Blackford?" The President smiled.

Blackford said yes, it sounded more presidential and "less like Ronald Reagan." Reagan liked that, and a few weeks later Blackford and Sally were invited to dine with the Reagans and the Caseys in the private apartments.

As he approached the Oval Office, Blackford thought back on his first visit there, led to President Kennedy by his brother the Attorney General. He took a republican pride in the room's modest dimensions. Five White Houses, someone had observed, would fit inside the Czar's Winter Palace. But it was perhaps exactly that, its modesty, that gave it its unique emanations. Blackford was never really ill at ease, but he was not insensitive to the magnetic pull of supreme authority. He was now in one of two rooms in the world from which instructions could be issued to launch a nuclear strike.

The President was seated, wearing a dark blue suit with the traditional white of a handkerchief showing above his breast pocket. He was reading a document that lay on his desk. He motioned Blackford to the chair at his side.

"Did I tell you about the scene in this room just after LBJ won his landslide in 1964?" the President asked. Blackford shook his head, No. "Well, it was the day after, and his visitors were Elizabeth Taylor and Richard Burton. And Lyndon leaned back like this"—the President leaned back exaggeratedly in his desk chair—"and said, 'Just think! Between the three of us, we've probably screwed the majority of the American people!'"

Blackford laughed. In fact he *had* heard it. It was funny all the same, and Reagan knew how to tell it. There was just a hint of a Texas accent when he imitated Johnson.

Reagan turned to him. "You got something?"

Blackford nodded. He reached for his wallet. "I have to tell you something first, Mr. President. This agent I'm going to quote to you works exclusively through me. He won't authorize *anyone* else to know his identity or read his messages, and he's been giving us valuable information, none of it ever proved wrong, for almost five years."

Reagan nodded.

Blackford unfolded the paper. "Here is exactly what it says: 'Blackford: I link with a small band of skillful determined young Russians who plan the assassination of M.G. No date set. If you instruct me to turn them in, use emergency access. I know and respect them and will give them over to torture and execution only if requested by President of the United States in cause of international peace. I trust you to share this information with him exclusively. Cyclops.'"

"Oh my goodness!" said the President. "Oh my . . . Oh my goodness . . ."

He looked up at Blackford. "You say I cannot consult anyone about this? Oh my." The President paused. "Let me ask you this. You are head of covert operations. Are you absolutely certain that there is no American involved in this operation to get Gorbachev?"

"I'm certain that nobody working for us is involved. I mean, no *American* working for us. It's entirely possible that one of our assets in Moscow is involved, but if so, it is not with our knowledge, let alone consent."

"You would be the final authority in knowing this?"

Blackford told him that no covert operation was undertaken without his knowledge of it. "Or, for that matter, your knowledge, Mr. President."

"Yes, yes. Gee whiz. This is a tough one."

Then suddenly, "You know, Blackford, you gave your word." He smiled. "I didn't give mine."

"No. But I did tell him he could trust me. Still, I can see your point, Mr. President. I myself would have to refuse to talk to anyone about Cyclops's message—for instance, I couldn't even tell Bill Casey about it, because that is our, well, sacred understanding. But I can't bind you."

"No," the President was talking to himself now. His voice was low, his head turned toward the center of his desk, his right hand gripping a pencil and scratching aimlessly on a notepad.

"No, you can't, that's right. This is a hell of a situation. I mean—I mean, we're not involved in any way, that's vital. But is it *our* responsibility to protect a foreign tyrant from his own people? Is that a diplomatic obligation? . . . Maybe if the foreign tyrant was an ally? But we're hardly talking about an ally, and it's a country that's waging aggressive war against Afghanistan, spending twenty-five percent of its GNP to threaten the free world. No, not an ally, for Pete's sake."

He looked up at Blackford. "Well, if I'm not supposed to consult anybody else, I am still free to consult you, aren't I? What do *you* think?"

"Mr. President, to quote you, that's a hell of a situation, me being the only person whose opinion reaches you."

The President's reply was suddenly sharp. *"I am asking you your opinion."*

"It would be to leave the matter alone."

The President sighed. He said nothing for a full minute. And then, the bounce of only a half hour earlier completely gone, "I'll get in touch with you tomorrow. Good night, Blackford."

"Good night, Mr. President."

The President was not in touch, the next day, with Blackford.

And Blackford did not use the emergency access procedure to be in touch with Cyclops.

CHAPTER 14

No. He shook his head at the steward, "No more, thanks." He took a cursory bite of the remaining apple pie but then put down his fork and dipped his finger into the teacup, lifting it out quickly—it was too hot. He remembered that Tip O'Neill had told him something he had got from Frank Sinatra. He liked to demonstrate it to friends and visitors, but at this moment he was quite alone in the master cabin. So he would content himself to demonstrate it yet again to himself. He lifted the same cup of tea, its temperature too hot for his finger, and put it up to his lips, sipped, and swallowed. The throat tissues did not flinch. There. That was the whole point—that whereas it is natural to suppose that your mouth and throat are infinitely more sensitive than your hardened index finger, the reverse is true!

He should have demonstrated to Gorbachev. How to stay out of hot water! Next time, maybe.

Next time! Ah yes. Now there would be not only one next time, but *two* next times! Old George Shultz had said to him in Washington that never mind the missiles, never mind the missile

99

testing, never mind the Star Wars, if we could get Gorbachev to agree to another summit, *this* summit would be a success. Well, Gorbachev had agreed not only to a second summit, but to a *third* summit.

Some things are really that simple and you don't need a staff of two hundred people to set them up for you. I said to him, Let's just you and me—and the interpreters, of course—I don't much like his interpreter. He tries too hard to convey the *feeling* of Gorbachev's words. He overdoes it. He could use a little time in pictures. Because Gorbachev says something in a loud tone of voice doesn't mean the *interprete*r has to yell his head off when he interprets it. I don't suppose I can do anything about that. Might start a war. (He smiled. And then he was solemn again.) Two more meetings with Gorbachev, one in Washington, one in Moscow.

Provided Gorbachev is alive.

Oh, I have prayed for guidance on this one. And I keep saying to myself, *"Sic semper tyrannis,"* maybe the only three words of Latin I still remember—no, I remember *"Semper fidelis."* Anyway, if ever there was a tyranny, that's the history of the Soviet Union. And Gorbachev, even if he is willing to come and talk to me in Washington and willing for me to go to Moscow to talk to him, what is he doing in concrete terms about that tyranny?

He picked up a clipping on the table, an article by Richard Pipes. Professor of Sovietology at Harvard. Former head of the Soviet desk in his own National Security office! And what had Dick written? "There is nothing that the Soviet government and Gorbachev have done to change its policies in any fundamental way. They are still arming at a pace that is frightening—both conventional and nuclear forces—they are still in Afghanistan, they are still doing all the things they have done until now. They are still arousing hatred against America inside the country. So I really don't see why one should believe that anything has changed."

It was fine of Gorbachev to grandstand in October about how he would cut one third of his force of SS-20s. And how many's he got? Two hundred and something SS-20s—Bud Mc-Farlane always uses exact numbers, drives me crazy. I could remember 225, 250, 275, but it isn't easy to remember something like 243. Marlene Dietrich tells a wonderful story about Hitler. Hitler didn't have any idea about numbers, what was the *important* number, what was the *less important* number. So in one of his speeches, Marlene said—I wish I could imitate her imitating Hitler—he said, "And what is mohrrr, the Churman steel industree has increased its production in chust one year from forty million five huntred and sixty thousand tons, to eighty million five huntred and SEVENTY-FIVE TONS!" Funny. So anyway, in the first place we don't know whether Yes, Gorby will reduce his theater weapons, or No, Gorby won't reduce them. But if he does, that means he is . . . well, down to about 150 SS-20s. Enough to take out every city in Europe bigger than Stratford-on-Avon. Big deal.

But Shultz is right, Gorby *has* moved. Up until this summer he refused to have any more disarmament conferences unless we removed our Pershings and cruise missiles from Europe. The sheer *nerve* of those people! And then what he keeps calling our "space weapons," and how they are designed for aggressive use, and I say to him, Look, you've got a lot of weapons that are designed for aggressive use, and you're engaged in an act of aggression right now in Afghanistan—

And he says they are *not* designed for aggressive use, so I say, Look, how, just *how,* can I ask the American people to believe *me* when I tell them that *you* won't believe *me* that our strategic defense is just for defense, but I am supposed to believe *you* when you say that all *your* . . . nuclear weapons—I'd have said exactly how many he has, except I always forget— are purely defensive? That awful interpreter shouted out Gorby's response, but I think he got my point, because he didn't say it again.

But I mean, if there ever *was* a tyrant, continuing their killing way, he certainly is one, and if there is a movement of citizens in that tyranny to do away with that tyrant—yes, execute him, which according to Oakes is what that little group plans—why should *I* do something about it? It would be different if beginning next month, on the first day of every month, Gorbachev promised to institute one of our freedoms in the Bill of Rights, one after another. Let me see, that means, beginning in December—one, two, three . . .—by September they'd have the Tenth Amendment. Forget it, we don't observe the Tenth Amendment, so we shouldn't make him do it. By August, the Soviet Union would be a nation of free people. But the point is he has no program that edges away from that tyranny, and though I kind of . . . like the guy, it just isn't any of my business to provide him with bodyguards against his own people.

There. I said that the right way. *It's not my business to provide him with bodyguards against his own people.* Suppose the people who tried to kill Hitler had started their operation before the war with England broke out and suppose that somebody went to Churchill and said, Look we've found out about a small band of resisters who are plotting to kill Hitler. Would he have done anything about it? Exactly. *Exactly.* I remember in *Man Hunt* when Walter Pidgeon had Hitler at his mountain hideout right in the crosshairs of his rifle—my heavens, how we all wish he had squeezed that trigger! Turn in Walter Pidgeon because he intended to shoot Hitler? That's *crazy!*

He had made up his mind. He pushed the buzzer. Instantly a steward materialized. "I think I'll try to get a little rest."

"I'll get your bed prepared, Mr. President."

"Thank you. Thank you very much.' The President picked up the *International Herald Tribune* and read about the conference he had just left.

CHAPTER 15

● SEPTEMBER 1986

NIKOLAI WAS SURPRISED BY the letter from the Ministry of Electrotechnical Industry and Equipment. Evidently such computers as were in use in Moscow had resolved that Nikolai Trimov, with his graduate degree in electrical engineering, would be more valuable to the People exercising his skills as an engineer than teaching English to teenagers. Effective September 8, he was to report to the deputy assistant of the MEIE at 28 Ogarova Street at 9 a.m. No word was given on the matter of a replacement. "Well," he said to Andrei as they prepared to view what passed for the television news, "I guess I'll just have to tell old Landau that he has to come up with another teacher."

"Is Tatyana up to taking on your classes?"

Nikolai smiled diffidently. "Actually, no. She's made strides, but she's got a way to go before she can handle third-year English. Last night she pronounced Trafalgar Square, *'tra-ffel ge-skware.'* You wouldn't get it in Russian, but it's funny in English." Nikolai's voice lowered now and he said, "I don't look forward to giving her the news. And I don't look forward to working every day in different quarters."

He thought for a moment. "Andrei, do you have your usual Thursday night date tomorrow?"

"Of course. I would not miss it. I would have that date with my little rosebud on Mondays Tuesdays Wednesdays and Fridays too if I were a little wealthier. If I were a lot wealthier. And scaring up those one-dollar bills becomes more and more difficult. It is a good thing I have my . . . contacts. Why do you ask?"

Nikolai was horrified to feel the blush on his cheeks. He looked down. "I thought to invite Tatyana to have dinner with me. Here."

"Oh ho! My little virgin Narodnik! The next thing we know we will have you drinking a little vodka! Well, you make yourself at home. I promise I will not return until after midnight. Do you need any practical advice?"

"Oh shut up, Andrei. But . . . thanks." He changed the subject. "There is the question of Viktor, of course."

"Will you be seeing Viktor?"

"Yes. We'll need to arrange other means of communicating, since I won't be at Pitkin every day. I have some ideas on that front. Evidently Gorbachev got on fairly well with Reagan at Geneva. He made the usual speeches about the American strategic defense—'space weapons,' he calls it—but Reagan was firm. But now they're having trouble scheduling a second summit. And the war in Afghanistan goes on. Seventeen months after Gorbachev came to power. The English radio puts at over one million the Afghan casualties, and more than ten thousand Russians dead, three times as many wounded. Have you decided finally about Pavel?"

"Yes, I have. But the time has come for you to meet him. In my judgment he belongs with us, with the Narodniki. And although I am formally his physical education teacher in the police academy, he studied karate independently and is formidable. When his training is finished he will begin work as a police sergeant because of the seniority he earned in the army."

"When does he graduate?"

"Next week. We have to hope that he is ordered to work somewhere in the vicinity of the Kremlin. Whether he is or is not, his contacts will be useful. But as I say, you must meet him. I have told him only that I share a room with a young veteran discharged on disability, and that you are very highbrow. Yes, that's how I put it: 'Nikolai is very highbrow. He knows everything about Pushkin, Shakespeare, Goethe, Dante—'"

"And the Narodniki."

"And the Narodniki. Okay to set up a meeting? Presumably," Andrei snickered, "not tomorrow."

"Yes, of course."

AT PITKIN after the first class-break, Nikolai showed up at the windowless office of the school director, having earlier made an appointment through his secretary. The most economical way to proceed was simply to show him the letter he had received the day before from the MEIE.

The director read it and sighed. "Typical. Absolutely typical. They remove a key member of my faculty without consulting me and with no mention of a replacement. And only yesterday"—he rummaged through a basket on his desk—"only yesterday I got this!" The director, reading the communication out loud, did a most remarkable imitation of Mikhail Gorbachev. "'*Notice to all school directors*. We are advised by the educational minister at the Kremlin that every effort must be made to interest more students in the study of the English language. You are authorized to grant extra credits for the study of English and the new budget will provide for extensive Russian–English additions to the teaching library done in cassettes.' Et cetera, et cetera, et cetera. Just fine. They don't tell you how, or who is going to *teach* English. Well, it is not your responsibility, Trimov."

"I am very sorry to leave you shorthanded at the beginning of the term, Comrade Landau. If you wish, after I am told what my schedule with the MEIE is, I can see if there are open hours during which I could come to you. Of course that would depend a little bit on how far away I am posted."

The director said he would be grateful for this, but that after a replacement was sent there would be no budget for him. They shook hands.

On the way to class Nikolai passed by Tatyana's classroom. The students were assembling, talking volubly. Her eyes brightened on seeing Nikolai. She got up from her desk, and Nikolai noticed that she was wearing a flower on her lapel. He commented in a whisper on how attractive it was, and how attractive she was. She smiled. And then said in English, "Are we going to lunch today you with me?" Yes, said Nikolai. He had some important news for her. She frowned. "Bad important or good important?"

"Both," said Nikolai. "See you at the cafeteria at twelve-fifteen."

When he gave her the news he saw tears spring to her eyes, and Nikolai was sharply reminded how expressive were her features. Her whole face was a wailing wall. He consoled her by saying he might be able to come to Pitkin and teach part-time. "And in any case, of course we will see each other frequently. And that brings me to ask you, Can you have dinner with me tonight? At my apartment?"

"With your roommate?"

"No, he will not be there tonight."

"I shall have to check with my mother."

"Would she raise any objection?"

"She would not want me to go alone to your apartment." Tatyana smiled. "I will tell her I am going to a faculty function. Don't worry. Just jot down," she handed him a used envelope, "the exact address and the stop. What shall I wear?"

"Nothing. I mean, anything." Nikolai was cross with himself for the levity. He wondered if she had noticed. He suspected that she had.

"I have discovered something very beautiful, and I want to share it with you." She reached into her bulky handbag and pulled out a slim volume. She spoke now in English. "These are poems by Edgaar Allan Po-ey."

"Edgar Allan POH," he corrected automatically.

"You know them?"

"I know some of them by memory."

"Recite one for me."

"Tonight. It is late. It is class time."

THROUGH HIS wide reading Nikolai had experienced many seductions. But never a seduction done by a virgin, though he had to suppose that these were common. Andrei had told him that he had been seduced when he was fifteen—by his teacher. "She was at least thirty years old. But she approached my ignorance exactly as she approached it when teaching me geometry. Her emphasis was on repetition." He had smiled.

Two things Nikolai must not do, he thought: hurt her, or impregnate her. Simple enough to take precautions against the latter. On the other, he was less certain. He would need to control the lust that had raged in him ever since, two days earlier, they had sat together at the movies and, in the dark, Tatyana had allowed Nikolai's hand to explore. He felt an urge he had a difficult time in controlling and when they left the movie house they were both silent. After he kissed her good night, he whispered, "Soon?"

She had answered, "When you say so."

They had both taken to sipping a little wine, and for this special night he had singled out a bottle of Tsinandali, a common dry white wine from Georgia he knew to be popular with the students at Kiev. It was available at the state liquor store, barren now of vodka ever since Gorbachev had launched his anti-alcohol campaign. The wine cost three rubles, a day's wages. He would let it freshen on the windowsill of number 6K. In the metro he found his mind blurring as he approached the Kievskaya stop, a few blocks from Kutuzovsky Prospekt. He gasped as, angling the bottle on the window of his apartment, he very nearly let it tip over the edge of the sill. He tied a piece of string around the bottle's neck and closed the window over the end of the string that protruded into the room.

There now, the wine was safe. But as the fever mounted in his loins he calculated that he could not risk waiting alone the

entire hour before she would arrive. He went down the stairs
and walked at a fast pace around the block twice. With only
twenty minutes left, he carefully sponged his body with water
heated in the tea kettle. He pulled up his cotton trousers, left his
undershorts in the drawer, and put on a clean shirt. He tried to
read, but the text was blurred. He blinked his eyes repeatedly
and then spoke the words aloud in a hoarse whisper:

> Why, such is love's transgression
> Griefs of mine own lie heavy in my breast,
> Which thou wilt propagate, to have it prest
> With more of thine: this love that thou hast shown
> Doth add more grief to too much of mine own.
> Love is a smoke raised with the fume of sighs;
> Being urged, a fire sparkling in lovers' eyes;
> Being vex'd, a sea nourish'd with lovers' tears:
> What is it else? A madness most discreet,
> A choking gall and a preserving sweet.

Tatyana arrived promptly. His radio brought in music, and
the apartment lights began to flicker in the compound. Nikolai
drew the curtains, first withdrawing the bottle of wine and filling two glasses. He told her how much he loved her. She began
to reply in English, but quickly abandoned it and said to Nikolai in Russian that she had never permitted herself to dream of
finding a . . . consort as intelligent as he, as well-mannered, as
wonderful to look at, as kind. Nikolai turned off the overhead
light, leaving only the two reading lights, by the couch and by
the bed. He kissed her deeply and soon was fondling her with
mounting urgency, easing her free of her blouse, and guiding
her hand. He nudged her across to the bed and carefully went
on with the disrobing. She gripped him by the neck and drew
him close, refusing to let him go. He whispered, "Let me,
Tanyusha, remove my shirt." He took it off, and then unbut-
toned and dropped his trousers and lifted himself onto the bed
beside her.

One hour later, as they lay wordlessly together, he found himself wondering for the first time since that night at Kandahār whether he was irreversibly pledged to give up his life, as the Narodniki had done, to pursue the dream they had in common. To give up a lifetime of what he now felt was possible with Tatyana? What madness. He probed and relished the thought of a hypothetical alternative—to slay the tyrant and to remain alive, alive to be with Tatyana for years and years.

"You are thinking things." He heard her voice, languorous but with a hint of gentle raillery, speaking English.

"I am thinking, Tatyana. You don't think *'things,'* you just *'think.'"*

"But," she persisted, "if you think, it has to be that there are things at the opposite end of your thoughts, no?"

Nikolai returned to Russian. "You are theoretically right. But in English, that's what they say, 'I am thinking,' and one supposes that that person is thinking about things that have to do with the conversation or with the activity he is engaging in."

Back to English: "Is the activity my Nikolai is engaging in quite . . . delicious?"

He leaned over and kissed her again, his ardor fully renewed.

CHAPTER 16

● SEPTEMBER 1986

THE GRADUATING CLASS IN which Pavel Pogodin, decorated veteran, karate expert, was prominent was given a week's vacation after the graduates received their diplomas from the police academy. Beginning on September 12, Pavel would report for duty to the 7th Precinct, north of the Bolshoi Theatre and the Kremlin. As a sergeant, he would be given a Lada, the standard-issue state automobile. With whatever subordinate was assigned as his assistant, he would go to whatever trouble spot Radio Control directed him to. When not on a headquarters-directed mission, he was to cruise up Dzerzhinskogo past the Turgenevskaya metro stop, turn left on Sadovaya-Sukharevskaya, and then toward headquarters down Neglinnaya Street until he arrived back at his starting point; and then continue as before. The loose square described to him was about four kilometers in length. It was just north of the Kremlin, from one of whose radio towers he would receive his signals. In normal traffic it took about ten minutes to complete the circle.

Pavel lived with his widowed mother in a large apartment building on Marshal Gretschko Prospekt, in an area reserved for first- and second-echelon diplomats, generals, and bureaucrats.

110

Iona Dorovsky had been a child bride in the last year of the war when she married the dashing three-star general who commanded the Soviet 16th Air Army, the bomber squadron charged with devastating the approaches to East Berlin in the bloody days of March and April 1945, during which Hitler committed twenty divisions in a futile attempt to save the capital. Informed by Radio Moscow that Hitler had committed suicide on the last day in April, General Pogodin resolved to celebrate the event by personally leading what would probably be the final Allied bombing raid on Berlin. This had been ordered by Stalin, finally to discourage the resistance, in anticipation of a formal surrender by General Jodl. General Pogodin's bomber was shot down by one of the surviving German fighter planes. He was seen by the pilots of two different Soviet planes to have ejected, his parachute to have opened up. He would have touched ground in the area of Poznan in Poland, a couple of hundred kilometers east of Berlin.

It was a full year before Iona Pogodin, only nineteen years old, would acknowledge any possibility that her glamorous thirty-six-year-old Grigori was dead. Moreover, it was convenient that he should continue to be listed as Missing in Action, inasmuch as she was therefore permitted to continue to live in the relatively luxurious apartment, the formal address of "General Grigori Pogodin." It had two bedrooms, a sitting room, a little dining room, and access to a private pocket-park reserved for residents of the building.

Pavel was born fifteen years after the war, when his mother was thirty-three. She was a woman of singular beauty, of great charm, beloved of her neighbors, whom she would spare no pains to accommodate, and entirely batty. Somewhere along the line, Pavel realized that other little boys had not only mothers but also fathers, and one day he raised the question at home. His mother drew her index finger to her lips and confided to Pavel that his father was the Czarevitch Alexis, who had escaped the slaughter of 1918 at Ekaterinburg and secretly married her—who produced him, Pavel, heir to the Russian throne!

Pavel was quite mystified by all this, but promised his mother he would keep her secret. He asked where his royal father was. This brought from Iona Pogodin another warning to be utterly quiet on the subject, as his royal father was every day engaged in activity that would restore the Romanovs to power. After which she, and Pavel, would move to princely quarters in the Kremlin. Meanwhile, Pavel must not expect his father to take the risk of visits home.

For about two years, between ages six and eight, Pavel was given an intensive introductory course in the great history of Russia under the czars. His mother spoke of the explosion of literature—of Tolstoy and Dostoyevsky and Gogol and Chekhov and Turgenev—under the czars' benevolent patronage. She took him a dozen times to view the treasures in the Kremlin. ("Remember," she whispered more than once, "these are all *ours!*") When Pavel got to be nine or ten he began to suspect that the whole thing was a hallucination, but he was utterly devoted to his mother and never saw any reason to interfere with a fantasy that made her dizzy with pleasure and anticipation.

And then somehow the historical orientation by his mother affected his view of Russian life. He was utterly absorbed by accounts of the last days of the czar and then of the death of the czar ("My grandfather!" he grinned, viewing the portrait in a book); and, in his teens, he felt the electrifying force of Solzhenitsyn, read in *samizdat,* and he read widely in great literature of dissent, wherever he could find it.

He was by nature cautious, never initiating antiestablishment conversation. But if others brought up the subject, which happened frequently when he was at the technical college at Gorky, he would with some delicacy evaluate the ideological temperature of the critic of the regime. It occurred to him along the way that he could be immensely valuable to the KGB, so pronounced had his skills become in inducing men and women of his age to say perhaps one quarter again as much as they'd have been prepared to say to others about their political grievances. He suspected that some of his friends, after a freewheel-

ing evening, woke the next day saying to themselves, "Oh my
God, did I tell Pavel *that* last night?" He laughed as he recalled
the underground story of the Russian who rushed to the offices
of the KGB to report that his missing parrot's political opinions
were in no way related to his own. Meanwhile, contemplating a
career in the police, he busied himself learning penology, a field
of study in which he found he had a stubborn interest, perhaps
traceable to his absorption with the last days of his "grandfather" and the royal brood, and the long ensuing history of
bloody oppression.

It wasn't until his return from Afghanistan, honorably discharged as a sergeant after a year's service with the artillery, now
feverish in his resentment of the slaughter and of the treatment
of the mujahedin, that he came upon Andrei, his physical education instructor at the police academy. Pavel, by coincidence, was
in appearance not unlike an adult version of the young czare-
vich: slight, his features aquiline, his skin a soft white, eyes light
brown, his mouth naturally set in a vaguely melancholy configuration. Andrei, on the other hand, was the robust outdoors
man: muscular, heavy-chested, and older by five years than
Pavel. Before entering the army, Pavel had persuaded a Japanese
student who was also studying penology to teach him karate.
Pavel had done his exercises regularly, even during his days in
the military, gradually achieving a considerable skill. Andrei,
learning of this avocation of one of his police cadets, persuaded
Pavel to teach him his special skills. They would stay after class
in the gymnasium, devoting an hour each day to practicing
karate.

After a few weeks, a hard intimacy generated, and under the
subtle ministrations of Pavel, the older Andrei confessed first his
disillusion with the regime, in due course his abhorrence of it.
But he stopped well short of sharing with Pavel his acceptance
of the mission of the Narodniki. To go that far he would need
the permission of Nikolai, so firm in his insistence that insurrec-
tionary sentiments be carefully suppressed when speaking to
others. Meanwhile, Andrei in turn took the interrogatory initia-

tive, curious to know how far Pavel's heretofore amorphous re-
sentments would carry him. He was startled to be told late one
night after karate practice in the gym, and after substantial re-
freshments, that on a day in March, at dawn, in Afghanistan,
before an offensive scheduled to begin fifteen seconds later,
Pavel had taken careful aim at the back of the head of a lieutenant who was peering over a foxhole fifty meters ahead.

The night before, Pavel explained, blowing cigarette smoke
through his nose, his voice faint and husky, he had walked by a
detention enclosure on his way to the food line. He stopped at
an unlit entrance to a command tent and saw the lieutenant in
question inserting a lighted cigarette into first one, then the second eye of a rebel whose arms were pinioned by two enlisted
officers.

Pavel doubted, he told Andrei, that he could ever efface
from his memory the screams of the now blinded peasant, a
young man about his own age. He learned later in the evening
from a crusty captain in the regular army that there had been no
tactical objective in the torture of the rebel. "The lieutenant just
likes to relax a little every now and then. And he thinks that it
does no harm for word to get out among the mujahedin that resistance to the Soviet army is very, very dangerous business."

"I waited until the general firing began," Pavel said tersely,
seated at a quiet end of the bar. "I needed plenty of cover. It
wasn't long, a minute, two at the most. There was firing everywhere, in every direction it seemed. I squeezed the trigger and hit
him in the neck. He jerked up and then fell down in his own
blood. The soldiers at either side were too preoccupied with the
firefight to bother with him. When a pause came, one of them
grabbed him by the helmet and drew his head back. He must have
decided he was dead. He just let him fall down again. If anybody
suspected the shot came from behind, we never heard about it."

THEY MET together, the six of them, at an abandoned barn at
Okateyvsky, one hour from Moscow, a short walk from the bus

station. The barn had not been used for several years, but the smell of dried manure was still there. The barn was on the farm where Mariya and Vitaly's parents had worked when they were growing up. Nikolai Trimov was the tacit leader, Andrei Belinkov, his deputy. Viktor Pletnev had become in effect the coordinator. Pavel Pogodin was their principal window on official Moscow.

The meeting began at eleven in the morning, and the whole day stretched before them. The purpose, Nikolai explained, was to become acquainted. Vitaly Primakov and his sister Mariya, devoted friends of Viktor, whom they had known since they were teenagers, would take on any duty assigned them, Nikolai explained. They both worked in the post office in Moscow's Lyubertsy district. The need now was to light again the fire of the Narodniki, a fire for liberty that had been doused by the regime against which they were now committed. The absolute requirement: Every one of them must be prepared to lose his life. If there was any hesitation on this point, it was imperative that such hesitation be expressed now.

Nikolai waited. No one spoke up.

They were seated on objects of convenience in the old building, Nikolai on a mound of hay, Viktor on a large log. Pavel and the Primakous—redheaded, with blustery complexions that belied their clerical work, long days spent indoors—on what was left of a long bench. Nikolai told the little band that Pavel, as a cadet at the police academy, had been formally instructed in some of the security procedures for guarding the chief of state. After considerable study, he and Pavel had come up with a plan.

On October 2, Gorbachev would attend the opening of the Bolshoi Ballet. He had done this the year before, his first year in office. It had become traditional for the chief of state to celebrate the ballet's annual opening. Chernenko had missed out, but then he was chronically ill. But Andropov had done it once; Brezhnev, year after year.

The procedure, Nikolai went on, was at once routine and carefully orchestrated. The procession of automobiles, eight or ten, drove into Theatre Square, the lead car gradually turning left on approaching the entrance to the old theater. The second car, and then the other cars, followed suit, and the caravan drew to a halt simultaneously when alongside the pavement that led up to the wide marble steps—sixteen of them, ascending to the entrance. The crowd that inevitably materialized to ogle was grouped by the police to the right and to the left of the spacious marble ascent, down the center of which the long red carpet would stretch, reaching from the top step to the bottom.

Nikolai turned to Pavel. "Tell us what happens then."

"What happens is that whichever car the General Secretary is in, and no one can know which it will be, is the car that parks directly alongside the red carpet. Four men step out of cars ahead and behind and approach the critical car. Gorbachev steps out. The guards flank him and he climbs up the red carpet. Everybody on either side claps and shouts. Thirty, forty seconds is all it takes to climb the stairs.

"But"—Pavel lifted his right hand to signal an important detail—"we were shown a film of the whole operation during our training, to give us an example of how his protection is effected. Brezhnev and Andropov never paused while mounting the steps. But Gorbachev likes crowds. This film of Gorbachev shows him responding to the applause. Suddenly he darted to the left, well ahead of his security guards, and took the arm of a girl who was waving at him. He shook two, even three more hands before moving back to the red carpet and up the entrance to the hall." Pavel paused now, deferring to Nikolai, who said:

"We have to be patient. But we must not lose any opportunity. My plan is to attempt the assassination *provided* Gorbachev does the same thing he did last year, which was, as Pavel told us, to swerve left and clasp hands."

Nikolai went to his briefcase and pulled out what, unfolded, turned out to be a large sheet of drawing paper, four feet square. He thrust one corner of the paper onto a rusty protruding nail in one of the wooden pillars behind him and asked Mariya to hold up the other end.

They could see his sketch of the marble staircase, the red carpet, the cordons on either side, a penciled line describing every stair. He pointed up to the twelfth step on the left.

"My plan is that one of us, armed, will be standing there right up by the cordon, wearing a police uniform. In the film Pavel saw there were policemen scattered on both sides of the staircase. Pavel," Nikolai's fingers moved two or three inches down, "will be here, approximately at the eighth step. If Gorbachev swerves to the left, our member"—he pointed back to the first position—"will fire as many rounds as possible into Gorbachev's head.

"And almost simultaneously . . ." Nikolai hesitated, his voice caught, affected by what he had now to say, "Pavel will aim his police revolver and kill our member."

There was silence.

"The objective," Nikolai cleared his throat, "is plain. If our Narodnik is caught alive, which almost certainly would otherwise happen, within hours all of us will be apprehended, tortured, and executed. He cannot be permitted to survive the episode." He watched them. The barn was still, except for the creaking of the bench as Mariya swung her booted feet gently.

"Now, is there disagreement on this point?"

Once again there was silence.

"In that case, it only remains for us to draw straws, to see who will be that person on October 2. We will do so at our next meeting." He decided to explain the reason, though they all knew. "It is prudent to allow time to go by, in the event any one of us wishes to rethink the plan or his commitment to the enterprise."

CHAPTER 17

NOBODY HAD QUITE ANTICIPATED the furor that arose from putting Blackford Oakes in jail. A festering popular resentment against what the *Wall Street Journal* labeled the "disestablishment of American security" became vocal. People here and there, on talk shows, in the letters columns of newspapers, hotly questioned the moral passions of Senator Hugh Blanton and the "elephantiasis of Senate pride," as Rush Limbaugh put it. The tabloids teemed with fanciful tales of adventures allegedly had by super-spy Blackford Oakes himself, or else done under his supervision. These included everything from seizing the minutes of Khrushchev's Twentieth Party Congress speech in 1956, denouncing the crimes of Josef Stalin, to hand-delivering the Stingers that had finally brought the Soviet juggernaut to a stop in Afghanistan. Blackford soon was linked to every turn of history in Soviet-American relations that benefited the West, including the defection of Nureyev, the escape to the West of Solzhenitsyn, the spotting of Soviet nuclear weapons in Cuba . . .

"Really, darling," Sally said to him in the one telephone call to her he was permitted every day, "I had absolutely no idea that you single-handedly managed to win the Cold War. Tell me, Blacky, did you hypnotize Gorbachev into instituting glasnost? Perestroika? . . . But I shouldn't tease, my love. To tell the truth, I'm rather enjoying it, because I think it must be some comfort for you in that awful place they have you. Oh darling, why don't you just swallow your pride, agree to appear, and take the Fifth Amendment?"

Blackford gently reminded her that the night before he turned himself in to the Justice Department ten days ago she had pledged not to argue that line again, for the sake of domestic tranquility. "To tell the truth," he said, "I don't particularly mind that the whole subject of covert activity is coming up a month or so before Blanton files his report. A few weeks ago I'd have predicted his no-covert-activity bill would sail through Congress. I'm not so sure anymore. What we need is a little friendly nudge from the White House. All the right arguments are being laid out, though of course the case could be made stronger if we could actually talk history, and talk about the uses of covert activity right now. But anyway, it gives me some-thing to do, watching it all. I don't have much to do except read the papers and watch television. If I'm in here another week I'm going to end up reading Norman Mailer's novel on the CIA."

"And doing your push-ups?"

"And doing my push-ups. I do those, and I say my prayers, and I miss you desperately, and might even reread Jane Austen. By the way, Sally, does anybody ever confess to just plain 'read-ing' Jane Austen? I know only people who 'reread' Jane Austen. Goodbye, darling. They're waving me away from the phone. I'll call tomorrow."

Blackford was glad he hadn't missed the David Brinkley program. The guest was Senator Blanton, the subject was the in-carceration of Blackford Oakes and all that it implied. George Will was now questioning Senator Blanton.

Will wanted to know why covert action should end just be-cause the Cold War had ended. Blanton said that since the sur-vival of the United States was not in question, we could certainly do without "CIA-sponsored lying, bribery, blackmail, and murder."

Will asked the senator to comment on a hypothetical situation. "A TWA airplane is hijacked by an organization called the . . . the 'Muslim Order for Justice,' a Palestinian-based terrorist group. Three Americans are killed, two are taken hostage, the Boeing 747 is destroyed. The hijackers disappear into the Libyan mists—"

Senator Blanton interrupted to say that he had always favored very strong legislation against hijackers.

Will went on without comment to say that the day after the TWA episode, the President meets with his National Security Council and wants to know about this Muslim Order for Justice. The Director of the CIA is able to tell him that it's a new outfit with headquarters in Tripoli, organized by Abu Ben Casa, a young firebrand previously with the PLO. Okay, the President says. Now what are you going to do about this outfit? The Director proposes a—Senator Blanton interrupted: "Covert plan?" Will raised his hand, and Brinkley told him to go ahead, and asked Senator Blanton please to listen.

What the CIA comes up with, said Will, pursuing his hypothetical situation, is a recruit anxious to earn a cash reward. His documents are in good order. He has grievances against Israel, and has had extensive training in anti-terrorist disciplines.

"Now skip ahead a year," Will said to Blanton. He describes a Delta 747 preparing to leave Zurich en route to Cairo. Suddenly six Swiss plainclothesmen materialize, in from the shadows. They quietly approach the boarding ladder and remove two passengers. Their briefcases contain dreaded, security-defying firearms and hand grenades.

How did this happen? "Well, the young recruit penetrated the Muslim Order for Justice. In order to get inside to its leader, he had to perform a ritual execution—which he did. He bribed several intermediaries, forged credentials, tapped phones, and got the details of the whole operation in time to get word to the Swiss police."

Will was ready now for his question: "Senator Blanton, in the case I have outlined, has the CIA *sponsored* lying, bribery, blackmail, and murder? Of the kind you would make illegal?"

Senator Blanton was visibly flustered. "Let me put it this way, Mr. Will. a) You cannot repeal the strictures against murdering and lying and cheating, and b) your hypothetical situations are too neat."

"My hypothetical situation, Senator, *happened*—in 1979. The reason you never heard about it is that the plane—it was PanAm, not Delta—left Zurich and landed in Cairo, and nobody there, including the pilots, knew what it was that almost happened."

Blackford leaned back in his chair. He remembered the briefing he had given the young recruit before he left for Libya. He was a very brave young man; living in Rio when last heard from, raising a family.

CHAPTER 18

● MAY 1995

W HEN MACK WALKED IN, Allie, who had been taking dictation, knew to get up with her steno pad and leave the office.

President Clinton came right to the point. "Can you tell me, is there anything else in the world other than his goddamn bill that Hugh Blanton would settle for?"

"I guess he would accept the Democratic nomination next year."

The President was not amused. "We've got a bum situation here." He reached down and picked up that morning's issue of the *Washington Post.* "Did you see the organizations lined up behind the Blanton bill? Which by the way he hasn't yet submitted, am I right?"

"You are right." Mack laughed lightly. "He's waiting for the testimony of Blackford Oakes. Actually, we know that his bill is already written out, word for word. But Blanton wants to give the impression that the testimony of Oakes is absolutely critical. Not, obviously, to the language of the bill, but as supporting material. He wants everybody to believe that the kind of activity he wants to outlaw damn near got us into a world war."

The President protruded his famous jaw. His bulldog pose. "That's crap of course. Isn't it, Mack?"

"Well, I'd say so. I've been brought up to believe that the Soviets didn't go to war because they didn't want their nice country turned into ashes by our stuff."

"So what then is Blanton talking about?"

"Arthur Blaustein—his chief counsel, and the Eagle Scout bent on driving that bill into law—thinks he's on to some caper Oakes engaged in which, he thinks, nearly got us into a hell of a mess. But he doesn't have the details, and apparently Oakes is the only person alive, with the exception of Ronald Reagan, who knows the story."

"Well, if President Reagan, under the intelligence laws, had to inform the congressional intelligence chairman about every covert operation, how come *they* don't know about it?"

"Don't know the answer to that, Chief. But Blaustein looked into every corner of every file and every computer being used in 1985–86. Couldn't find anything."

"Exactly what did they look for? What'd he say, 'Dear Computer, please give me the file on the covert action that almost precipitated a nuclear strike, sometime around 1985, 1986?'"

"The key word is 'Cyclops.'"

"Oh. Well, did Blaustein approach Reagan?"

"He sent him a very nice letter, you know, full of duty-honor-country language, lots of praise for the Reagan administration—"

"Bombed?"

"Yeah, sort of. Reagan was very polite. He said, What did Senator Blanton's committee want to know? Blanton said he wanted to look into a covert operation called 'Cyclops.' The President replied, Sorry, have no memory of Cyclops. He added a postscript, that he remembered when Boris Karloff was asked to play Cyclops in a horror movie, but said no, because he couldn't stand one of his eyes being pasted over all day."

The President, who smiled on the least provocation, did not now do so. "Okay, so Reagan is out. Wisely. What about the Soviet end? Have they tried—hell, have they tried Gorbachev?"

"Interesting you came up with that, because that's exactly what Blanton now plans to do."

"Through whom? Our guy? Has he got the authority to ask my ambassador to forward that inquiry?"

"He'd have to go through the Secretary of State."

"And the Secretary of State, theoretically, has to ask me, right?"

"Right, unless he simply assumes that you would say yes as a matter of executive-legislative cooperation."

The President paused. "Let's think that one over, going to Gorbachev. Let's just take the obvious things, okay? One, Mikhail Gorbachev is not going to tell a United States senator that he came close to ordering a nuclear strike against the United States, and that's what it was, agreed?"

"Agreed."

"Two, if Gorbachev was actually tempted to act against the United States in a really aggressive way during '85-'86, that would have been because we either threatened him or aced him in some critical situation. Agreed?"

"Agreed."

"We *know* we didn't threaten him. Well, we threatened him in the sense that we made it impossible for his army to win in Afghanistan. But that story is public, and sending over the Stingers was a covert operation only at the beginning. By 1985, we were doing that pretty openly. But there was never any ultimatum there. So what are we talking about? Something that just pissed the hell out of Gorbachev? Soviet leaders don't threaten nuclear war when they're pissed off. If they did, we'd have had a nuclear war in 1949 . . . You know what I think?"

Mack had got used to the phrase. When the President used it, either he followed it immediately with what it was that he really thought, as in, "You ass, it's *that* obvious . . ." or else he followed it with a pause. When he paused after using the locution, that meant he wished his interlocutor to jump right in and say, "What?" Or, even better, "What, Mr. President?"

"What?"

"I think the whole thing is . . . crap. Whatever Cyclops was, whatever he did, there's no way he could have threatened war. So what we come down to is: What are we going to do about the Blanton bill? I started to ask you, did you see the ad in the *Post?*"

"Same thing appeared in the *Times.*"

"Who's financing that drive?"

"Oh, the usual people. If you get a few thousand signatures, it doesn't cost that much per person."

The President picked up the paper and began to list the Blanton bill endorsers. "'The People's Peace Front.' Is that the San Francisco group?"

Mack nodded.

"'The Committee for International Justice.' Is that the committee that wants us to try the South Korean gang as war criminals?"

"Among other things, yes. They'd also like it if we strung up Marcos."

"Marcos is dead."

"That doesn't bother the Committee for International Justice."

The President went on, reading out the names of the backers of the Blanton bill. He stopped. "'The Gay-Lesbian Liberation Frat'—What in the hell does covert operations have to do with—"

"Maybe they think the CIA goes undercover in drag."

The President put the paper down. "What do *you* think, Mack?"

"Mr. President, I don't think you can stop the bill unless you come out on it. You don't have to oppose it. Just suggest a compromise, the effect of which would be to dilute it. Why not say that perhaps covert action should be permitted only with the backing of the committee chairmen in the House and in the Senate, except when, in the opinion of the Executive, the national interest supervenes?"

"What do you mean, 'supervenes'? Doesn't that require me to describe a situation in which the national interest can't be confided to the two chairmen?"

"Actually it does, but it never needs to be stated that bluntly. If a bill was passed with that proviso in it, you would have the same authority you now have. You would simply have to make a finding that this situation and that one are situations in which the national interest . . . supervenes."

"You know something, Mack, Blanton is not only the darling of the left wing of the party. He also *owns* Illinois. The difference between Blanton working for me next year in Illinois and Blanton spending the campaign giving anti-covert-activity lectures in Frankfurt or—or Hiroshima could mean the difference of twenty-four electoral votes."

Mack nodded. "We can always go back to my original suggestion."

"Which was?"

"Give him the bill, and then ignore it."

"You tell me it's very tightly written."

"So's the Ninth and Tenth Amendments."

The President nodded. And then said, "By the way, if Blanton doesn't relent on the Blackford Oakes front I expect the National Guard to come down and release him. Christ, they might as well have put Lindbergh in jail, or MacArthur."

"You're right, Chief. That's coming to a boil."

"Maybe I should call Blanton in here?"

"Wouldn't work. Nothing works with Blanton." Mack looked at his watch. "Unless you want me to postpone it, Mr. President, I called a staff meeting for ten minutes ago."

The President waved his fingers toward the door. "See you later, Mack."

CHAPTER 19

W HEN, AT REYKJAVIK, THE news was given out to fifty attend-
ing newsmen that General Secretary Gorbachev would be
coming to Washington before the end of the year, and that not
long after, Mr. Reagan would be paying a reciprocal visit to
Moscow, there was spirited talk in Congress on the general question of security. It had recently been disclosed that the new U.S.
Embassy in Moscow was a hundred-million-dollar piece of
Swiss cheese, designed primarily to oblige Soviet eavesdropping.
Congressman Dick Armey characterized the new building as "an
eight-story microphone plugged into the Politburo."

Where exactly would the U.S. delegation meet, Senator Dole
wanted to know, in order to discuss the disarmament treaty? Nor-
mally, he explained to television interviewer Larry King, when in
need of maximum security abroad U.S. diplomats retire to the
"bubble." That is a kind of electronic bunker within which, it had
generally been supposed, not even one's guardian angel can over-
hear you. But, Dole said, it turns out that even our bubble in
Moscow had been successfully bugged. "And that which is
bugged," said Mr. Dole, "does not get debugged merely by the
touch of a sweeper's wand. The estimated cost of debugging the
new embassy has been put at twenty-five million dollars."

The bubble not being secure, one congressman gravely suggested that the Secretary of State bring to Moscow his own

traveling van, "something on the order of what CBS News trots out when there is a local situation to be filmed." But then a reporter released the judgment of an expert: Such vans could easily be made to emit the sounds even of whispers within. Columnist William F. Buckley suggested that U.S. staff meetings be held in a helicopter a couple of thousand feet over Moscow, but he was not taken seriously. Another congressman solemnly deliberated that perhaps the Secretary should retreat every evening to his Air Force jet and use *it* as an office, but the unspoken consensus was that this would not be dignified. The Senate reacted by voting 70–30 its conviction that in protest against this violation of privacy, Secretary George Shultz should postpone his visit to Moscow, where he was scheduled to meet with his counterpart to do the advance work on the proposed disarmament treaty.

At the daily meeting of the CIA's senior staff, Blackford and Bill Casey discussed the uproar over the new structure in Moscow with some amusement, quite apart from the general alarm the Agency felt over the progressive porosity of U.S. security. Blackford reminisced that, as a boy listening to the Metropolitan Opera over the radio one Saturday afternoon, he had been fascinated by what the listening audience was told by Milton Cross, the master of ceremonies, during an intermission. He had spoken of receiving a letter from a listener in Chicago. The listener wanted to know: Who hears the opening strains of the *Tannhäuser* overture first, the people sitting in the balcony of the Met in New York, looking down on the stage—or me, in my living room in Chicago? The question had been turned over to the technicians, and now their verdict was in. Given the speed of sound (1,088 feet per second) contrasted with the speed of light (186,000 miles per second), which is the speed at which radio transmissions travel, the man in Chicago heard it first.

"I wonder whether Secretary Shultz, addressing arms control adviser Paul Nitze across a ten-foot table, will be heard first by Nitze, or first by the KGB and then by Nitze." Casey reported that our diplomats throughout Eastern Europe and the Soviet Union were frequently reduced to communicating with each other by handwritten notes and on children's blackboards with easily erasable chalk. "With denuclearization," Casey said, "comes maybe the return of the palimpsest."

And then, a few days after the Senate vote, it was revealed that two United States Marines—and then it was three U.S. Marines—and then it was four Marines—were accused of reciprocating a Russian woman's frequent gestures toward glasnost with their own opening: of the embassy safe. The State Department declined to specify what exactly lay in the safe, merely that it contained "precious secrets." Speculating on what these might be, columnist William Safire said that the safe might have disclosed, for instance, our fallback position if, at the bargaining table, the Soviet Union said that it would consent to a reduction to XYZ intermediate range missiles, and not one more; but also a whole lot of other sensitive material. The safe in Moscow was not, a former ambassador said, answering a reporter's questions, the major repository of United States secrets. Congressman Speath, a close student of the continuing spy saga, wondered whether there was any repository of United States secrets to which the Soviet Union hadn't achieved access in recent times. Since 1984, the *New York Times* reported, "at least" twenty-six people have been convicted of charges of spying. Among them were spies whose findings "reached monumental proportions." An estimated "billions" of dollars would be required to compensate for the damage.

"And we don't know how to put a dollar figure on the damage done at another level," Congressman Armey concluded his speech on the floor of the House. "There are, within the borders of the Soviet bloc, a few men and women who struggle against their tyrants by covertly helping the western alliance, even as what we called the Resistance struggled against the Nazis forty-five years ago. How many of them were fingered as 'assets' of the United States by these spies?"

It was a feverish few weeks, but eventually the uproar died down, and eyes fastened instead on what, if anything, would come of Gorbachev's rejected initiative at Reykjavik.

BLACKFORD ANSWERED the ring on the private phone in his office. It was Kathy. "He wants to see you. Same time, same place. Five forty-five. Okay?" Yes, Blackford said. He had no appointment (he smiled) that he would put ahead of a summons by the President of the United States to a private meeting.

At lunch in a secluded corner of the CIA dining room in Langley, Blackford talked to Anthony Trust. He hadn't seen him since the news of Reykjavik, two days earlier. Trust greeted his old friend exultantly.

"By golly, as our leader would put it, our guy did it! He came through!" Anthony Trust spread his fingers in a V-for-victory sign, then grabbed his Coca-Cola, poured it into a Dixie cup as though it were a champagne glass, and ceremoniously touched it to his lips. "Old Gorbachev thought he'd take the Gipper to the cleaners. Abolish all nuclear weapons! Terrific idea. Take ten years or so—but, so what? Oh, and of course, beginning ten days from now you, Mr. President, will cease all work on Star Wars. So our guy says—I wish I had been there— Oh, by the way, No. *N-y-e-t*. And the unilateralists weep at this great loss of an opportunity to be the President who said good-bye to all nuclear weapons. And incidentally goodbye to our deterrent force."

"Yes," Blackford said, biting into his ravioli. "That session was dynamite. I look forward to Casey's reading on it. You knew he headed straight to Florida? A week's relaxation. He needs it. Have you read the cables?"

"Oh sure. Pretty much what you'd expect. The wimps are wimping. The smart money is pro-Reagan. Neil Kinnock threatens to commit suicide, and Margaret Thatcher suggests a national plebiscite on the question."

They chatted about this and that. Blackford did not disclose that before the end of the afternoon he expected to hear directly from "our guy." The commander in chief.

His mind turned to the question, Why had he been summoned? Amiable though their relations were, Blackford Oakes was not regularly consulted by the President on sundry matters.

And if the purpose of the visit were social, it would not be at that hour, in that office.

It had to be Cyclops.

TWENTY-FOUR hours after returning from Iceland, the President was looking entirely fit. He bounded up from his desk and shook hands. Blackford reasoned that it would probably not be good form to congratulate the President on doing what he had done in rejecting Gorbachev's proffered "exchange." As chief of covert operations for the CIA, Blackford was not a lobbyist for one or the other position in foreign policy. So he put it to the President in the form of an intelligence report. "Our friends in Europe are very pleased with the action you took."

"Well you know, Blackford, I made that decision quickly, granted. Because among other things it was a straight-out violation of the terms of our coming together. He had agreed we wouldn't discuss his idea of suspending the anti-missile missile. But I got to tell you this: The idea of a world without atom bombs, that is a real dream. It won't happen while I'm sitting here, but I wish I could be the President who did accomplish it.

"You know something?" The President looked up as if he were going to surprise Blackford with a state secret. "There are people around, I mean, people on *our* side, who are against eliminating the bomb altogether. Shultz, for instance. Henry Kissinger. Jim Baker. Of course, it's true we have to have a defense against one of those wacky third-power people, Qaddafi types, coming up with a bomb. But if the SDI goes well, then we'll *have* protection against the little powers, the kind of protection that doesn't require Mutual Assured Destruction— the dumbest, most immoral policy I ever heard of.

"I said to Gorbachev, 'Mikhail'—you know, we call each other by our first names. Not a bad idea. Helps to break the ice—I said, 'Mikhail, let me tell you exactly why I would hand over to you all the technology we develop when we go after an

SDI. You know why? Because between the time we develop that technology and the time we deploy it, you—I don't mean you, Mikhail, I mean, some successor to you—might figure: This is the only moment we have left to launch a first strike against America. Tomorrow is too late, because tomorrow they'll have their missile defense, and when they have it, they'll be in a position to dictate to us anything they want, because our nuclear missiles won't be a threat to them any longer.

"So I said, if we give you the whole technology, then the moment will *never* come when we could threaten you while safe under our SDI umbrella."

"What did he say?"

"Oh, the usual thing. Ronald, he said, you know SDI is an invitation to another arms race, there would be weapons floating around in space . . .

"But you know something, Blackford? *I* know—hell, you've got to know, you're the people who assemble all the information—*we* know why he is so insistent on this point. It's just this easy: *They can't afford to continue to spend money,* and more and more money, on a space defense race. Because they are up to their keisters in debt.

"But that isn't what I asked you to come in about." The President leaned forward and began to doodle with his pencil on the pad. "Have you got anything in the last few weeks from what's-his-name, our contact in Moscow?"

"Cyclops?"

Reagan nodded.

"No sir. The routine once-every-three-weeks message. If there was any change on the question of the assassination plan, he'd have told me."

"So it's still being organized?"

"Presumably."

The President swiveled around on his chair. "You know something, Blackford, something really interesting? The day before we left—Sunday—we were in one of those diplomatic waiting rooms, waiting to go in for dinner. Just the four of us.

Gorbachev and me at one end of the room, Nancy and Raisa at the other end of the room. And he was talking about this and that, and then he pointed at Raisa—they couldn't hear us, it's a big room—and he said, 'She is an atheist.'

"I didn't get it. I mean, if I pointed at you and I said, 'He is a Republican,' doesn't that mean that I'm *not* a Republican? I thought what the hell, could it be possible that the *head* of the Soviet Union is telling me he is a believer? Well, you want to know what I did? The next day was when we said our formal goodbyes, and we have those little exchanges, you know, before we drive off, so he said his usual thing about the peace of the world, and what I said was something my father used to say when he went off on a trip. I wanted to push the Christian thing. So I watched him very carefully when I said, 'As my father used to say:

> May the road rise up to meet you,
> May the wind always be at your back,
> And may you be in heaven,
> A half an hour before the devil knows you're dead.'"

"Did you get any reaction?"

"None that I could see. On the other hand," Reagan laughed, "he didn't spit. The whole thing is pretty interesting. And that gets me to my point." Reagan was silent again for a moment. And then, slowly, "We've got to stop the Cyclops business."

Blackford drew a deep breath. "Are you telling me I'm to tell Cyclops to turn them in to the KGB?"

"I'd just as soon not get into details of that kind. I don't know whether they've got to be turned in or not and I don't want to know. I'm just saying that I think Gorbachev is different enough as a Soviet leader that we shouldn't let him be derailed. That's my conclusion."

"You mean you want me to call the whole thing off."

"Well . . ."

"You know, Mr. President, this isn't an operation we control. It isn't *our* plot."

"Yes, I know that."

"I'm not even sure, I mean, I have no idea whether Cyclops can control them. He can try to talk them out of it, I guess. But that might not work. Probably wouldn't work, if they're as set on it as I'd guess they are. I mean, Cyclops might get himself killed just trying . . ."

The president said nothing. Blackford paused. And then said, "The only sure way is for Cyclops to turn them in to the KGB." He waited. The President said nothing.

Blackford got up. The President did not move his gaze from his desk. Blackford extended his hand. The President looked up, and took it, and Blackford saw the sadness in the eyes. It meant that he knew the full consequences of his decision.

Blackford walked out of the office, down the staircase to his car.

HE ENTERED the study of his house using the back door—he didn't want to see Sally before he made the phone call. He dialed a number at the Agency, spoke to a deputy at the Operations desk, and instructed him on several matters. He told the deputy to book him to Moscow the following day with "the Harry Singleton documentation, including 'Jerry Singleton.' And get in touch with . . . Jerry and tell him he's taking off with me."

He yearned to discuss the matter with Sally. But under the circumstances he was glad to find her note telling him she had accepted an invitation to a lecture at the University of Virginia and would not be back until after midnight.

He poured himself a drink, sat staring at the bookcase. And then went to the telephone.

"Anthony? I need you. Urgent. Right away. Thanks."

CHAPTER 20

● OCTOBER 1986

A S HE MADE FINAL arrangements to leave Washington, Black-ford faced the first of what he knew would be a distressing series of problems. What was he to tell the Director? Whatever, it would need to be over a scrambled line to Palm Beach, where Casey was vacationing.

The Director was accustomed to Blackford's absences from Washington, though these were now less frequent—as chief of covert operations he needed to spend most of his time in the cockpit at Langley, supervising the activities of agents in the field. It was a time-consuming job. Only he and the Director knew how many agents and assets the CIA had, and what the financial overhead was, though this item others knew—specifically, the President. Blackford felt somehow . . . unfaithful, leaving Washington on what Casey's office would think was a routine meeting with intelligence centers in London or Paris or Rome or wherever, when in fact he was on a mission personally directed by the President.

But he had never broken his promise to Cyclops, a promise so solemn that even the President had felt bound by it—if indeed Mr. Reagan had not consulted anyone; Blackford would never know. He concluded that he had no choice. He had to continue with the subterfuge: Tell Casey now about Cyclops? Tell Casey about the six-year bond with Cyclops, from any knowledge of which Casey had been excluded? Tell Casey about the impending assassination of Gorbachev and the presidential noninvolvement? The sheer load of such information, previously unknown, unassimilated, would deeply disturb Bill Casey, and humiliate him. Might very well, as a matter of fact, cause Casey to dismiss Blackford, though of course this would not be practical until after Blackford had contacted Cyclops.

Blackford stopped for a moment before starting the motor in his car. He posed to himself an interesting, anfractuous question. After giving it some thought, he concluded that in all probability if he, Blackford, were Casey, and Casey were Blackford, and Casey had held out on Blackford as he, Blackford, had held out on Casey—he, Blackford, would almost certainly fire him, Casey! He was invigorated and amused by the sternness of his judgment at his own expense. It was as if he had suitably punished himself for his insubordinate independence. He drove off from the Agency, after an hour with his deputy, with a conscience considerably eased.

In FACT, Blackford Oakes need not have worried. When first advised about Cyclops, just over one year before, the President had taken confident advantage of the loophole: He, the President, had never given his word to Cyclops that he would consult no one about the secret tie. That evening he had laid out the whole situation to Casey, who agreed that it was not the business of the United States to interfere. And they both agreed to spare Oakes the embarrassment of knowing that his own pledge to Cyclops had not been sustained. At Reykjavik, before they parted, the President had drawn Casey to one side. "Been thinking. It's time to call off Blackford Oakes's Moscow people, you agree?"

Casey had nodded, resignedly.

HE MET "Jerry," his "son," as arranged, in the Pan American waiting room at Dulles Airport. Serge Windels was a cheerful twenty-eight-year-old, blue-eyed and freckled, tall, but not basketball-player tall, with abundant hair that was once red, now a rusty blond, usually straying over half his forehead, some of it reaching to his horn-rimmed glasses. Half the time Serge looked over the glasses, half the time through them.

"Why don't you get those half-moon glasses, if you don't need them for distance?" Sally had once asked Serge at a picnic at the farm.

"Don't know, Sally, I guess it's a good idea. On the other hand, by the time I get around to getting new glasses, I'll probably have lost my distance vision." Sally smiled and said later to Blackford that Serge was the most wholesome thing in the entire Agency, as far as she was concerned.

"I'm pretty wholesome, no?" Blackford said.

"No. You're not wholesome Any more than Rudolph Valentino was wholesome, or Clark Gable, or Cary Grant. You are still beautiful, exotic Blacky."

"Well, okay. I'll give up my wholesomeness for that. It is funny, though. Serge, I mean. He strikes everybody that way, Andy Hardy."

"Like Tom Cruise or Tom Hanks, you mean. You're dating yourself."

"Tom Hanks? Who is he? Lincoln's nephew?"

Sally's look said, Forget it; eloquently, dispositively.

"You wouldn't know he left the Ukraine at age fourteen."

"Fourteen? I thought he was a baby. What happened to his accent?"

"Our wholesome little boy has no accent. And when he speaks Russian it's the same thing—he has no trace of a graduate of the University of Iowa."

"Does he also kill people? I mean, wholesomely?"

Hers was a thirty-five-year-old act—it had become something of an act, Blackford thought, though for many years it was far from that. In fact, Blackford's occupation as an agent of the

CIA had been primarily responsible for the long delay in their marriage. When in those days she had referred to Blackford's covert activities, the exact nature of which she usually knew nothing about, it was with the high seriousness of the Vassar branch of the Committee for a Sane Nuclear Policy, to which Professor Sally Partridge had belonged for years. She was coming close to endorsing a statement advocating unilateral nuclear disarmament when Blackford actually sat her down, went to the telephone, called Edward Teller at the hotel suite where he had just left him, pleaded with him to come to the country for lunch the next day, made Sally promise that she would listen for one hour to Teller's analysis of the consequence of unilateral disarmament, and then made himself scarce. The lunch had been a quite unpredictable success, in part because Teller had lost none of the Hungarian polish which even his devoutest enemies conceded was utterly seductive.

But what had done it for Sally was Teller's total analytical seriousness. She had rather hoped that he would be condescending to her, a mere Doctor of Letters, author of two books on Jane Austen, and an Adjunct Professor at the University of Mexico. That would have encouraged her defiance. It was not so at all. He dealt with her as he might have dealt with Oppenheimer, or Leo Szilard, or—"God, Blacky, he sometimes made me feel I was Einstein, asking my judgment on this point or that one."

So she gave up on unilateral nuclear disarmament, but stuck to a sane nuclear policy, provoking Blackford into asking whether he was supposed to deduce that he, Blackford, advocated an insane nuclear policy?

The moment he spoke the word he regretted it. Because, of course, she replied, "Exactly."

HARRY AND Jerry Singleton sat side by side on the flight to Frankfurt. Harry let down the tray from the back of the seat in front of him. "Let's check out our papers." He pulled out the passport from the floppy plastic case in his pocket. He was the senior Singleton, born on December 7, 1925, in Akron, Ohio. His permanent address was 3025 P Street, N.W., Washington. The inside of the passport showed that he had traveled around South America on what must have been a cruise, since the dates of the customs stamps—Venezuela, Brazil, Argentina, Chile, Peru, Ecuador, Fort Lauderdale—were two or three days apart. The passport indicated one trip to London and one to Paris and Geneva, returning three weeks later to Washington.

He handed the passport over, inviting Jerry to scrutinize it. In turn he opened Jerry's. Jerry was born on September 28, 1958, in New York. He had traveled about more than his father, with a trip to some part of Europe every year or two beginning at about college age—his passport was almost ten years old. Jerry's permanent address was in Chevy Chase, Maryland: 28 Quincy Street, another CIA safehouse.

"Are you going to tell me what this is all about—Dad?"

Blackford leaned back in his seat, letting it recline slightly. He thought back on the briefings he had received from Rufus in his long career, how exemplary they were in clarity and purpose, how fastidiously the risks were defined. Blackford's problem was delicate here because he could not give Serge a briefing that revealed the principal objective of the trip. Serge (who had pursued native Russian in college) was along to translate and to perform errands, vital and trivial.

But some background was needed, and Blackford began to speak. Quietly. Serge had to lean over toward him. He raised his glass of beer to his lips for an occasional sip. He asked a few questions. Blackford was able to answer most of them.

Their apparent objective in Moscow was to visit that city, where neither of them, their passports indicated, had been, and to make one final effort to establish whether Jerry's aunt, Harry Singleton's sister-in-law, was alive or dead. Neither father nor son had ever laid eyes on her. Harry had pledged to his dying wife, Natasha, Jerry's mother, that he would make a diligent effort to find her. Natasha Singleton had all along assumed that her Ukrainian-born sister Avrani had died during the war—until only a few months before, in June, when on her deathbed the letter had reached her from an old family friend telling her that he had reason to believe Avrani was alive and living in Moscow.

"You got the letter?"

Blackford pulled it out of the passport case. Serge read it carefully. "It's good. Got a couple of expressions you'd expect to run into from a Muscovite in his seventies. What about the return address?"

"It's there. But, unfortunately, soon after writing the letter the old family friend passed away." He picked out a frayed air mail envelope marked, in Russian, RETURN TO SENDER ADDRESSEE DECEASED.

Serge murmured his admiration for the skills of the CIA's technical resources department. And then, "So. We're in Moscow on a benevolent family mission. And we pay a visit or two to the museums, that kind of thing. What then?"

"That depends. I have to find somebody, and you have to help me do that because my trail is very cold. That's how the man I'm looking for wanted it. But he also wanted me to be able to get to him in an emergency."

"You're supposed to operate through a third person?"

"I'm supposed to find out from a third person what I'm supposed to do."

"Do you know where Mr. Third Person hides out? Is he also related to me?"

"It involves putting up a notice in the Cheryomushki post office and waiting until something happens."

"Who is the notice addressed to?"

"To your aunt Avrani."

CHAPTER 21

● SEPTEMBER 1986

ONE WEEK BEFORE THE Bolshoi Ballet opening, Vitaly and Mariya Primakov signed on for the evening shift at the post office, a shift that ran from four in the afternoon until midnight. Such were their instructions from Nikolai, and they were not hard to implement—there was always a shortage of night workers to sort the mail. If when the cards were drawn to single out the assassin the jack of spades was dealt to either of the two, it would be as simple as that he/she, the designated assassin, would not show up for work that day.

Pavel Pogodin's assistance was of course critical. During the final days before the event he would cannibalize an appropriate police uniform and the accompanying accoutrements. He had already, weeks before, got hold of a police badge and the papers of a defunct colleague—nothing that could withstand intensive scrutiny, but good enough to pass routine inspection while approaching the cordons leading to the Bolshoi Theatre. And, the day before the event, he was given the special identifying pin to be worn the next day. The design of it in hand, it was not difficult to produce a facsimile in his workshop. An entire day was set aside during which Pavel would instruct the chosen Narodnik on what might be expected of a policeman ordered to auxiliary crowd-control duty designed to provide supplementary protection for the General Secretary.

Nikolai would spend a diligent day at the offices of the MEIE reviewing blueprints for electrical systems planned for over fifty buildings in the quarter to which he had been assigned, on Ogarova Street, not far from the Bolshoi Theatre. On D-Day Nikolai would detain a subordinate draftsman after hours to amend a blueprint scheduled to be put to use in the immediate future. This practice was not unusual, especially among the young engineers seeking to make an impression on their superiors. He and the assistant would do their work in the main drafting room, where as often as not other engineers were working late. They would not leave the building until sometime after 8 p.m. No one would ever be able to say that Nikolai Trimov had been anywhere near the scene on October 2. Of course, if Nikolai himself drew the black jack, he would simply desert his station.

THE DAY had arrived for the drawing. The six young Narodniki met again at the abandoned stable at Okateyvsky. The ugly wet-cold weather comported with the heavy mood of a band of brothers met to decide which one of them would be dead four days hence. The plan had been rehearsed in minute detail. No concertmaster put any string section through its paces more insistently than Nikolai had done, detailing contingency after contingency, elaborating what was to be done in each case. It remained entirely possible that Gorbachev would this time swerve to the right to greet his crowd, not to the left, in which case the operation would abort. And it was of course not only possible but perhaps even probable—who knows, Gorbachev might have been severely reprimanded by his closest associates for what he had done the year before—that Gorbachev would walk directly up the red carpet to the entrance hall; in which case, once again, the operation would abort.

On the other hand, Gorbachev might just reenact last year's walk to the left, to cuddle with the crowd. At the summit conference in Geneva, the television showed, he had twice abandoned his car to make company with the cosmopolitan crowd.

They sat in the same rough circle as when the plan had first been discussed two weeks ago. The wind outside was shrill. Nikolai drew from his army sack a pack of playing cards.

That was the signal for Andrei. He cleared his throat and stood up, leaning back against an old wooden stanchion. "Nikolai," Andrei cleared his throat once again, "on behalf of my companions, I am to—I have to—I am directed to report to you the resolution that we have made."

Nikolai looked up with alarm. He had not authorized any meeting by his five associates. No meeting by more than two of them at one time was authorized by the rules he had carefully laid down. What did Andrei have to say?

But Andrei had fallen silent, so that it was Nikolai who finally spoke.

"What is it, Andrei?"

"It is this," Andrei blurted it out: "We have decided that you are not to deal yourself a card. If you go, our Narodniki will fall apart. You are, in our judgment, indispensable as a leader."

Nikolai was stunned. The very idea of a self-serving discrimination seemed to infect the purity of the Narodniki, among whom no one was spared, no preferments tolerated. He could not entirely suppress a biological and spiritual jolt at the fleeting thought that he might at once see his mission through and live to spend a lifetime with Tatyana. But the clarity of the ruling idea, the compelling feel of total collegiality, instantly suppressed all other thought.

"It is out of the question, Andrei. We will proceed."

Andrei said, "We feared that might be your reaction. Here is ours."

He turned his head, looking over the circle of his confederates. They all stood up. "If you don't agree, we will leave right now and disband the Narodniki."

Nikolai was silent. Slowly, tears came to his eyes, tears of frustration, of awe, of uncomplicated love and gratitude. He was forced to acknowledge his own singularity.

Andrei was correct. Nikolai *was* central to any truly coordinated effort. They could, each one of them, do as Ragozinikova had done, each of them place dynamite on his person and walk in on one or another petty tyrant. But to assassinate the leader, making possible a chaotic state in which an entire oppressed people might arise—that took sustained thought and discipline and coordination.

So he approached first Andrei, then Viktor, then Pavel, then Mariya, then Vitaly, embracing them each in turn. He went back to his little mound of hay and sat down. The rest then sat, and the circle reformed.

Nikolai cleared his throat.

"We will proceed. Pavel is, by the design of our plan, excluded. I will deal the cards then clockwise, beginning with Andrei, then to Viktor, then to Vitaly, then to Mariya, and continue to deal until the jack turns up."

He had privately decided, in his nightmares about this moment, that he would deal the cards swiftly, rather than slowly. He remembered the passage in Solzhenitsyn's *Gulag* about the guard who, when administering a flogging, paused for as much as ten seconds between strokes, the better to prolong the victim's pain. Accordingly he dealt out the cards rapidly. It seemed as if half the deck had been exposed before the jack of spades materialized, in front of Vitaly.

Mariya threw her arms around him and sobbed. Vitaly whispered in her ear, but they could hear him say, "You must not, Mariya, you must not. One thousand times we said this to each other, one thousand times, that we would give our lives as Narodniki."

The remaining four walked out of the stable to make possible the privacy of brother and sister. After fifteen minutes they reassembled. And now the conversation was mostly between Pavel and Vitaly. What Vitaly was to do exactly, where he would meet Pavel, when to put on the uniform, when he would be told the code and given the lapel pin for that day.

Had he sufficient practice in aiming and shooting a pistol? Yes, but in the army was he using a revolver or an automatic, because the standard police pistol in Moscow was a revolver . . .

It was nearly sundown when they reached Moscow, separately. The sense of mission that sustained them all sustained even Vitaly Primakov.

CHAPTER 22

P AVEL WATCHED THE MOTORCADE slowly winding down to a
full stop. He felt the subdued exhilaration of the crowd.
Tired Muscovites, doing a little gawking, waiting to see their
leader in the flesh on this fall evening, benign with light and
warmth. Pavel was a veteran and had seen action at the front,
but the excitement he now felt was without precedent. In a few
minutes he might see the end of the life of the head of what the
President of the United States had accurately labeled an "evil
empire." And if so, he, Pavel, would cause the death of a
brother. Fratricide. He clenched his fists, seeking to dominate his
body's muscles. Then he saw the security official open the door
of the car that had parked by the red carpet, saw Mikhail Gorbachev step out and begin to climb the stairs, waving first to the
right, then to the left at the applauding crowd—he found himself hoping, hoping desperately that Gorbachev would not turn
left to greet the crowd on this side of the great stairs, because he
knew that otherwise he would in fact do what he had to do.

But Gorbachev did just that, turned left, did so swiftly, embracing an elderly lady a mere two steps above Pavel. Pavel saw
Vitaly draw his pistol and aim at Gorbachev. But there was a
moment's hesitation—if Vitaly pulled the trigger instantly he'd

kill the old lady with whom Gorbachev was for that split second entwined. Pavel lifted his revolver and fired three times at Vitaly, who had got off two shots, one of them grazing Gorbachev.

Although Pavel had brought Vitaly down, he was surrounded now by a half-dozen guards and there was the sound of an Uzi automatic weapon going off, then the cry, "Stop! We want him alive!"

But it was quickly evident that the would-be assassin was dead.

Gorbachev was lost within a human cordon that rushed him back into his car. The motorcade zoomed off, fifteen sirens sounding. What seemed a full company was suddenly standing at intervals of two or three meters, bayonets fixed, facing the crowd on both sides. The captain of the guard approached Pavel. "Come with me, sergeant." He gripped Pavel's shoulder. "You did a fine job."

THE KGB major thought it time to have another session with Mariya Vitaly and motioned to the burly sergeant on duty to follow him to her cell. As the jailer turned the key, the major called out in the relative dark—his eyes hadn't accustomed themselves to prison dimness—"Mariya, we've come back for another visit. This one won't be as pleasant"—he entered the blackness of the cell—"as the last one, so you had better prepare to tell us more than you have about your brother's counterrevolutionary companions. Do you hear me?"

There was silence. He gave the signal, and the sergeant leaned over and smashed his closed fist against Mariya's right cheek. Her head merely twitched to one side.

The sergeant leaped to turn on the overhead switch. He and the major stared down on a lifeless body.

It was absolutely the case, they said to each other much later, that there had been a trace of a smile on that mutilated face. Because Mariya had long since resolved that if Vitaly drew the jack of spades, she would, beginning at 8 p.m. on October 2, carry the cyanide capsule in her mouth.

CHAPTER 23

S ERGE CAME BACK FROM the post office. "Our notice," he told Blackford, "was removed. Maybe by the guy you've been looking for, maybe not. I put up a new one, same thing. What are we going to look at today?"

"I thought we might drive over to Zagorsk. It's one of the two or three seminaries Stalin left open. Khrushchev breathed a little threatening hot fire into it at one point, but then let it stand. It's where the Orthodox catspaw hangs out. I'm told it's interesting."

"Why not?"

As they walked past the desk toward the hotel entrance the concierge hailed them. "Mr. Singleton," he called out to the older man, "the telephone is for you."

Blackford went to the booth. He heard now for the first time in five years a voice he had first heard in 1952. The speaker was, as usual, laconic.

"I will be, beginning at six tonight, at—memorize this address, Blackford—226 Kalinin Prospekt, apartment 1412. Do not be late. You will, of course, be alone." The telephone clicked off. Blackford rejoined Serge. "It's set. Thank God. We can go on to Zagorsk. My date isn't till six."

They were back at midafternoon, after walking about the historical seminary, which seemed now more like an old monks' home. "It looks like they're eyedropping holy water into hell," Serge commented as they left in the hired car with the Intourist driver. Freedom of religion, Soviet style.

Back in the hotel in their little sitting room Serge carefully read the afternoon paper. An item on page 7, a mere inch or two, caught his eye. "Dad!"—Serge had got into the habit of calling him that, and rather enjoyed it. "Listen to this. 'Two weeks ago a young man fired a pistol shot that grazed the ear of General Secretary Mikhail Gorbachev, doing absolutely no harm. The dangerous man was shot down by a policeman and by security. An investigation revealed that he was an escapee from the Vronsky Health Institute, an asylum where danger-ously unbalanced citizens are treated. Security delayed in publi-cizing the event because they have been looking for the next of kin.'

"Oh, well," Serge shrugged after finishing the story, "so there are crazy people everywhere. Except that here they usually get shot, I gather. Hinckley plays basketball every day." The ref-erence was to the would-be assassin who five years earlier had shot President Reagan. "And get that 'two weeks ago' business! The reporter will probably put in for a Pulitzer for finding out, just two weeks after it happened, that somebody took a shot at the chief of state."

Blackford said nothing. But when Serge was finished with the newspaper, Blackford asked him to clip the story. Serge looked up at him. The embassy would routinely clip it and wire it in to Langley, so why would Blackford want it? But he said nothing and, using his fingernails, ripped it out, jaggedly. "Say, Dad, is it okay if I call the embassy? There's a girl there I went to college with."

"Not tonight. Maybe tomorrow. And if you visit with her, it'll have to be at the embassy. You can get lunch there at the PX."

"Okay," Serge said resignedly. "I'll just walk around a bit, maybe stop in somewhere. It's fun to use my Russian. My record so far is ninety-eight percent. And the guy who wondered about whether maybe I wasn't really a native wondered on account of my clothes, not my accent." Serge could tell that Blackford was not quite taking it all in. His mind was elsewhere.

Blackford was giving thought to the route he had memorized, the route that would take him to 226 Kalinin Prospekt. He calculated that to walk there would take forty minutes. Conveniently, at this meridian, he could arrive just after the sun had set.

THE ELEVATOR at 226 Kalinin did work, and at exactly six Blackford depressed the button for the fourteenth floor. The elevator creaked up and finally stopped. The door was not automatic. Blackford pushed it open. But when the elevator door closed behind him he found himself in total darkness. The overhead light was not working. He reached into his pocket and pulled out a penlight. He saw that he was standing outside 1404. He walked carefully, stopped at 1412, and knocked on the door. There was a moment of silence and then a voice, two words in Russian.

Blackford decided to reply in French, a language he knew his host to be familiar with. *"C'est moi. Avec qui vous avez fait le rendez-vous."*

The door opened. Blackford slid in and let it shut. He put out both arms and touched them down on the old man's shoulders. "Well, you scoundrel, you'll outlive us all."

He led Blackford to the tiny living room/dining room, motioning him to sit opposite at the table covered by a French-style red-and-white-checked tablecloth. On the table there was a bottle of wine in a dull aluminum cooler, a bottle of vodka, and a tray of *zakuski*.

Boris Bolgin had aged since their pivotal meeting in Geneva. How many times, over the years, they had crossed paths, Blackford reflected. And on two of those occasions Bolgin's very specific objective was to shoot Blackford; a third time, to kidnap him.

Blackford was talking to the man who had headed the KGB in Great Britain and briefly in all of Europe. Bolgin's figure was plump; what hair he had left was totally white. He bore on his face the scars of Siberia's frostbite. Bolgin had been seven years in Siberia when the Nazis marched. His knowledge of languages, vital to the war effort, rescued him from the Gulag. He began translating for the KGB, and six years after the war was chief of station in Great Britain, where he first crossed swords with Blackford.

But the last encounter, the one in Geneva, was Appomattox time. Boris handed Blackford his sword.

They had spent a long evening together. Bolgin did not volunteer to tell Blackford what it was that finally affected him. Blackford suspected he knew the reason why. It would seem so trivial, after all that had come before. Like defecting because of the Twentieth Congress speech against Stalin: why did anyone need to wait to hear it said by Khrushchev, three years after Stalin had died? He did not press Bolgin, who many years before had privately abjured first Stalin, then Stalinism, then Marxism, then communism. But he had not engineered the moral will actually to pull out—even to assert his right to retire, now that he was nearing age eighty. He hadn't thought to do what, finally, he was doing, across the table from a much younger man, but a venerable antagonist.

But Bolgin had come to the conclusion, whatever had driven him to it, that he could seek to compensate for the damage he had done in a lifetime's work for Soviet communism only by using what resources he had to seek to hinder its march, however erratic, through history. He did not wish to talk about the analysis he had made, and it did not occur to Blackford to inquire. So that the evening boiled down to the mechanics of the new life. From then on, Boris Bolgin became Cyclops.

Now, in Moscow, Blackford thought to ask immediately: "Boris, how much time can you give me?"

"I have as much time as you wish, Blackford. I will need to get home eventually. I do not live here. It is the apartment of a friend who is out of town."

Blackford let out a deep breath, then reached over and took the wine bottle, aiming it at Bolgin. "Or are you sticking to your vodka, you old lush?" Boris replied by reaching for the vodka and pouring himself a generous drink. With his other hand he advanced the wineglass to Blackford, who filled it.

"First things first, Boris." Blackford reached into his pocket, pulled out the clipping from the afternoon paper, and put it in front of Bolgin. "Was this business last week our gang? I mean, your gang?"

Bolgin looked down at the clipping, then raised the vodka to his lips and took a deep swallow.

"Yes," he said.

"Jesus Christ, Boris."

Boris chose this moment to talk at discursive length about high moments in the Bolgin–Oakes marathon. This was vodka time for Boris Bolgin, and at this time, usually spent alone, Bolgin was glad to talk to someone else. He wanted to know: What was the clue, back in 1951, that had led Blackford to trail the British viscount to the confessional in the little church in Mayfair at which, without ever being seen by Boris, the Queen's second cousin revealed through the priest's screen his nation's most delicate secrets? What was it that had prompted Blackford to arrange the kidnapping of the Soviet scientist in Paris, when he had to have known that the abduction could not hope to escape detection? Wasn't it, really, a breach of professional protocol when Blackford had refused to act as the executioner in the case of Count Wintergrin?

Blackford spoke frankly, gave to Bolgin everything he wished to hear, factual details sparing only continuing intelligence operations; he was glad to talk to Bolgin about what had motivated him, Blackford, to do this, or to do the other— intimacies which he had never felt free to share with any of his own countrymen. Sally, by mutual agreement, was generally excluded from details of his operations. The code within the CIA prevented him from talking about details extraneous to the operation, including those that touched on Blackford's frame of mind. But he could share these with his archenemy, because Bolgin needed no familiarization with the tangential perspectives. They were in the same business and could talk to each other as professionals. The code that barred a CIA agent from divulging to another CIA agent who did not need to know the particulars of an engagement did not operate here. There was no code detailing what you could or could not reveal to a defector who would remain in Moscow, and work from there for what had been the enemy. And Bolgin was glad to talk about his own experiences. Blackford learned details he hadn't known, and shivered over the closeness of past escapes.

And of course there was, finally, the business at hand.

It was ten at night when Blackford went to the elevator. Boris said he would allow fifteen minutes to pass before leaving to go to his own apartment.

CHAPTER 24

S ERGE THOUGHT—WHY NOT?—he might as well walk down Tchaikovsky Street and go by the embassy; maybe Gloria was working late, might just run into her. That wouldn't mean defying Dad's orders, exactly. And anyway, he wouldn't mind seeing what the derelict embassy looked like. It had received a lot of attention in recent weeks in America. In documenting the vulnerability of the unoccupied new embassy to intrusive Soviet intelligence, the State Department did not proceed to drop its objections to the old, inadequate embassy. The decision to abandon it for a more modern building with adequate facilities had, after all, been reached in the late sixties.

Moscow's street lights flashed on as Serge approached it and discerned the two Soviet guards at parade rest outside the large iron gates. He stopped to observe one of the guards leaving his post to open the gates and let a limousine slip out. The ambassador, presumably.

Serge approached the guards and spoke in Russian. "Hello, my name is Serpei and I am visiting from Kiev. This is the U.S. Embassy, is it not?"

They did not answer him.

"Oh come on now, tovarich. I would not treat *you* that way if *you* were visiting in Kiev. Our security guards there are very friendly. It isn't as though I were a threatening character," he laughed.

He succeeded. One of the guards said, "We are not supposed to speak except to people who seek entrance into the embassy. I will pretend that you are asking me to let you go in, so I can speak to you. Yes, it is the embassy. The hours are nine to twelve and two to five. But a Russian from Kiev—why would *he* want to visit the U.S. Embassy?"

The guard snorted, or at least that was what Serge made the sound out to be. "Maybe they would give you a tourist visa to visit America, but would our ministry give you an exit visa?" The other guard joined in the raillery.

"Well," said Serge, "I am in Moscow for the first time, to take the art course with the curator at the Kremlin museum. I like to wander about and see this fabulous city."

"You are allowed to come in during official hours by simply requesting to look at the U.S. Information Agency library, which has books and foreign periodicals. Many students do that. But we would then take your identification papers and put them in the registry."

Serge chuckled good-naturedly. He did in fact have an emergency I.D., a Kiev graduate student's university pass, but not with him. The rule was that he must never simultaneously keep on his person that I.D. and also his conflicting U.S. passport. He was now carrying his U.S. passport. "Well, maybe I'll come around tomorrow and have a look at their library. I studied English also at Kiev and can read it without difficulty." But the guard he was addressing had turned and was opening the inner gate to let someone out.

Serge caught a glimpse of her as she passed under the light over the guardhouse. He stepped back into the shadows. The young woman, wearing a light wool coat with a narrow fur collar, turned left and began to walk down Tchaikovsky Street. Serge lingered only long enough to avoid any impression that he was following her. He repeated to the guards that he would probably come in, if not tomorrow, one day soon. He said good night and sauntered off in the same direction as the girl. Once out of sight of the guardhouse, he quickened his pace until he was abreast of her.

"Gloria Huddleston! It's me, Serge Windels! What do you know!"

The woman stopped under the street light. Gloria Huddleston looked up at the man she had first known as the college senior who had attracted her in sophomore year at Ames. They had dated frequently during that spring and when Serge left to do graduate work at Georgetown she missed him greatly. They had corresponded for several months. But for the last five years they had settled down to Christmas-card exchanges. It was from her last card that Serge learned that Gloria was being sent to Moscow as a librarian for USIA. He had told her that he was working for IBM and spending a great deal of time traveling.

Her delight at seeing him was authentic and effusive, sentiments reciprocated by Serge, though it slightly bothered him that Oakes had told him not to make contact with her until further notice, and then only within the embassy. But . . . how, really, could it matter? It was, after all, a coincidence.

They walked happily down the street, laughing and asking about friends in common, until at one point Serge asked, "Hey, where are you walking to?" She said she was going home, "to cook a dull supper. Do you want to share it?"

Serge replied that sharing was the happiest conceivable way in which he could spend this uncharted evening. "Do you have everything you need, I mean for dinner for two?" Gloria reminded him that there was never any shortage of anything when one shopped at a United States Government PX. "And you can even have all the caviar you want to eat. It costs me, like, well, like next to nothing. But it's funny," she laughed. "When I first laid eyes on you at school I thought, Gee, this guy is a real authentic American hayseed—with your red hair and your freckles, and your Gary Cooper build. I wouldn't have guessed, that first time, that you would even know what caviar was. It wasn't till our third date that I found out you were as fluent in Russian as in English! Say, I'm getting pretty good at the language myself; you can try me out later if you want."

It was a tidy little apartment, nicely appointed by Gloria in a lively chintz purchased and sent by her mother. A single bedroom, then the living room with a little dining room at one end and a utilitarian opening to the kitchen. The walls were lined with books and prints of prerevolutionary Moscow. There was a framed front page of the November 9, 1917, daily, then also called *Pravda,* announcing the formation of a government in Petrograd by Vladimir Lenin. Gloria brought out a bottle of red wine and one of white wine, and they had vodka with their caviar, and then some Virginia ham with pickles and toasted dark Russian bread. They enjoyed themselves with mounting gaiety and nostalgia and lust, and soon after sipping the cognac Serge led her into the bedroom. In the muted light she was still the cheerful, nubile sophomore who never thought to disguise her delight in every aspect of carnality. Serge recalled that in the past there had never been a moment in their protracted unions when the smile left her face. This had not changed either, and it was all just as it had been back at college, fortified by manifest experience—so to speak, Serge even whispered it to her—"experience accumulated on the road."

"Jerry Singleton" was glad that Dad was not sitting in the living room when he got back to their hotel and opened the door to their two-bedroom suite. But Blackford could hardly be expected to be up at three-thirty in the morning.

CHAPTER 25

● OCTOBER 1986

MAJOR VASILOV FINISHED THE file. He had read every word in it. There was nothing there—*nothing*—to suggest that Vitaly Primakov had been a Soviet dissident, let alone that he would one day attempt to assassinate the leader of the Soviet Union. He and his sister Mariya were children of two farmers, both of them dead, who had worked in a collective in Okateyvsky. Vitaly had served honorably in Afghanistan, was discharged as a corporal. Vitaly had worked in the secondary school as a clerk-assistant to the director, who was most vigorously interrogated and could come up with not one incident in which Vitaly ever manifested any grievance against the regime. He then left Pitkin, as the administration referred to it, to take another job as a clerk, working alongside his sister. No one at the post office had any reason to suspect any subversive inclinations in Vitaly. Mariya's record was as clean as her brother's.

But the cyanide business!

"Let's face it, Bibikov," he addressed his assistant, "you do not find post office clerks who have handy supplies of cyanide. Mariya was not the daughter of a chemist. Her doctor advises us"—Vasilov picked up the folder and flicked it open—that "'the patient Mariya Primakov came to me on July 2, 1985, to request an abortion. A routine examination revealed that she was in good health. She was admitted the following day to the local clinic where the procedure was successfully performed. She was discharged later the same day.' That is her *entire* medical record. Our representative did not ask the doctor whether, by any chance, he had cyanide pills lying about for dissatisfied clients."

"It's the pill," Bibikov said, "that gives it away, doesn't it?"

"Well now hold on, Bibikov. I agree that the pill absolutely suggests that the woman was in on the assassination. But unless we have leads to someone else, just because we can't find out how she got the cyanide doesn't mean she couldn't have got it on her own. We can't assume there's an incriminated doctor or chemist on the scene. Who knows where? . . . How? . . . Why?— No, we know *why*. That's now obvious. The medical report says that the plastic sheathing enclosing the cyanide is the kind used in capsules designed to dissolve slowly, and they're routinely available. To have got one of those and then filled it with the cyanide does not require any special skill. But getting possession of the cyanide in the first place has to mean that someone in the medical business let him, or her, have it. On the other hand, its location having been accidentally spotted, it might have been stolen."

Konstantin Vasilov lit a cigarette and inhaled deeply. Lieutenant Bibikov reached for his own pack, but before lighting up said, "May I, Major?"

"Yes, yes." He paused. "The pressure from the Kremlin is very great."

"What are you going to recommend, Major?"

Vasilov stubbed out his cigarette, stood up, leaned back against the window, and spoke in a voice almost theatrically resolute. "I'm going to tell Krivitsky, uh, General Krivitsky, I am going to tell him, General, you have to go in one direction or in the other. You cannot achieve the effects you desire from Course B under conditions only Course A will promote. Either we let the matter go and assume Primakov and his deranged sister were lone assassins, or we publicize Vitaly Primakov."

"What exactly do you have in mind, Major?"

"If we are fully to attempt to trace everyone with whom he kept company, then obviously we need to know everyone with whom he kept company. And we can do that only by putting his picture in the newspapers and in the post offices."

"What exactly would you put on the picture?"

"Here is where I believe I can satisfy Krivitsky. General Krivitsky. We do not need to say that this is the picture of *the man who tried to assassinate the chief of state*. We can simply say that the Bureau of Missing Persons urgently desires to meet with anyone who knew this person, Vitaly Primakov. What does that let out? Merely that he is missing; not that he tried to kill Gorbachev. Of course, the people around the post office where he worked—they know, they've heard about it. But it isn't likely that we're going to find his confederates in his place of work. We will need to count on someone showing up who saw him in extra-office, extra-home situations, and see what kind of a lead we can develop there."

"Would it be wise to offer a reward? I mean, what incentive would there be for someone to go to the bureau otherwise?"

Major Vasilov looked up at his assistant. "I think that is a good idea. But then the whole operation will need to be decided by Krivitsky. General Krivitsky."

CHAPTER 26

B LACKFORD WAS UP EARLY. Systematically he explored his alternatives.

Boris Bolgin had been frustratingly noncommittal. But one thing he ruled out at the outset of their long conversation: Bolgin would not reveal to Blackford the identity of the ringleader of the new Narodniki—the term he used, explaining to Blackford the historical reference.

"I have betrayed enough people in my life, and have lost completely the appetite to betray any more."

Blackford had reminded him sharply that in his original message, advising Blackford of the small group bent on assassinating Gorbachev, Bolgin had said he would interdict the operation if the President of the United States asked him to. "Well, Boris, okay, for a year there was no such request from the President. But now there is. Aren't you committed to abort?"

"Blackford, Blackford, be careful with your language. I am not in a position to 'abort' the operation, as you put it. Yes, one of the members of the young group has taken me into his confidence, and some of the information he has given me I have relayed to you via our computer channel. But if I were to say to him that he and his confederates must abandon their enterprise, I know very well what he would say."

"What?"

"He would say, 'You are an old man, with very little in the future to look forward to. We are young people, and have not lost our idealism.'"

"Which means?"

"Exactly."

It wasn't necessary to spell out Bolgin's ultimate weapon, which was of course that if he failed to persuade the young Narodniki to abandon their objective, there was always the alternative of turning them in to the KGB.

"Exactly. The one alternative I flatly reject." He had poured another vodka and then said to Blackford, "This doesn't mean that you must give up any hope of forestalling another attempt on Gorbachev's life. I'm not saying that I can succeed, but I can certainly attempt to succeed in persuading my contact that the mission should be abandoned. As I say, there is no reason to believe that they will heed my counsel. But they *might* do so. And in any case, they will listen to me—my contact will listen to me, and he will relay my thoughts to the others. May I remind you that it has been more than one year since I gave the President the option of interceding? Since he did not take up that option at the time, I have to reason that he decided that, between the young Narodniki and Gorbachev, it was an internal affair. Well, why does his reasoning suddenly alter? Why should I consider myself bound by your President's revision of *his* position? It is not as though you had come to me with evidence that Gorbachev is in fact opposed to communism and determined to put an end to it."

Bolgin paused after taking another gulp from his drink.

"What would be *most* useful for me, Blackford, is any confidential evidence that Mikhail Gorbachev is truly prepared to lead our country away from communism. He reiterated publicly his faith in communist ideology as recently as a month ago."

"Yes. But isn't that more or less required? In fact his willingness to talk about disarmament, even if it is only incremental, does mean *something*. And the press is somewhat freer than it has ever been."

Bolgin had waved that argument aside, reminding Blackford that the history of the Soviet Union was punctuated by spasms of liberalism, in every case of brief duration—the New Economic Plan of Lenin, the "spring" of Khrushchev ("which lasted about eighteen months"). "When, after Chernenko died, Gromyko nominated Gorbachev for his present position, he said to the Politburo, 'This man has a nice smile but he's got iron teeth.' I regret to tell you that he was, I think, right. Gorbachev has teeth of iron."

Blackford, abandoning the wine, had taken the proffered cup of tea. He acknowledged to himself that his heart was not entirely in his commission. But he also recognized that in fact he had the power to overrule Bolgin. By betraying him.

So that when he woke that morning in the hotel and looked out of the window at the Bauhaus drabness of the big office building across the way, beyond which the eye could only barely discern the onion domes of the old churches within the Kremlin, Blackford Oakes put the question to himself: *Would my failure to betray Bolgin be the equivalent of my betraying the President of the United States?*

SERGE WAS later than usual in going out for his morning jog. Blackford stopped him at the door. "Sit down a minute, Serge."

Dressed in his running shorts and T-shirt, he did so.

"Okay, here's how it stands. I'm going to schedule another meeting with my man. He will contact me when next he sees our little notice in the post office, but the new one should include the phrase, 'So anxious—please help.' Post it on the bulletin board early tomorrow. That means tomorrow afternoon he will tell me where to report that evening. You are to follow me to where the meeting is. It may last a half hour, maybe three hours.

You are to look for me to come out of that building. I will have prearranged where you are to wait for me, not more than one block away. We will both watch the apartment building and when my man walks out I'll point him out—*'That's him.'*

"You have two jobs. The first is to follow him back to his own apartment, so that we know where he lives. The next is to devise a way, if you can, to identify anyone who goes to his apartment to call on him. And to trail that person when he leaves the building, and find out where *he* lives. This can be a long, arduous job but it's one we have to take on. I'll take the flight to Washington the day after tomorrow, after meeting with my man. I have to straighten out an urgent matter. That means," Blackford pulled out his counterfeit engagement book, "that I'll be back on Tuesday, October 28. Meanwhile, the story is that you are staying on here, taking in the sights of Moscow and hoping to turn up a lead on your aunt. I had to go home temporarily because . . . because my sister has been hospitalized. If we have any luck, when I get back you will have a few names, if possible photographs, of people Bolgin is seeing. My hunch is that he sees very few people, and if that's true, we may make it real fast to the guy we're looking for."

"What do I say if some Moscow cop spots me spending a few uninterrupted hours staring at one apartment-building entrance?"

"You'll have to elaborate on how we have a lead that maybe that's where your aunt is living. She may be dotty, which is why she's not taking the initiative in identifying herself."

"Well, Dad. I may as well go and have a good jog. Obviously my next few days—weeks?—are going to be pretty sedentary."

CHAPTER 27

IT WAS ON THE Friday after Bolshoi that Nikolai gave out the word that there would be another meeting of the Narodniki, usual place, usual time, the following Sunday.

Philosophically they had prepared themselves to discount the loss of Vitaly. But they now knew that there was no way to prepare emotionally for such a loss, let alone cope with the unexpected suicide of Mariya. She had confided to no one that she would swallow the cyanide pill with which, two months ago, Nikolai had supplied each of his confederates, after Viktor's successful operation.

Viktor had befriended a graduate student in the department of chemistry. While being given something on the order of a guided tour, Viktor had been introduced to the cyanide bottle, among the forty or fifty chemicals on the long shelf. Late one afternoon, dressed in a technician's smock, Viktor had brought down the bottle from the shelf and poured twelve grams out into a vial—two grams constituting, he had established, double a lethal dose. It was safer, if bent on suicide or poisoning, to take more than the single gram, though one gram, historian Viktor had ascertained, was all the cyanide that had been needed to kill that glob Goering, found dead the morning he was scheduled to hang. Twelve grams was an unnoticeable reduction in the powdery chemical level inside one of the dozens of laboratory bottles, each one holding a hundred grams of the sundry powders.

Nikolai told the diminished company that there were matters to explore after the Bolshoi experience. The most obvious one was that security was not possible where two Narodniki lived together, let alone were brother and sister working together. "I take responsibility for it. I should have thought the matter through, the almost certain apprehension and torture of Mariya. Her survival made Vitaly's death irrelevant. We had him executed in order to protect the rest of us, ignoring that Mariya would be left alive."

Andrei disagreed. He said that tragic though Mariya's death was, there was a significant dividend that came from Pavel's having shot Vitaly. "If we had just let Vitaly take the pill, they'd still have gone after Mariya, and she'd still have had to take the pill. But since he had to die, it was grim but good tactics that he should die from Pavel's pistol. After all, Pavel has now been promoted to lieutenant and made a part of the Kremlin security detachment. We can't disregard our new advantage, can we?"

Pavel agreed that he was superbly situated to expedite the next advance on Gorbachev, whether by himself or by someone else.

At this point Viktor said that the episode of the Bolshoi Ballet had caused him to think deeply about the philosophy of the original Narodniki. Those heroic young people had given up their lives in order to kill individual tyrants of the third echelon, he said. None of them conspired against the Czar. But it was precisely against the equivalent of the Czar that Nikolai's band was conspiring, and the reason for this was their profound belief that an assassination of that magnitude could trigger a convulsive political uprising, counter-revolutionary in its implications. "And if that's the case," Viktor said, "then we're entitled to give a little thought to our own survival. Maybe we can live to see a new Russia the old Narodniki never dreamed possible."

Pavel said that a change in philosophical strategy of that nature would clearly benefit him, in his present situation. "After all,

I've become, so to speak, a part of the Imperial Guard. I don't pretend to be close to Gorbachev every few minutes, but I laid eyes
on him three times in the last couple of days. And if it were to be
as simple as a dual death, Narodniki style, I probably would have
the opportunity sometime soon to approach him, unsuspected,
whip out my police revolver and pump it into his brain. Before I
was through I'd be dead from Uzi fire from other guards. But if I
were less than dead, I would certainly bite down on my cyanide
capsule rather than face what I'd be faced with, which would almost inevitably lead to the betrayal of—you." Pavel paused, and
here his voice broke. "You, my blood brothers."

Nikolai acknowledged the force of these arguments and said
that grave thought should be given to them. Viktor interrupted
him. "Dear Nikolai, you are very scholarly in inclination, I know,
since I am myself an academic. But we really don't have to have
eternal seminars on this subject, do we? Why not proceed on the
revised understanding, and consider only assassination strategies
that give the assassin a reasonable opportunity to escape?"

Nikolai said nothing. Clearly the framework of his strategy
had been moved to another plane. His companions respected his
vision as well as his responsibilities.

"Among other things," Andrei contributed, "if we are going
to outlaw Narodniki who live together, then you and I, Nikolai,
would have to cease sharing an apartment. And since you're the
wounded veteran entitled to it," Andrei let out a chortle, "that
means I would have to move. And pray, dear Nikolai, where
would I move to? I cannot afford to move in with Nina seven
nights a week. Only a millionaire could afford that."

Nikolai looked up. His sense of authority had returned.
"Yes, of course, there is always a reason to survive, in the hope
of enjoying a better country—a better country in part because of
our efforts. Perhaps you are right, Viktor, that we should vote to
change our constitution to read, simply, that we are prepared to
die for our cause, rather than that we plan to die for our cause."

Viktor grinned. "As they say in parliamentary countries, 'All
in favor, say Aye!'"

Pavel's hand went up, as did Andrei's and, finally, Nikolai's.

They brought out their lunch from the little individual knap-sacks. Viktor produced four bottles of Pepsi-Cola. "You are aware," he said, handing each of his companions a bottle, "that Gorbachev is sending vodka to America in exchange for making Pepsi-Cola here?"

"Perhaps," Andrei said, "he hopes the Americans will all be-come alcoholics, like people who live under communism."

"To accomplish that," Pavel said, "he'd have to export com-munism along with the vodka. I don't think there are many signs that the Americans are willing to accept communism, however drunk they are."

After the lunch wrappings had been carefully put back in their cases, Nikolai brought the meeting to order: He had evolved a plan for the second attempt. "But after our conversa-tion today, I can see that there is a missing part. That part has to do with arranging escape strategies. Because the plan I have in mind would certainly lead the KGB to me and to Pavel. And if they begin to look for me, they will begin also to look for you, Andrei. So—I won't outline the plan. And we will not put it into effect until the escape strategies are formulated. And here is one very important element of those escape strategies: It is that each of us is to work out his own design and under no circumstances reveal what it is to any of the others.

"So that if one of us is caught, and for whatever reason doesn't succeed in taking the cyanide, then he will not have the information the torturers will be working to pry out of him."

"But," Viktor made the qualification, "he would know our identities."

"Yes. In the situation we envision, the prisoner, incapable of absorbing further torture, would give out our names. But ours is a very large country, and it is something else for the KGB to track us down. In making our individual arrangements to escape we must assume that the KGB will have our names and photographs—Viktor, have you been officially photographed?"

"Of course. Just like you and Andrei, by the army."

"Right. Yes. So that anyone caught who revealed the names of the rest of us—the names would lead to photographs, which would lead to television exposure of our faces. Not easy to escape detection from that kind of a manhunt."

"We would have to hope that before the information was given out, the captured one's cyanide would be taken."

"Yes," Nikolai said.

Andrei spoke. "It is getting a little late. I take it we will not hear the plan at this session, Nikolai? We will hear it only—we are not to implement it until—until when? How long are you giving us to arrange the escape plans?"

Nikolai thought. "Unless someone here is contemplating cosmetic surgery, which," he grinned, "would make it difficult to continue in our present jobs, any disguise we consider would have to be theatrical. That would be the first priority, to devise a convincing disguise. The second would be false papers. And the third—"

Andrei supplied the answer. "The third is money. Money is most awfully useful, as I think I mentioned to you, Nikolai, the first night we met. Back when you were a virgin." Instantly he regretted his slip: only Andrei knew that Nikolai, their leader, had a girlfriend. Perhaps Viktor suspected it, since he'd have seen Nikolai and Tatyana lunch together so frequently before Nikolai went over to MEIE. He bit his tongue.

Nikolai ignored him. "On the matter of identification papers, we all know that superficial counterfeits are pretty widely available. The kind you can buy for twenty rubles will maybe work to get you an extra ration coupon to buy vodka. But we will want high-quality papers. Each of us has different ties in different directions. Let's agree that one week from now we will each have got satisfactory counterfeit identifications.

"Now. On the matter of money, I have to confess that short of bank robbing, which isn't my line of work, I have—no ideas, offhand."

Viktor broke in. "How much money are we talking about?"

Pavel spoke. "I learned from the police academy that passports can be got for one thousand rubles from master forgers."

"That would be the basic expense," Nikolai said. "But if those passports are going to be used to leave the country, we'd need travel money. How much?"

Viktor again volunteered. He said that a fellow student in the History Department at the university went for a three-week academic stay in Helsinki for less than five hundred rubles. "Obviously there were people there to look after him, make things cheaper in food and lodging. But would it be safe to say that for double that—say, one thousand rubles—you could leave the country and subsist for a while?"

"Sounds about right," Pavel said. "So that makes: two thousand rubles, half for papers, one quarter for travel, one quarter for subsistence."

"I have twenty-five rubles," Andrei grinned. "Granted, I could save at a faster rate if I curbed certain appetites. In . . . two years I might be able to save two thousand rubles."

Pavel spoke again. "Two thousand rubles and there are four of us, which means eight thousand. I can supply that sum. I'll hand over to each of you two thousand rubles next Sunday, if we are to meet on Sunday."

The effect of his announcement was electric.

Nikolai broke the spell. "Dear Pavel, you are not to expose yourself to criminal activity. The Narodniki are not about robbing banks."

"I propose only to rob from my dear mother, Nikolai."

Pavel took a few minutes to tell them the story of his mother's grand hallucination. "But when I was six years old and she told it to me, she led me upstairs to her bedroom, where there is a safe. A quite large safe. She opened it and brought out a truly remarkable jewel case. I am relying on my memory, but I was so fascinated by it I fondled the bracelets and the necklaces and the rings and earrings one by one. I asked her where she got them. She whispered to me that they had been given to her by the Czarevitch as a wedding gift a year or so before I—the Czarevitch's son—was born."

"Where did she in fact get them?"

"An old family retainer, who was my nurse for a while, told me when I was growing up that my mother's family had left her some jewelry. Also the general she was briefly married to."

"How is it that she hasn't disposed of them?" Nikolai asked.

"Because," Pavel smiled eagerly, caught up in the romance of his youth, "she has sworn not to wear them until the Restoration takes place. As she put it, 'When I step out with my jewels on, the people will look at me and say, "How appropriate that the Czarena had such magnificent jewels."'"

Andrei asked, "Have you any idea how much her collection is worth?"

"Well, no, actually. I don't know what jewels go for in the black market. But it is not in the least a problem to find out. My offhand guess is that they are worth much, much more than we need. I'd be surprised if they fetched less than one hundred thousand. On the other hand, I needn't sell them all. Though probably it would be good if we each had three thousand instead of two thousand rubles. A little money for bribes would prove useful."

No one of the Narodniki was so indelicate as to dispute that point. Nikolai said that given the press of events, they would meet again the following Sunday. But that he and Pavel, who had been cooperating on the plan, would not waste any time in the interval in moving forward, to the extent they could do so.

"Let me ask you this," Viktor wanted to know. "If you disclose the plan next Sunday, is it likely that it would go into effect within a week? Because in coming up with an escape strategy it would help us all to know whether we are talking about the immediate future or . . . or next spring, or whatever."

Nikolai said that if the plan could be effected at all, it would be effected in the following week, or fortnight.

CHAPTER 28

S ERGE DECIDED AFTER THE first day of his reconnaissance activ- ity that perhaps on day two he should take a few precautions and come up with successive disguises. Tomorrow a hat, a mustache, a pipe, and some utterly forgettable clothes.

On the first day he had done as much as he could to make himself inconspicuous and at the same time to keep his eyes relentlessly on the entrance to 1005 Dimitrova Street, into which, the night before, he had tracked Boris Bolgin (finally, Dad had confided his name to him) returning from his engagement with Blackford. In the relative dark—there are no street lights on Dimitrova—he quickly cased the street opposite the building and was glad to find that it harbored several little state-run enterprises: a fish store, a cafeteria, a shoe store, a barber shop, and a post office. He could reasonably spend a certain amount of time at each of these while keeping an eye on the building opposite.

And indeed he did, especially trying the patience of the shoe store clerk who, to begin with, didn't care whether Serge bought a pair of shoes or not, but became impatient when he rejected one pair after another, having tried on about twenty. But the shoe testing was good for using up a whole hour, Serge's eye on the target across the street as he sat trying on the shoes. And he was able three times to patronize the cafeteria, always seated so that he could see across the street.

It was prudent of him to think to wear a disguise, but the difficulty was that his decision to do so came too late.

ON HIS second visit to the restaurant, on day one, two men were seated at a table in a corner, one of them facing away from Bolgin's apartment building. Diagonally, he faced Serge Windels.

Yegor Bolsky was short and squat and kept his fedora on mostly to cover a head very nearly bald. After several discreet stares at Serge Windels, he whispered to his companion, *"Supov. Keep talking to me. I am reaching in my pocket for my Minox. I want to take a picture of a man; for heaven's sake keep your eyes looking at your plate or at me. Don't turn around. I am quite certain I remember him from Berlin. If I am right, he is an American agent. Right, keep mumbling to me. My fingers are on the camera and in a second I will draw it out and cover it with my left hand. When I do that, take a match—there—"* he pointed with his nose, *"and lean toward me as if you were going to light my cigarette. I will quickly remove my hand from the lens and snap a picture. I am not certain whether, during the Berlin operation, he ever actually saw me. But since you were not in Berlin, he would not recognize you. So when he leaves I will nudge you, and you leave a few seconds later—I'll take care of the bill. Keep your eyes on him, follow him wherever he goes."*

The photography completed, Bolsky returned the camera to his pocket. "I will take this over to the lab and go then to the Berlin file—I am talking about an operation in . . . 1983. Yes, February and March 1983."

SERGE FELT that for so long as other diners still sat in the cafeteria, he could safely continue to kill time by sitting there, reading his newspaper and monitoring the building across the street.

But Bolgin did not once leave his apartment building. At the end of the day, Serge would know whether there had been any inbound traffic—assuming the hall porter at the building was diligent in logging visitors to Bolgin's apartment. Serge had told the porter that he was with the Ministry of Veterans' Affairs and needed to verify whether Bolgin had any relatives who might look after him, as the veterans' retirement homes were terribly overcrowded, and although Bolgin had applied for a veteran's apartment and claimed not to have relatives, his record listed several. The Ministry was investigating, and to do this required confidentially logging those visitors who came and went.

For almost one-half hour, only the two men at the corner table were left in the cafeteria. Meanwhile, the imperious, buxom waitress, who had taken away his sugar bowl after Serge had got from it only a single teaspoonful, was talking, ostensibly to herself, about customers who are so thoughtless as to treat the cafeteria as a waiting room.

So he got up and left. And was followed.

Yegor BOLSKY got his picture developed. He took it to archives at KGB Research and told the captain he had reason to believe there was an American agent in Moscow, and if this picture—he put it down in front of the captain—corresponded with a picture that would be found in the Berlin repository under Operation Halmstrasse, then Yegor Bolsky was indeed onto something. "Meanwhile," he said in a tone detectably self-satisfied, "I am having the suspect followed."

The Operations file came up with a photograph. There was a marked likeness between the lanky American pictured slipping the envelope to the Russian defector in Berlin on February 10, 1983, and the lanky American who had been reading the paper at the cafeteria on Dimitrova Street only two hours earlier. The brass upstairs showed interest. A deputy to General Krivitsky, no less, came down to take charge.

"Very unusual," he nodded his head solemnly. "But does the Halmstrasse file tell us who the American agent was—is? Or do we know only that this was the man who slipped the money to the traitor, Wallensky?"

"I have not personally examined the entire file," Bolsky said. "Do you wish me to do so?"

"Well, you're the logical person to do so, Bolsky. After all, you snapped the picture back then."

But the search was fruitless.

Which meant that all the KGB had to go on was a plausible conviction: that the American spy who had been caught feeding a Russian defector in Berlin an envelope, later established as containing five thousand marks, was currently in Moscow, presumably up to no good.

It was with some eagerness that they awaited the return of Bolsky's assistant, Supov, who would tell them where the American spy had gone. The deputy instructed Bolsky to call him at his office when Supov showed up; if the deputy had left his office, he would leave word with the duty officer, and Bolsky could reach him wherever he was.

It was after eight when the fatigued Supov, an elderly man, almost professionally unnoticeable, with a colorless face, clad in his colorless suit, sat down in Bolsky's office. He didn't even think to ask whether the photograph had validated Bolsky's suspicion. He launched right into his report, reading from a notepad.

"The suspect left the restaurant and went to the shoe store two doors down," he read in a monotone. "He was there for almost an hour. He went then to the fish store, which is two doors down, and was there for over a half hour. He did not come out with a package in his hand, so we assume that he did not buy any fish. He went to the post office at the corner. He was there until the post office closed at five-thirty. He returned to the cafeteria and ordered a cup of tea. At six-fifteen he crossed the street and entered 1005 Dimitrova. He reappeared ten minutes later and stopped a taxi. I succeeded in getting a second taxi, gave the driver my credentials, and instructed him to follow the cab ahead at a distance that would not alert the occupant, and told him when the cab we were following stopped to discharge its passenger, he was to continue driving for fifty meters, stopping at the opposite side of the street to discharge me.

"All of this was done. The suspect left his cab at Krasina Street. I stopped one block further. Walking at a good clip I could soon see the suspect in the apartment building vestibule of number 68 Krasina, and I could actually note which of the buttons he was depressing. After he went up the elevator, I walked in and wrote down the name corresponding to the button he pushed. It is, first 'G.' Then I will spell the last name: 'H-u-d-d-l-e-s-t-o-n.' I decided to come back home. It is most probable that the suspect is still in that apartment. Indeed, it is possible that he occupies that apartment."

Bolsky wondered at first whether the information elicited was dramatic enough to warrant rousing the deputy, who, it being after 9 p.m., was almost certainly at home or at some function or other. He would decide based on what the duty officer told him. If he was at a ballet, or at a meeting of high commissioners, Bolsky would wait until tomorrow. If, on the other hand, he was at home, Bolsky would go ahead and ring him.

The deputy was home, and Bolsky did ring him. The deputy reacted immediately.

An agent was to be sent immediately to the apartment where the suspect was last seen. Supov must stay with that agent until the American left the building, in order to identify him. The suspect must then be followed in order to establish where he was living—his address in Moscow, so to speak, if different from the current address. The deputy was to be informed the following morning where the suspect had spent the night. The deputy would then decide how to proceed.

All this was set in motion. It proved a most fearfully long watch for Supov, whose instructions were to stay with the new agent until the suspect reappeared; because at six in the morning, daylight imminent, the suspect *still* had not left the building. Supov had been up now twenty-four hours and was ready to collapse. He told his replacement, finally, that he was going to go home, and that the agent should, at eight promptly, report to Bolsky that obviously the suspect was living right there, at 68 Krasina, under the name "G. Huddleston."

All this information was dutifully communicated to the deputy, and 68 Krasina was put under permanent surveillance, the KGB detail, armed with the photograph taken the preceding day, assigned the responsibility of trailing the suspect when he finally appeared.

The man of the photograph never did come out of the apartment building. One agent was placed inside the building, where he could survey the occupants' panel, carefully monitoring anyone who rang the bell for G. Huddleston. A second agent discreetly patrolled the hallway into which apartment 803 emptied.

But no one rang the Huddleston bell downstairs until about 7 p.m. It was a man who then rang, but not the suspect. This man wore a mustache and a shapeless hat and had a pipe in his mouth.

The agent on the eighth floor reported that a man with a mustache and a Tyrolean-style hat had a few moments later knocked on the door of 803 and been admitted.

The deputy thought all of this interesting enough to bring to the attention of General Krivitsky himself. The general listened with characteristic patience. He then acted with characteristic decisiveness. "It is obvious that the apartment at 68 Krasina is being used by at least one American agent, perhaps more. You will," he turned to his deputy, "organize a break-in at eleven tonight. Give Bolsky three men. Armed. Their story is that we have information that the apartment is being used by a drug merchant. Bring in whoever is there, and leave one man to search the apartment thoroughly."

At 11:03, with the passkey obtained from the superintendent, the door to 803 swung open and four swirling flashlights came to rest on a couch in which a tall young man, quite naked, was copulating with a young woman, also naked. The lieutenant spat out a few words, the flashlights were deflected to one side, the clothes on the floor were flung at the couple, who were gruffly instructed to dress and prepare to accompany the police to headquarters.

After a decent interval, Bolsky turned on the overhead light and then looked at the couple, dressed now and holding hands. It was both surprising and gratifying that the man was the suspect whose trail had been temporarily lost.

Pavel ZELINSKY led a drab life. His wife had left him, taking along his twelve-year-old son. She was unwilling, she said, any longer to put up with his alcoholic fits, during which he would often batter his wife and his son. He had submitted to a cure, and after six months' treatment at the terrible sanitarium/detention center near Zagorsk, to his wife's disgust he—a reformed alcoholic—had taken a job as a bartender!

Now, Galina and the boy gone, Pavel had nothing to look forward to, nothing to occupy him. He paid listless attention to the humdrum television programs in the morning before going to work; another two hours of television during his time off in the afternoon, then back to the dingy bar that served neighborhood clerical workers, night workers, and a few schoolteachers. Until closing time, at ten.

The one exhilaration came weekly. It was then that his nervous system came, however briefly, to life. This happened in the post office when he received the weekly letter from his wife—postmark illegible, no return address—reporting on how things were with her and with their son. These letters invariably arrived on Tuesday mornings, and after several months' experience Pavel could anticipate that the letter would be inserted in his box between nine and eleven. Accordingly, he would appear at the post office at nine, the hour it opened. Every five minutes he would peer into his little window, waiting to see whether the postal clerk at the other end of the wall of boxes had inserted his letter. His letter from Galina.

Until it arrived, Pavel would kill time by running his eyes over the notices pinned on the bulletin board. Mostly they were notices to boxholders, announcing one new regulation or another. There were also announcements of forthcoming public events and neighborhood artistic doings and gallery openings.

And there was a section devoted to men and women wanted by official Moscow: the police, the Ministry of Veterans' Affairs, the Missing Persons Bureau. He had become familiar with the photographic gallery, but today he saw a fresh face. He approached the photograph. It was of a face he knew, someone he had frequently brought a drink to, him and his wife, and his friend. He read the text carefully.

This man, Vitaly Primakov, was wanted by the Bureau of Missing Persons, who would give a "substantial reward" to anyone who came in with information on the basis of which the Bureau could locate the said Primakov.

Pavel Zelinsky had come upon something vaguely interesting, interrupting the miserable routine of his miserable life.

But it was time to check his window, and—it had arrived! He pulled the key from his pocket, opened the box, tore open the letter, and read hungrily the two-page note from Galina. She was well etc. etc. etc., Petya was doing well at school etc. etc. etc. Pavel was waiting always for that one word that she missed him, that she loved him, that she would permit him to write to her, that she would consider returning to Moscow if he was cured. But no. Petya's grades at school. Her work hours had changed. They had had meat for lunch Thursday, on the birthday of the mayor. He stuffed the letter into his pocket.

And then thought suddenly of Vitaly Primakov. Pavel Zelinsky had, God and the angels and saints knew, absolutely nothing else to do until work time. So all right, he would report to the Bureau of Missing Persons. He approached the bulletin board to get the address: 1010 Pavlovsky Street. Convenient, right by a metro stop.

He was there in less than half an hour and was momentarily put off by the humming bureaucracy, though the clerks, mostly women, were engaged, or seemed to be, primarily in talking with one another. He waited by the long counter until one of them took note of him. To her he said that he had seen the notice asking for anyone who knew Vitaly Primakov. Well, Pavel Zelinsky knew him.

The clerk, a chubby woman whose fingernails were so long she had difficulty opening the file, found the right page and dialed the number of the officer who should be called in re Primakov. Pavel was told to go to the third floor and to ask for Comrade Valerian.

He did so. Valerian took notes as Pavel Zelinsky spoke. Vitaly and his wife—at least, Pavel took her to be his wife because she was very affectionate toward Vitaly—came quite often to the bar at Vernadskogo Prospekt. They met there often with a young man. No, he didn't know the young man's name but he had gathered from a conversation overheard that he was a teacher at the Pitkin School nearby.

Would he be able to identify that man, if he were shown pictures of the faculty at Pitkin?

Oh yes, that would be quite easy to do.

An official car drove Pavel Zelinsky to the KGB and he was taken to the cluttered office of Major Konstantin Vasilov. A second car came in from the Pitkin School, carrying the superintendent's dossier of photographs of the thirty-six men and women who had taught at Pitkin at any point during the academic year. Major Vasilov instructed Pavel to examine the pictures.

He did so.

The major spoke anxiously. "Do you recognize him?"

"Yes, Comrade Major."

"Well. Which one?"

"I have a favor to ask."

"You will get your reward, you have my word on it. Which one?"

"No, Comrade Major. I wasn't talking about the reward. Well, perhaps you can call it a reward, in a way. I wish the help of the Bureau of Missing Persons."

Major Vasilov looked at Pavel. An unappealing figure, perhaps forty years old, half of one front tooth missing, his hair scraggly, his shave irregular. Major Vasilov was not accustomed to being treated this way.

He decided to be stern. "Are you telling me that you refuse to identify this man unless I put the Missing Persons Bureau at your disposal?"

"Well, Comrade Major, I did not mean to sound quite so demanding. It's just that I wish to locate my wife, to find out where she is. I am in a position to give the Bureau a great deal of help, because she writes to me every week, and perhaps the letter could be traced. For instance, last Thursday, the birthday of the mayor of the town she lives in took place. I know that."

Major Vasilov reasoned that he had two alternatives. One was to have one of his men rough up Zelinsky—there were ample facilities to get that done, here at number 2 Dzerzhinsky. But it would be messy, and there was a distinct intractability he detected in this unprepossessing bartender. The second alternative was to grant his request. What did he, Konstantin Vasilov, care?

"I shall grant your request." He turned to Lieutenant Bibikov. "Lieutenant, get me on the telephone Comrade Zagrev." He turned to Pavel Zelinsky. "Zagrev is the chief of the Bureau of Missing Persons."

Zagrev was on the line.

"Comrade Zagrev, it is Konstantin Vasilov. Major Vasilov, KGB. Calling on behalf of General Krivitsky. I wish to make a formal request on behalf of the KGB. Comrade Pavel Zelinsky will come by your office this afternoon to identify a missing person and to give you information on the basis of which you can be expected to locate her. Is that agreeable, Comrade Zagrev? . . . Yes. Well, good day. And yes, I shall pass along your regards to General Krivitsky."

He turned now to Pavel Zelinsky. "Point to him."

Pavel pointed to the picture of Viktor Pletnev.

CHAPTER 29

● OCTOBER 1986

IN THE INTERVAL SINCE the Bolshoi episode, Lieutenant Pavel Pogodin had made important inroads with, no less, General Secretary Mikhail Gorbachev. A week after Bolshoi, Pavel was called into Gorbachev's private office and there, in the presence of Pavel's immediate superior and of the three principal officials concerned with Kremlin security, he was decorated with the Soviet Order of the Red Star. Gorbachev informally instructed him to stand at attention while he pinned the red star-shaped medal on his chest and read the citation commending him for extraordinary diligence and speed of motion in a critical security situation.

Gorbachev then told Pavel, who had been standing at attention, to go to parade rest. Pavel did so. Gorbachev informed him that the decoration must not be given any publicity until after the Kremlin officially took note of the attempt on the life of the General Secretary. "That of course is a day that may never come. It will depend on comprehensive security considerations." But the citation would be noted in Pavel's official record, and when it was made public, Pavel would be entitled to wear the little red star on his uniform. Gorbachev then formally embraced Pavel, and dismissed the company.

Pavel had already been relieved of his automobile radio beat. He was now posted in the principal headquarters security office at the northeast end of the Kremlin, where he was one of thirty-six men and four women. It was here that arrangements were made to provide for contingency security precautions, such as for the visit of an American President, or a May Day parade, or a trip by the General Secretary to the Caucasus. Pavel was assigned as an aide to Major Slavitz.

And very soon he learned that subordinate officers in the security unit were primarily used for the simple convenience of Politburo brass. Comrade Shevardnadze's chauffeur having complained of bad radio reception, a junior officer was sent to "do something about it." First Deputy Foreign Minister Kovalev's secretary was tired of waiting for Procurement to bring in the new electronic typewriter—a junior officer was assigned the job of expediting the order.

What happened three times in the fortnight after Pavel's posting was a request by General Secretary Gorbachev's office, but a request in which the services of Pavel were specifically requested, by name.

Gorbachev maintained a small personal suite, a short hallway's distance from his imperial office. He used it mostly for quick naps, for an occasional shower in the middle of the day, and as simple shelter against bureaucratic din. He wanted, he told Pavel on leading him into it, a television set "of the kind they have in modern hospitals." One that came down on a metal arm that would suspend the screen at whatever distance from the eye the user wished, so that he might lie relaxed in bed and view a program or the news. The television must also accept videotapes, presumably inserted in an accompanying unit that would sit on an appropriate table.

Pavel said he understood exactly, and would see to it.

Major Slavitz was curious as to what it was the General Secretary had asked for. When told, he snorted that Pavel hardly had the background to supervise such an installation. Pavel readily acknowledged this but said that frankly he had been rather intimidated when the General Secretary pointed at him and said, "I wish *you*" to see to this.

Slavitz decided he would not interfere. But he resolved at the same time not to go out of his way to introduce Pavel to the resources of the Kremlin's Engineering-Architectural Department. Let Pavel figure it out.

Pavel found the Soviet bureaucracy extraordinarily obliging when told that the petitioner was on a mission for the General Secretary. At three in the morning, Pavel was working with an electrician and a television engineer in the General Secretary's hideaway suite. By 8 a.m. the metal arm was bolted to the ceiling, the little Sony television sat on its cradle, and the movement of a protruding arm positioned it wherever one desired, the springs in the arm locking it in place. A discreet cable running under the carpet connected it to a VCR unit.

Pavel had not slept at all. When at 10 a.m. the General Secretary strode into his office, his executive secretary, Maritsa, handed him a note. It was from Pavel, requesting permission to see whether the installation was acceptable. Gorbachev summoned him instantly and Pavel accompanied the General Secretary to the little room and pointed to the television over the bed. Gorbachev howled with glee, threw himself on the bed, face up toward the set, reached out for it, pushed the Power On button and viewed all four Moscow channels, one after the other. His face lit up with pleasure.

"Why can't my other aides be like you, Pogodin! I say, well done."

Pavel thanked him, saluted, and withdrew to his post. He would not ask Major Slavitz for permission to take even a half day off. He did what he could to stay awake until his duty watch was over, at four in the afternoon. He reached his mother's house with his eyes half shut.

Two days later, Major Slavitz told Pavel that the General Secretary had called again for his services. "Perhaps, Pogodin, he'll ask you to build an anti-missile missile system." Pavel smiled demurely and walked out across the northeast courtyard past two detachments of guards. He was ushered in by the private secretary.

The grand private office of the General Secretary had not lost its imperial impact on the eye since last used by a reigning czar. There was the porticoed doorway. Fresh flowers sat on lunar-shaped marble tables on either side, pointing up toward the exuberantly painted ceiling with its great vault of puffy clouds and flying geese framed by an Italianate balustrade. On the left, an enormous chinoiserie screen, blending with the paneled walls and crystal lights, the whole of the room giving the impression of a red-carpeted avenue toward the throne at the other end of the room. Once upon a time it had been that: now in its place was an eighteenth-century gilt-edged desk, the cockpit of the de facto chief of state. Gorbachev motioned to Pavel to approach the desk. Pavel did so, saluted, and stood at parade rest.

"Relax, Pogodin. There is something I want. It is of a highly private nature. I have a remote . . . cousin. He is not altogether right"—Gorbachev pointed to his head, and tapped it lightly. "An accident, as a boy. But I like to humor him. He saw recently at the house of a friend one of those . . . French . . . tapes. I would like to present him with a little library of such videotapes of a relaxing . . . erotic nature. They are very widely viewed, as you may know, in Europe and in America especially. I could not personally be linked, you understand, with any official request for such tapes. But I am not ashamed to indulge my poor cousin with a little visual entertainment. These tapes I know are available on the black market."

Pavel squinted his eyes, and cocked his head skeptically.

"How do I know that, Pogodin? Because I know *everything* is available on the black market." Gorbachev found himself delivering a stock sentence or two from one of his speeches to the price control commissioner. He calmed down. "I need someone I can absolutely trust, and you have earned that trust, to bring me, oh, a half-dozen tapes? Now you will find in the envelope on my desk, directly in front of you—" Gorbachev reached over to snap on the table lamp, but the bulb did not light. "That accursed lamp. In any event, take the envelope over there and put it in your pocket. You will find more rubles there than you need, I am sure, to buy a little collection of the kind I am talking about. For my cousin. I wish you then to have constructed a dozen or so labels, *War and Peace*, Part 1, Part 2, et cetera. Affix those labels on the tapes on the outside. And inside, remove any indication of what the tapes actually depict. I would not want my cousin's housekeeper to know about this. Do you understand me?"

"Yes, Comrade General Secretary. But I do have one question."

"Yes?"

"If the tapes I am able to find are not in the Russian language, does that matter?"

"Well, I am sure he would prefer them in Russian. But I suppose the kind of tapes he enjoys speak in Esperanto." He smiled. "If they are truly . . . clever, I imagine it doesn't matter if they are in Italian or in French or in English."

"I understand, Comrade General Secretary."

"And understand this, Pogodin. I am holding you personally responsible that no human being should ever know about this transaction. Upon your honor?"

"Upon my honor, Comrade General Secretary."

It was necessary, on this occasion, to inform Major Slavitz that Pavel would need to leave the Kremlin in order to perform a private errand for the General Secretary. Major Slavitz was now resigned to it: In effect, Pavel had become a kind of all-purpose aide to the General Secretary. There wasn't any point in giving vent to his resentment or his jealousy over Pogodin's privileged position.

Pavel knew that pornography was not permitted in the Soviet Union, but he knew also—Andrei had made references to it—that it was to be found. Like everything else in Moscow, if you had money, and if you were willing to run a risk.

Not much of a risk, he assumed: He was not even aware that Stalin had sent to Gulag the incidental merchant caught with "dirty pictures" in the folds of a bookstore or whatever front the smut merchants used.

He walked down the pedestrian mall of the Arbat, training his eye to look for telltale signs. There was no equivalent in Moscow of what he had read about Times Square in New York City or Soho in London. But as he strolled down the wide street he felt the cosmopolitan bustle, men—and women—going this way and that, often entering doors not marked as merchandisers of anything in particular. There were, as always, the stores that sold hard-to-get food delicacies. He passed by several movie houses featuring films not widely spoken of in the official newspapers. One woman, bent over with age and presiding over the Russian equivalent of a little kiosk, beckoned to him; would he like to see her supply of "foreign magazines"? She brought up a copy of *Penthouse* and opened it to the center spread, which he found himself looking at inquisitively, his mind turning to Freda, a recent girlfriend, a furtive comparison crossing his mind.

He asked if she had any videos. She said no, but for a few rubles she would give him an address. He gave her two rubles and she pulled a pen from her bosom, a scratch pad from the counter, and wrote out an address at the Tishinsky Market. He asked for directions. She offered to sell him a map of Moscow. Smiling, he took the map from her, giving her a few kopeks. He opened the map and studied it. The address was a short cab ride away.

There he rang the bell. It was promptly answered by a lightly clad young woman of voluptuous dimensions. She looked him over, without a word. She asked if he was a policeman, because "if so, you may know my brother. He is a policeman." Pavel understood her point, and assured her he was not on official business. "In that case," she said, "come in."

He walked into her dingy quarters, past a little utilitarian kitchen, into a bedroom. "Ten rubles for one-half hour," she said, slipping off her blouse. Pavel stopped her. He wanted videotapes, he said.

"Why not the real thing?" she countered.

Pavel was embarrassed by his brief hesitation. He asserted self-control, repeated that he wished only the videos and had been told she had a supply. She buttoned her blouse, walked to a corner cupboard and asked, "How many? They are twenty rubles, each one."

How many did she have?

She smiled. "As many as you have rubles to pay for."

He bought ten.

This was one half of his duty. He went then to a job printer, picked out the type design, and ordered the appropriate labels. They were ready by late afternoon. At his mother's house, in his study, he affixed the labels with care, eliminating all traces of the erotic descriptive matter.

The following morning he appeared at the security office with a cardboard carton. It was loosely packed, so much so that it was possible to discern one of the labels on the exposed tape, a video edition of *War and Peace*. Pavel telephoned to the private secretary of the General Secretary, gave his name, and said that he had succeeded in accumulating the research material he had been asked for. After a moment or two he was told to come with the material at 11:10.

Gorbachev dismissed the guard at the end of the room. Pavel approached the General Secretary, holding the carton in his left hand, saluting with his right hand.

"At ease. You succeeded?"

"Yes, Comrade General Secretary. And if after a while your cousin should desire more, you have only to advise me. There is a fairly large supply." Pavel then reached into his pocket and pulled out an envelope, putting it down on the desk. "The excess rubles, sir."

Gorbachev reached over to switch on the desk lamp. It flickered on. Then off. Then back on. "Cursed lamp. Thank you, Pogodin."

"Sir?"

"Yes?"

"Would you like me to get your lamp fixed?"

"I most certainly would. I have twice asked that it be done. You may know that the wiring for this whole unit of the Kremlin is being redone. For that reason, I suppose, they have postponed fixing it effectively. If you can have it done, more power to you. I am beginning to believe you can accomplish anything, Pogodin. Perhaps I should turn foreign policy over to you."

"Thank you, Comrade General Secretary. I shall see to it."

CHAPTER 30

THEY ASSEMBLED AGAIN ON Sunday morning, as planned. It was not easy to reach Okateyvsky because huge rains coming on the heels of the big electrical storm the night before had caused flash floods. Bus drivers welcomed every opportunity to bring service to a halt, and Andrei had walked to the front of the bus and made an unambiguous threat to his driver. Intimidated, and talking loudly to the crowded bus travelers, among whom two Narodniki sat, about the high probability that they would end up spending the night in a bus stuck in the mud, he eased his vehicle over on the left bank of the road and made his way past a water trap. Pavel, coming from the south with Viktor, was a half hour late. The storm gathered force again. The four conspirators were grateful for the mounds of hay that seemed to insulate them from the pelting rain, battering against the old building's rotting eaves.

Nikolai, with some forethought, had wrapped a large bath towel under his shirt and he offered it now to his sodden companions, who, stripping, did what they could to get dry. Andrei undertook to light a fire in a cavity near the entrance to the stable. He took dry hay and bits and pieces of wood and then a half-dozen loose egg-sized stones. It produced a modest and welcome blaze. He dragged from the corner an old bicycle wheel and placed it over the stones. Now there was a grate of sorts, over which the especially wet clothes were left dangling to dry as Nikolai called the Narodniki to order.

He told Pavel to recount the extraordinary experiences of the past week. He did so, leaving out the episode involving the pornographic tapes. He had given his word of honor, and although Pavel was prepared to assassinate Gorbachev, he would not dishonor a promise made to him. Pavel concluded by telling them that he had promised the General Secretary to fix his quirky desk lamp.

"I told Nikolai about this when I went off duty on Friday. Saturday morning, I brought Nikolai to the secretary in the outer office and told her that my friend Nikolai Trimov, the electrical engineer, would need to inspect the area around the desk in order to ascertain exactly what was needed to fix the lamp. With her and a security guard closely observing him, Nikolai did so. After the inspection, Nikolai specified what he would need to do."

Pavel continued: "It must be done by Tuesday. We want to give the General Secretary immediate attention. I have an excuse for not getting it done tomorrow, Monday, when he will be occupying his office all day. But the General Secretary has the weekly Politburo meeting on Tuesday afternoons. I told Maritsa that my friend Trimov would come in prepared to fix the lamp when the General Secretary was absent from his office."

Pavel deferred now to Nikolai.

Nikolai turned to another point. Inasmuch as none of his companions had advised him to the contrary, he said, he assumed that each had made his own escape plans.

Viktor said his plans were made but that his forger would not actually give him his documents until he paid for them. Nikolai turned inquiringly to Pavel.

"Yes, yes, I'm sorry. I should have begun with that." He reached into his sack and pulled out three hefty manila folders, giving one each to his companions. "Three thousand rubles," he said, with a routine voice. "My dear mother's jewels are indeed worth well over one hundred thousand. I wouldn't be surprised if they are worth twice that, even more."

Nikolai said he thought it appropriate to thank Pavel. "Perhaps one day we can make it up to your mother."

Pavel replied, "You will make it up to her in full on Tuesday afternoon. Nikolai will explain. Though God knows," he laughed heartily, "what would happen to my dear mother if after the Soviet Union were overthrown and Restoration declared, they failed to tender me the throne."

The laughter was general and their perspectives returned. The bourgeois debt to Pavel and to his mother faded in importance.

Nikolai spoke again. "You are not electricians, and you needn't know in detail what I plan. Suffice it to say this, that a) if Gorbachev leaves his office, b) if the Kremlin's electrical utility workshop has in it what I am almost certain are parts of its regular inventory, c) if the Kremlin security leave me alone under the desk, then d) I will proceed to wire the metal rosette handle that pulls the drawer open to a strip of copper under the drawer, so that anyone who pulls on the handle and simultaneously on the bottom of the drawer will receive a mortal load of current. I have gone through all the motions. I know exactly what I have to do under the desk, the measurements I need to make before going to the workshop. Pavel will accompany me, explaining to anyone, as required, what it is we are doing. Pavel has the complete confidence of Comrade Maritsa, who dominates that office. The desk's front is solid, so that what I am doing when on my back in the desk's kneehole will not be visible to any of the security wandering about."

"What if he comes back in less than one hour?"

"I am in a position simply to fix the connection and leave undone the electrocuting link."

Viktor wanted to know if anyone was likely to bring about a premature electrocution.

"It is unlikely that anyone would sit in the chair of the General Secretary and then, one, slide open the drawer, and two, tug at the drawer from the base. There would be no need to tug at it until I bind it to make it stick. These simultaneous acts are necessary to cause the electrocution."

There was a general silence.

Nikolai went on. "Pavel and I will leave the Kremlin together, and separate. From his mother's house, Pavel will telephone to Viktor, who will report to his contact that the plan has been consummated. That is vital. We do not know any details, but we must assume that Viktor's all-important contact has a cadre that will take the assassination as the signal to move for immediate reforms. Andrei and I will go our separate ways. No one of us knows the plans of any of the others. And that is as it should be."

They were silent. The rain had stopped and the wood splinters in the fire continued to crackle.

"Perhaps," Nikolai said, "we will one day all meet, in this . . . venerable building." He smiled.

They gathered up their clothes. Nikolai started to leave, but stopped and embraced his fellow Narodniki, each in turn; then, wordlessly, each walked out toward the bus stop, at five-minute intervals.

CHAPTER 31

Y OU CHECKED IT WITH Mitchell?"

"Yes. Yes sir."

"And of course Dole and Moynihan and Boren?"

"I regret to tell you, Senator. Not only will they go along, that phone call made them happy men."

"I need happy women too. Okay with Roberta, I assume?"

"Oh sure. Needless to say, the whole committee is for it."

"Anything beyond thirty days begins to look like cruel and unusual punishment. But you know something, Arthur, I think the defiance by Blackford Oakes is in a funny way working for us. Sure, we're preparing to let him out of jail even though he won't testify—so theoretically he hasn't purged the contempt that put him in there. But the punishment imposed on him affirms the rights of congressional investigating committees. There are people out there, I have a feeling—Alice, for instance, feels exactly this way—who are thinking that, okay, so the great Blackford Oakes will not tell us what we want to know, even though we stick him in jail. So we let him out—he wins that one. *But,* we win the *big one!* By passing a bill that denies the Executive the authority to authorize covert activity. So that

Blackford Oakes's keeping the secrets to himself, Cyclops especially, gets him—exactly where? So his secret is still secret—it'll
come out one day, you bet. But his tactics, which were clearly
designed to obstruct the legislation he opposes, will not be permitted to prevail. See what I mean?"

"I do, Senator." Blaustein was a little put off by the disorderly thought of the orderly chairman. But it was momentary,
surely. "I see what you mean. And you may very well be right."

"Did you see the MacNelly cartoon in the paper this morning?"

Arthur Blaustein had seen it, but he pretended he hadn't.

"You remember that, protesting against the Mexican War,
Thoreau committed an act of civil disobedience and they put
him in jail. The next day Emerson visited him, spoke to him
through the prison bars.

"*'Thoreau, what are you doing in there?'*

"*'Emerson, what are you doing out there?'*

"Well, you can imagine what MacNelly did with that. I'm
the Emerson, and Oakes the Thoreau. The trouble is, with these
funny cartoons, nobody submits them to any *reasoned analysis.*
MacNelly is saying, in effect, that everyone who opposes covert
action ought to be in jail, like Thoreau. Isn't that the plain
meaning of what that cartoon says?"

"Well, Senator. Not *exactly* that. But I see what you mean."

Hugh Blanton decided to drop it. He picked up the *Wall
Street Journal.* "See this? The editorial that ends, 'Somebody
should engage in a little covert action and escort Senator Blanton and his dream team into the real world, but to accomplish
that would require an effort on the order of a Manhattan Proj-
ect or Normandy landing.'"

"Senator, the *Wall Street Journal* is on the wrong side of
every issue, so why should you be surprised?"

"Well, that's true. Arthur. Let's quickly go over it, one more
time.

"At two-thirty I ask for the floor. Gore's been tipped off to
be in the chair, and the leak's got around about springing Oakes.

I think we'll have a pretty full house. The senators want to be able to say they voted to let Jack Armstrong out of jail.

"So. At two-thirty I announce to the Senate that, speaking for a unanimous committee, I call on the honorable senators to vote to release Blackford Oakes from prison. We are not"— Senator Blanton was suddenly addressing the full Senate chamber, not just Arthur Blaustein, his chief counsel—

"We are not expunging the contempt of Mr. Oakes, fellow senators. No. We have made our point, that when a duly constituted committee of Congress seeks information on the basis of which it can most responsibly recommend a piece of legislation, we need—we are helped by—the cooperation of expert witnesses. We have made our point. Mr. Oakes chose an act of constitutional defiance. It is the judgment of the committee which I have the honor to serve as chairman that two insights have crystallized during the past thirty days. The first is that the integrity of the Constitution and of this body has been affirmed. The second is that the legislation sought by the committee majority by no means stands or falls on the basis of what one man, one civil servant who has worked many years for the Central Intelligence Agency—on what one man can contribute to the argument. It does not matter, really, what Mr. Oakes now does. What matters is that the United States guard against the corruption of the basic democratic practice of open covenants, responsible deeds, accountability."

Blaustein thought it wise to break in. "But before you get into your bill, you'll let them *vote* on Oakes, won't you, Senator?"

"Oh yes. Of course. So I'll do that. 'I therefore move that Senate Resolution such and such voted on such and such a day'—you have those citations in my manuscript, right?"

"Right."

"So the vote is taken. It will be unanimous."

"Not quite."

"Why? Who?"

"Senator Wellstone loathes the CIA in general, and Oakes in particular."

"What did Oakes do to Paul?"

"Senator Wellstone appeared with Oakes on the MacNeil-Lehrer show a few months ago, on the general subject of intelligence activity. Oakes's demolition of the senator's arguments was not covert."

"Oh, yes. Yes, I remember reading about that. That was . . . incautious of Paul. It should have been I, not he, on that program. You need to know how to take care of yourself in this business, Arthur."

"Yes, sir."

"All right then, we'll have a virtually unanimous vote to let Oakes out. I will then say that I am introducing a bill to prohibit covert activity by any branch of government. I'll make the arguments, which are not difficult to make, and which appeal to the basic sense of decency of American legislators. I will then read the concise table of historical atrocities we've assembled—that will take, I figure, oh, twenty minutes—"

"More likely forty."

"All right, forty. Then we'll do the historical bit, the long struggle against secrecy, et cetera—about fifteen minutes. Then I'll read a list of organizations backing us and Nobel Prize laureates—how many of them do we have lined up to support us?"

"Four hundred and thirty-six."

"I didn't know there *were* that many laureates."

"I didn't either."

"Then I'll give them the final crusher: the enormous leverage imprudent acts can have in a nuclear age. And that's when I'll hit them with the Gorbachev bit. That he actually considered a nuclear demonstration strike, to the best of our knowledge, though we cannot pin that one down."

"If anything will do it, that ought to."

"Right. And we'll do the usual pleading against a filibuster. It won't work. We're going to have to win this one *after* a filibuster. All right. So we have to fight. The civil rights struggle took a hundred years. We're prepared to give it a hundred hours—right, Arthur?"

"Right," Blaustein said wearily. "Right on, Senator."

CHAPTER 32

● OCTOBER 1986

S EATED IN HIS OFFICE, Blackford waited patiently for Kathy to call back. She did so, an hour later. He listened.

"So that's the way it is?" Blackford's voice was grave.

After she replied, he said, "Well. Thanks, Kathy. I'll be in touch."

The presidential rebuke ringing in his ears, he drove his car out of the space reserved for it and headed for Westminster, an hour's drive north of Langley.

HE HAD arrived from Moscow late the afternoon before, had a long talk with Sally in Mexico and a few happy words with Tony. What exactly were his plans? He couldn't say, exactly, at this point . . .

Sounds like the old days?

Well, not quite, but there is something rather important . . . Yes, I suppose I *have* said that kind of thing before . . .

And then he tried to read the Sunday paper, but soon went into a fitful sleep. He must be at his office early enough to file his request for a presidential audience, a top priority.

He called Kathy at nine. He had driven the forty-five miles in the hour since her return call, had reached the little town of Westminster and driven onto the private driveway. In front of him now, at the end of the drive, was the modest white country house, beyond it the rose garden where, Blackford assumed, he would find Rufus, even at age eighty-five bent over his beloved, demanding flowers.

Indeed he was there. He stood up, not without difficulty. Blackford stooped down, picked up Rufus's cane and handed it to him. Rufus beckoned Blackford to walk with him into the house. One hand on Blackford's shoulder, Rufus walked slowly. They sat down in the screened veranda. Rufus called out for Micaela. She would bring them iced tea.

"You will have a sandwich with me in an hour or so?" Blackford said yes.

"It has been a while, Blackford. And I am ever so happy to see you again. Can I safely assume that you have a problem to discuss with me?"

"Yes, Rufus. A problem I swore to the principal I would not discuss with any living human being except the President of the United Sates. I am breaking my oath. But I think it would be worse—for all of us—to fail to take counsel with you." Blackford looked down for a moment. "Maybe you won't mind my telling you, Rufus, this one has really got me down."

Rufus took his glass from the tray, Blackford reached for his, and Micaela left them.

Rufus's voice conveyed a tenderness of feeling. "Black, let's start from the beginning, shall we?"

AFTER THE smoked salmon sandwich, the glass of white wine, and the lemon sherbet, Rufus was ready:

"Do you know, Blackford, Mr. Reagan is a very shrewd man. And he shows that shrewdness sometimes by simply refusing to think through the implications of a dilemma he's uncomfortable with. He does not want you in his office to tell him

what is likely to happen to Cyclops and then to your young
Narodniki—your Cyclops did let it slip that they are young . . .
How pleasant, by the way, to come upon that sacred designa-
tion, after all these years. I was in my teens when the original
Narodniki were in battle dress.

"*So?* So he says, in his uncomplicated way, that he will not
see you until you have consummated his instructions."

"That's not the word Kathy used. What she said exactly
was, 'The President says, Mr. Oakes, that he doesn't really think
there's anything to talk about until you've carried out his instructions. If you already have, I'm authorized to give you an
appointment. If not—not.' But I see your point. And as I've just
finished telling you, I left Serge Windels in Moscow to try to
track the Narodniki. I expect to return tomorrow. Maybe he'll
have done that, though the odds are against it, which means—"

"Yes. Bolgin. —Cyclops, as you properly refer to him."
Rufus engaged now in one of his characteristic, legendary
pauses. All who knew him knew not to interrupt him. Finally:

"Blackford, you have no alternative.

"You must first establish whether Serge has established who
the leader of the Narodniki is and where he is, and can take you
to him. If so, you plead with him, then threaten him. But if Serge
cannot, you must go through Cyclops. And tell him that he has
forty-eight hours in which to give you proof that the assassination is called off—or you will report him to the KGB."

Report Boris Bolgin to the KGB!

It was on the order of turning in Solzhenitsyn to the KGB.
Blackford found himself needing to climb this ladder one rung
at a time. So he asked specifically:

"What kind of proof would you settle for, Rufus, if it were
you talking with Bolgin?"

"Only one thing would serve. The names, occupations, and
addresses of the members of the Narodniki band. Otherwise he
could deceive you."

Blackford stood up. He felt an impulse he hadn't felt since
that day in Berlin when Michael was shot while protecting

Blackford from bullets intended for him. It was the impulse to be sick. Sick at the prospect of betraying—he would not permit himself to use a kinder word—a man of the same age as Rufus who had risked his life every day for six years for the same cause Rufus and he had fought for. And being prepared to do as much to the three or four or thirteen young men and women brave enough to risk their lives to advance the same cause.

But he reminded himself why he was here. It was because Rufus always knew to draw down the relevant perspectives. In 1952, Rufus had given serious thought to causing Blackford's fighter plane to explode in the air with Blackford at the controls, after the mission was done. His decision not to do so wasn't a manipulation of perspectives under the impulse of sentiment. Rufus's decision had been made only after he fully collated all considerations, one of them that Blackford, age twenty-six and marvelously endowed, would likely be a valuable asset to his country over a long period of time. Blackford came to know in the thirty years after that mission, during which he so often worked hand in hand with him, that Rufus suffered personal pain as much as anyone when pain was visited on friends of the West, and although he struggled for the most part successfully to shield himself from any appearance of a personal involvement with any of his colleagues, Blackford knew with the power of his senses that this wasn't so. Rufus cared. Cared, among others, about Blackford. But he would not allow the structure of his thought to be hostage to such priorities as Blackford himself would have constructed, if the priorities had been his to arrange.

Blackford felt a sudden release.

Rufus was right. And Blackford's treatment by the commander in chief was right. It was not an act of discipline, a gesture designed to humiliate. It was a structural affirmation, and his thought now was no longer disheveled. Blackford's head was heavy—but now clear.

CHAPTER 33

BLACKFORD SWALLOWED ONE OF Sally's Mexican killer sleeping pills five minutes after the Pan Am flight took off nonstop to Moscow. He had a premonition that tomorrow would be a long day.

Indeed it was, beginning with his signing in at the receptionist's desk at his Moscow hotel. He had wired "Jerry" that his arrival time would be in midmorning, instructing him to wait at the hotel until he showed up. When he stretched out his hand to receive the key to the suite he saw an envelope in his box. He asked for it.

It was his telegram to Jerry Singleton, unopened.

He didn't know what to expect upstairs in their suite. The living room appeared to be untouched. He went into Serge's room. His suits were in the closet, underwear and socks in the drawers. Blackford gave the bathroom a professional inspection, of the kind he had been trained to perform thirty years earlier as an apprentice agent. Look carefully at every item. Serge's toilet articles were, so to speak, comprehensively there. Missing were a razor, a toothbrush, a tube of toothpaste, a comb. Serge—or someone else—had withdrawn exactly the articles Serge would need in order to spend one (or even more) nights sleeping elsewhere. Presumably an appropriate supply of shorts, shirts, socks, and T-shirts were gone. The lot could easily fit in one paper bag, or even in the pockets of a raincoat. Either Serge had voluntarily decided to spend one or two nights somewhere else, or else someone had been let into the room to collect Serge's bare essentials.

He telephoned to the receptionist at the desk. He spoke slowly, deliberately, attempting to surmount the language problem. "My son, Jerry Singleton, did not spend last night here. He is perhaps traveling. Do you have a record of when he checked out? Or if he did not check out, do you know if he spent Sunday night in the hotel, or Saturday night?"

The woman muttered something in perilously insecure English, which he interpreted as instructions to stand by the telephone. She reported back what seemed like a full ten minutes later that there was no record of Jerry Singleton's having checked out. Blackford despaired of explaining that he was curious whether there were records that showed that the bed had been used on Saturday or Sunday.

He had no alternative than to go to the embassy.

There he had no trouble with the rites of passage. He breezed by the guards outdoors, spoke the right language to the receptionist, who led him promptly upstairs to a private waiting room, where in a matter of moments the right man from the embassy materialized.

"Mr. Singleton? I'm Fred Horne, cultural attaché. Would you come into my office?"

Blackford transacted the special rituals through which CIA officers establish each other's authenticity. Fred Horne, a man in his early forties with graying hair and heavy glasses, was awed to find himself talking not to Harry Singleton, but to Blackford Oakes, the Deputy Director for Operations of the Central Intelligence Agency. What could he do for Mr. Oakes?

"I came to Moscow on a presidential mission. I came with an agent. He is posing as my son, Jerry Singleton. He speaks fluent Russian. I am just back from a two-day trip to Washington, and he is missing. Do you have any reports on him?"

"We sure do, Mr. Oakes."

Fred Horne left his office and came back in a minute or two with a folder. "Ambassador Hartman is on top of the situation and we expect to hear from Langley within an hour or so after the office there opens up, which would be 5 p.m. our time, as you know. Your friend was picked up by the KGB. He is being held incommunicado. The ambassador plans to make a major fuss on that point sometime this morning, but of course now he'll consult you on it."

"What are the charges against him?"

"That's something else that's bothering us. They're not specified—beyond this, that he entered the country using false papers—"

Blackford interrupted him. "Listen, Fred, hold up on everything for now. Get somebody on your staff up here instantly. I'll give him the key to our suite at the Rossiya Hotel. He should go into both bedrooms—you'd better send two people—pack everything in Jerry's room—he has bags there—and then take everything from my room—most of my stuff is still packed, but bring the dirty laundry bag and pack the toilet articles. Pay the bill, tell reception we've been called out of town. Take the clothes and put them in whatever safehouse you plan to put me in. It may be too late, but there's a chance."

Horne got on the telephone.

Ambassador Arthur Hartman was an old hand. No crisis would rattle him. He had met Blackford several times and addressed him by his first name. "I would guess this isn't something you want to give me any details about, am I right?"

Blackford managed a smile. He was right. "And meanwhile, I need all the details I can get."

"Well, Blackford, I can give you the general picture. Your friend Jerry was keeping company with one of our USIA librarians. Her name is Gloria Huddleston. Seems they were at college together. They were, Miss Huddleston reports, chatting in her living room, drinking a glass of wine, when these three or four armed heavies moved in, said they were investigating a drug charge, put handcuffs on them, led them out into separate cars. She never saw Mr. 'Singleton' again. She was left overnight in a single cell, questioned the next morning, and then turned loose."

"I suppose she was asked who it was she was . . . chatting with late at night?"

"Yes."

"So that blew *his* cover in a hurry. Any charges filed against Huddleston?"

"No. At least, not that we know of."

"Now, listen, Arthur," Blackford spoke gravely. "You must go to the Foreign Ministry and demand to see Jerry. I assume you'll take legal counsel with you. But here is an item of enormous importance. Whatever we wind up doing about Jerry, we have to get one thing from him, something he can whisper to you if he has to."

"What is it?"

"Ask him simply: *Did you get an address?* I have to have that information."

"Anything else?"

"He's a bright guy, except for that bloody-minded business of moving in with the girl, which I told him not to do. We don't know what line he's taken. It's most likely that he has simply refused to talk, insisting on legal counsel. It's also conceivable he has hidden from them his knowledge of Russian, in which case he can tell you a great deal they may not want us to have. Seems to me the most they have is a deportation case. The critical situation that brings me here, Jerry knows nothing about. The absolutely necessary link I have to have is that address. If he doesn't have it, I'm going to have to revert to a procedure that won't work for another twenty-four hours, and every hour may count heavily. I'd need help with that, but let's see if meanwhile you can get the address."

Ambassador Hartman knew how to make a truly fearful, first-class diplomatic fuss, and he proceeded to do so. Within two hours, he was told that he and legal counsel of the embassy could interview "the defendant, Windels," at four that afternoon, at the Lubyanka.

At 5:30, at the safehouse on Seslavinskaya Street, a garage apartment where Blackford had been placed, the doorbell rang.

"Who is it?" Blackford asked without opening the door.

"Jeff Bell, legal counsel, embassy. I have what you want."

The door was opened. Bell, who had spent ten years teaching Soviet law at Columbia University Law School, extended his hand. And then said quietly, "The address you want is 1005 Dimitrova Street, apartment 1012."

Blackford closed his eyes. The address was now on his hard disk.

"Tell me quick, because I've got to get going. Is Serge okay?"

"Yeah. They haven't sorted out whether he's just the college boyfriend of the girl he was screwing when they moved in, or the CIA agent they photographed in Berlin three years ago paying off an informer, or probably both. We're taking the line that the Berlin picture is another guy. Hell, they know he's here on assignment, but they also know they're not going to find out what that assignment is. So, along about, oh, Friday, Saturday, we'll agree that they can put him on a plane and send him home, even though to do that is a grave injustice against an innocent person."

"What about 'Jerry's' father?"

"Your name hasn't come up, and Serge has declined to tell them what hotel he sleeps in when he's not sleeping with Gloria Huddleston."

"Okay, thanks. Now, depending on how it goes with me tonight, I may need help tomorrow. I'll check in with Fred Horne the way I did this morning."

"Good luck," Bell said.

They walked out together. Bell asked if he could drop him at "the address."

"Sure. Thanks. To a corner nearby."

BORIS BOLGIN was apoplectic when he saw who was standing at the door. Blackford let the old man curse uninterruptedly for a full minute, which Bolgin did while simultaneously gesturing

Blackford to come in to his cramped living room stuffed with books. Eventually he stopped swearing. His normal color returned to his face, he went out into his kitchen and returned with the Oakes–Bolgin staples: vodka, wine, and zakuski. Boris Bolgin could be feverishly angry, but he could not be inhospitable.

Blackford spoke for the first time. "I did cheat on you there, Boris. Followed you the other night to discover this address. And I hope you will forgive me. But your security has in no way been jeopardized. Only I," he lied, "know your address. But this is an emergency."

"You are here to talk about my friends, Blackford?"

"Yes. And I am here with fresh instructions. Boris, you must remember this, that I am not at liberty in situations when my instructions are absolutely explicit from the commander in chief. I am here to tell you one thing: We are no longer in a position to permit you to weigh whether to bring about the disbanding of the Narodniki. My instructions are to take any means required to put an end to the assassination plot."

"Blackford," Boris took a good draft of vodka, pushing the bottle of wine in the direction of his guest, "you explain clearly, as always. But you are not in a position to abort the operation."

Blackford drank down one half of his glass of warm sweet white wine. "No, Boris, I am not. But you are."

Boris stared at his old antagonist, for five years now his closest professional confidant, to whom he had entrusted not only his life, but the integrity of what was left, at eighty-five, of his body. At eighty-five he could not survive what he had endured in his twenties. But at eighty-five he was as sensible to pain as he had ever been, perhaps more so. Boris knew the exact meaning of Blackford's words.

"You would do that?"

"I have no alternative. I want you to act within twenty-four hours."

Boris paused. Then he raised his hand. "There is no way, Blackford, in which I can be in touch with the leader of the Narodniki until the day after tomorrow. On my word."

Blackford chose to believe him. More accurately, he felt that an extension of a mere twenty-four hours could not be thought unreasonable. But this was the moment to express the harshest terms of the ultimatum. "All right, Boris. But then let me tell you what I will ask of you Thursday at"—he looked at his watch— "7 p.m. I will need to have this security from you: The names, professions, and addresses of all the players. All the players."

Boris looked up at Blackford, his expression pained. *If I were a younger man,* he was saying to himself. But then Boris too was a professional. And he understood the excruciating logic of what Blackford had said, and had to deliver.

"Very well. But now I no longer choose to eat and drink with you."

Blackford rose, sadly.

"I understand, Boris." He hesitated in extending his hand, pausing to ascertain whether Boris would accept a handclasp. Boris's arm remained stiff at his side.

"I will see you in forty-eight hours," Blackford said.

Bolgin nodded, and as he closed the door and walked back to the table he said to himself, "In forty-eight hours Mikhail Gorbachev will be dead."

CHAPTER 34

● OCTOBER 1986

PAVEL AND NIKOLAI WAITED, beginning at 2:45, outside the office of the General Secretary. Nikolai was not dressed as an electrician—he was, after all, an electrical engineer and such differences in station were respected, even in a classless society. He had been introduced as such on Saturday to security, and to Maritsa.

Nikolai wore, then, a jacket and tie, but brought along a large electrician's tool kit, borrowed from someone at the MEIE. The kit was carefully examined by two security guards. After they had done so, Nikolai said to the senior of them, "You do understand that I will need extra materials from your utility shop? But I won't know exactly what until I examine and test the defective unit."

And then, addressing Maritsa, "I am afraid that if the trouble traces to the receptacle at floor level, we will need to turn off the electrical circuit in the office. But for no more than a half hour at the most, I'd judge." He smiled, relaxedly. "I hope that doesn't immobilize too much of the Kremlin!"

Maritsa found Nikolai's informality engaging. She said there would be no problem, if it was only for a half hour.

A few minutes after three she emerged from the inner sanctum and gestured to Nikolai and Pavel to come in.

Nikolai went directly to the desk, took off his jacket, and laid it on the chair. He took a flashlight from the tool kit and dove into the cubbyhole. "First thing I got to do," Pavel and Maritsa heard him from his catacomb, "is see if the receptacle is damaged. I'll have to take the retaining plate off." His voice was muffled.

There was a moment's silence, after which Nikolai clambered out, looked about in his tool kit, and pulled out a small screwdriver and pliers. He edged back into the cubbyhole on his back. Pavel and Maritsa could see the strain in the wire leading to the desk lamp—obviously Nikolai was examining it. Yes, and simultaneously he was measuring with the length of his forearm two critical distances. First the length of wire running from the floor receptacle up to the small hole in the desktop through which it passed to the desk lamp. Second, the width of the desk drawer and the distance between the lamp cord and the drawer front's bottom lip. A few seconds later he edged out from under the desk and said brightly, "I know what we need, Pavel," he said. "Take me, please, to the utility shop."

Pavel turned to Maritsa. Would she be good enough to call the steward at the shop—yes, thanks, Pavel knew where it was located—and inform him what this was all about? Maritsa nodded, and after letting the two men out sat down at her desk and took up the telephone.

Pavel and Nikolai were admitted into a subterranean chamber of very large dimensions. It had once been an armory, was now still that but also many other things, including the repository for several hundred ornate chairs used at state functions. In a far corner there was the equivalent of a large hardware store.

Nikolai took out a notepad. He looked about and got hold of a reasonable length of two-conductor cord. He proceeded, while the steward looked on, to strip the sheathing from one end of the cord, exposing two separately insulated conductor wires of copper strand. One of these he cut back, removing a length equal to one half the width of the desk drawer.

The overseeing steward lost interest, returning to his desk.

Nikolai turned to the next task. He prepared a strip of copper. It would be about the width of two thumbs, designed to fit across the bottom of Gorbachev's desk drawer, directly behind its bottom-front lip. Into this copper strip Nikolai drilled several holes. Small wood screws through these holes would fasten the strip to the drawer's wooden bottom. He equipped himself with electrical tape for insulation and disguise.

Back in the General Secretary's office, under the desk and on his back, he quickly screwed the copper strip into place. Turning onto his stomach, he worked at the floor receptacle's metal coverplate, removing two screws.

Emerging from under the desk, the coverplate in hand, he explained that part of the problem had been the fault of one of the two screw anchors, which had broken in the floor. Briefly waving the plate in the air, he said he would drill another hole in it so that a new screw could secure it solidly to the floorboards.

Snatching the battery-powered hand drill out of the toolbox, he fitted a drill bit into the chuck. Now, shifting position on the floor, he gave the impression that he was at work on the coverplate.

Leaning against the drawer front, he pressed his shoulder firmly upward to hold the drawer steady. Pavel and Maritsa heard a brief whine from the drill. A hole now existed reaching from the rear of the drawer front, diagonally up through the wood to the back of the brass rosette handle.

Nikolai shoved himself around again on the floor, murmuring out his discomfort. He asked Pavel to come around and help by putting his foot on one end of the coverplate to steady it against the drill. Together they held the metal plate firmly while Nikolai quickly drilled the necessary extra hole.

He dropped the drill back into the box and, spraddling back down onto the floor, slid underneath the desk. Thrusting his legs about to give the leverage necessary to slide in under the desk on his back, Nikolai caused Pavel to step to one side, by Maritsa, both avoiding the thrashing legs. They heard an exasperated grunt from Nikolai. He inched his way back into view, took a couple of deep breaths and muttered, "I'm glad I'm an electrical engineer, not an electrician!" And then, to Maritsa: "Sorry, but we'll need to cut the current now. I have to fix the wiring down inside the receptacle."

The guard had been alerted and the lights in the big office now went off.

With his flashlight, Nikolai started back under the desk but paused briefly, apparently preparing his equipment. In that moment he slipped a long, thin woodscrew through the hole he'd sunk moments before. He felt the long screw jam securely against the rosette. He took the extra two-conductor cord and tightly wound one of its exposed copper strands around the screw's protruding extra length. He then bedded the rest of the insulated wire across a taped-over portion of the copper strip, bending the wire further and leading it leftward along the strip's far side. There he jammed the conductor's raw metal between the copper strip and the drawer bottom.

Rolling quickly on his side, he stuffed the remainder of the new wiring up alongside the drawer, back to where it could drop down to the floor receptacle. Nikolai screwed the coverplate back in place. Less than a minute later, the desk lamp's plug was sharing its electrical connection with the new wiring to the drawer.

He called out to Pavel that the current could be reestablished.

The room lit up.

Nikolai crawled out and turned the desk lamp on and off three or four times.

"Looks all right. I'll bed it down at the receptacle." He disappeared again. In a few moments he was back up. In his left hand he held a large woodscrew. To distract attention, he pointed to a plug at the far end of the room. Pavel and Maritsa turned their eyes to it. "Might not be a bad idea, somewhere along the line, to have that looked at." Swiftly he plugged the large screw between the side of the drawer and its mounting, jamming it in firmly.

Maritsa told Nikolai that all the electrical circuitry in this wing
of the Kremlin was scheduled for an overhaul.

What Nikolai cared about was the woodscrew, now safely
inserted. When Gorbachev next attempted to open his drawer
he would find it stuck. His right hand gripping the brass rosette,
his left hand would reflexively grasp the drawer's bottom edge,
seeking extra leverage. The hidden copper strip would propel
current up his arm through his chest to his firm grip on the
rosette, the shock spastically curling both hands to tighter contact with the conductors. His heart would stop.

Nikolai took his voltmeter. "One last test," he said. He
touched one of the prods of the voltmeter to the rosette, as if to
bid it goodbye. His body hid his other hand, which touched the
second prod to the copper plate. His meter read 220–240. The
operation was done. Time consumed, forty-two minutes.

When Nikolai had completed the electrical circuitry, fasten-
ing together the trigger mechanism, he was sweating. Sweating
markedly more than might have been expected of a young technician simply because he had to work a while under a desk. He
thought it prudent, while still lying on his back, to give himself
two or three minutes to quiet down before emerging from the
cavity and announcing that the work had been successfully completed. He would substantiate this by turning the desk lamp on
and off a few times for the benefit of Maritsa and the security
officials standing by.

Accordingly he delayed his reappearance, and in a few minutes felt his heartbeat returning to normal. Emerging from
under the desk, he plucked several sheets of tissue from the box
at the side of the huge desk and used them on his face. He addressed himself then to Pavel Pogodin, most formally.

"I think that settles that problem, Lieutenant."

Pavel helped Nikolai pick up his tools, scattered about between the desk and the chair.

They both bade good afternoon to Maritsa, who thanked
them, and they walked, Nikolai carrying the electrician's tool
kit, to the door.

"I thank you very much, Trimov. I know that the General Secretary will be relieved not to worry about that little nuisance anymore. Good day. Ah, you are going out the northeast gate? I will accompany you. I am headed there myself."

GORBACHEV BEGAN to raise his voice, something he didn't often do at meetings of the Politburo. Obviously Colonel-General Nikolai Chervov was opposed to the INF treaty. Just as obviously, Colonel-General Chervov was not prepared to express that opposition categorically. His technique was the detail, the little detail. At first Gorbachev dealt with this by patient confutation, item by item—always he was well briefed in military matters. Now the General was arguing—at 5:10 p.m., after more than two hours of general discussion—that after the INF treaty was consummated, the day might arrive when the submarine power of the United States, carefully coordinated with the power of France's *force de frappe,* could succeed in a first strike against the Soviet Union. Such a strike would be devastating. And Soviet diminished nuclear resources would leave the U.S.S.R. with insufficient nuclear heft for a retroactively deterrent second strike.

Gorbachev, preemptively anxious to meet any such argument from his active military advisers, had consulted, no less, General Vassili Pankovsky, retired but still revered as a Russia-firster who throughout his illustrious career had always demanded an almost excessive degree of Soviet military capability. That very morning, Gorbachev had received the analysis by General Pankovsky of the INF treaty, in which he gave it as his opinion that nothing contemplated by the treaty could conceivably diminish the deterrent strength of residual U.S.S.R. nuclear forces. Gorbachev had meant to bring with him the folder with General Pankovsky's analysis. But, distracted by the hovering electricians who were going to fix his accursed desk lamp, he had left the folder in the middle drawer of his desk.

"Nikolai Andreyevich. I assume that you respect the judgments of General Pankovsky in these matters. Well, I received

from him this very morning—he is living in the Caucasus, as you
probably know, but I have kept him intimately informed on all
disarmament proceedings—I received from him, as I say, this
very morning, a three-page analysis directed exactly to the questions you raise. I stupidly forgot to bring it along, but"—he motioned for one of the three aides seated directly behind
him—"Dmitri, come here." Dmitri was instantly at his side. "Go
to my office. Open the middle drawer of my desk. The folder directly on top is labeled 'Pankovsky.' Fetch it right away."

Dmitri needed no further instructions.

It was a matter of what—three minutes? Surely less than five
when the alarm shrieked.

It halted the heated talk at the table, even though most of
the fourteen participants were unaware of the alarm's exact
meaning. They sensed, of course, an emergency of some sort.
But it had never once been sounded since its installation by
Stalin during his last, paranoiac years. Stalin's idea, someone
dimly recalled, was that the general alarm they had all just now
heard would signal the gravest kind of threat, for instance an
approaching air raid, even a nuclear strike.

Gorbachev blanched, stood up, and went to the door. By the
time he reached it a half-dozen security officials had rushed
there. The man at their head was breathless. "Comrade General
Secretary. A terrorist assassin plot—to kill you! Your desk was
wired! Dmitri is dead! Scorched!" He gulped in breath. "If you
had been sitting at your own desk and opened the drawer, you
would—! Oh, Comrade General Secretary!"

"Stop sniveling." Gorbachev was now the general, utterly in
command. "What security precautions should be taken by the
gentlemen in this room? Quick now, be specific."

The security chief composed himself. "I am sorry, comrade.
There is no reason to panic. Let us proceed methodically." He
turned to the stricken members of the Politburo, still seated
around the massive table, silent, waiting to be told what to do.
"Comrades, the security reserves of the Kremlin are being summoned in full force. You will be met at the entrance of this build-

ing by your individual security agents in ten minutes. You are not
to enter your offices until the detachment from the bomb squad
inspects them and certifies them as safe. Comrade General Secretary, I must request that you depart the Kremlin immediately.
Contingency 'C' is now in effect. Your automobile and escort ve-
hicles will be waiting for you in the courtyard at . . ." he looked at
his watch, "five forty-five. Colonel Glinka will accompany you on
your way to the assigned destination. You will have minute-by-
minute reports on the security investigation upon arrival."

The leaders of the Union of Soviet Socialist Republics did
exactly as they were told. When Gorbachev was advised that his
caravan was ready and waiting, he left the Cabinet Room. He
asked his escort officer, Colonel Glinka, whether it would be
feasible for them to go first by his own office, as he was anxious
to see with his own eyes what exactly had happened. Colonel
Glinka was absolutely stern on the matter. No.

"The forensic unit and the security investigators will be in
meticulous control of the area, Comrade General Secretary. My
orders are inflexible as to Contingency 'C.' There is to be no de-
viation in the route we take to remove you. And the Zeta Case
will be, as usual, by your side."

The Zeta Case was the Soviet equivalent of the U.S. "foot-
ball," the name the Secret Service years ago gave to the electronic instrument and codes through which the President of the
United States can order a nuclear strike.

Gorbachev said nothing. But when he reached the automobile he stopped suddenly. He lifted his finger to Colonel Glinka.
"Can it be possible that this is the work of Pogodin?"

The colonel said that every possibility was being examined.

PAVEL AND Nikolai had walked out side by side, exchanging not
a word. They passed through security, into Manezhnaya Street.
They went to the Borovitskaya metro station, a half block away.
The first train came by. It slowed down for passengers headed
on Run B. Pavel turned to Nikolai.

"We may never meet again. But if I live, and if I can be there, I do not care how long it is, five, fifteen years, I will, on the October 2nd after liberation, come by our stable at Okateyvsky. We will have a reunion in a free Russia."

They embraced.

Pavel took the second train and in twenty minutes was at his mother's house, listening to the police radio. It was 6:15 when he heard the solemn notice on channel Z, to which only sets carried by police officers could tune in.

An attempt has been made on the life of the General Secretary. The device intended to kill the Soviet leader has instead killed an aide. Two suspects are being pursued by the security police.

Pavel picked up the telephone and dialed Viktor, who was anxiously awaiting the call.

"It didn't work," Pavel whispered, hoarsely. "Someone else sat down at the desk. Go immediately to your contact and tell him. He must leave the city. Goodbye, Viktor."

"Goodbye, Pavel."

Pavel's mother was ready. She had been ready since four in the afternoon. This was a most exciting moment for her. She understood completely why her son must dress up like an old, bearded man of holy orders. Security above all, Pavel had told her. The great moment was approaching when the Restoration would come about. And they must both be in Leningrad—in St. Petersburg—when it came about. It was vital that Pavel, the Czarevitch, should be thoroughly and safely disguised. He was now transformed into a retired priest of the Russian Orthodox Church, escorting his younger sister on the eight o'clock train to Leningrad, where they would spend a few days with a cousin. Deep inside her large suitcase was the jewel box. "Very important, Mother, the jewels. For when you are first publicly identified, you must be appropriately dressed." Pavel's mother agreed. They climbed into the farmer's truck Pavel had arranged for and made their way to the Leningrad station.

As they filed into the line of passengers headed for the railroad cars, a policeman, inspecting Pavel's papers, asked the holy man kindly to step aside. The policeman wished to ask a few questions. Pavel said that he was anxious to oblige, but might he first deposit his sister in the carriage, two cars ahead? The policeman accompanied them, the bags were stowed, the sister seated. "I'll be right back, Ilsa."

The policeman led Pavel to the guardroom opposite the walkway to the train. "I just need to check your identification number with headquarters, Father. There has been a singular disturbance in the Kremlin." He took Pavel's I.D. card and began to dial a number.

The call was never completed. The old priest yanked the telephone wire from the wall and administered a severe karate chop on the policeman's throat, dropping him to the ground. Pavel's necktie served as a noose. Pavel applied a commando strangle to choke life away from the inert body. In less than five minutes, the necktie hidden around his own neck, beneath his clerical collar, he opened the constabulary door and rejoined his mother in the train.

VIKTOR TOOK the metro to a station three blocks from Dimitrova Street. He was breathing heavily when he knocked on the door of 1012. There was no answer. He doubted that Boris would leave his room on this tumultuous day. He looked about the long dark hallway, smelling of garlic and old tobacco. There were no signs of life. He moved back to the opposite side of the hall, raised his leg, and with all his force smashed his heavy workman's shoe directly above the door handle. The panel splintered. He reached in with his hand, unlocked the door, and burst into the little salon.

Boris was there. Sprawled over the table, a bottle of vodka, half empty, a few inches to one side.

Viktor grabbed him by the head and chin, saw the blood, looked down on the floor, saw the pistol. He paused only long enough to utter a silent prayer for eternal peace for this brave old man.

He went down to the street and back to the metro, headed this time for the locker in the far corner of the university gymnasium. A half hour later he emerged from the building wearing a goatee and glasses and carrying a briefcase with his papers, a biologist with the University of Novosibirsk, to which he was now returning with handbag and books after several weeks' research at the university.

He took the bus for the airport, looked at his watch. Plenty of time, though he didn't want to idle anywhere. It was almost an hour later that the flight to Novosibirsk was called. Like most flights within the Soviet Union it was crowded and late. There were two buses outside to take the passengers from the terminal to the aircraft, two hundred meters away. Individual tickets were being carefully checked, and the passengers in front of him directed to the first bus. When it came Viktor's turn, he showed his ticket to the agent who examined it.

"Please go to the second bus, we will begin filling it up," he was told. Viktor walked with his bag and briefcase to the bus. Only two other passengers were in it, both standing, holding on to the handrails. The door was open and he stepped up, lugging his two pieces of hand baggage with him. He set them down on the rack and suddenly the bus lurched forward. The two men wheeled and dived at him. He was pinned prostrate on the floor, a foot on his neck, as his wrists were handcuffed. A shout from the driver's section roared back. "Pin his mouth open! Stick that wood between his teeth! Pull out his tongue. Don't let him get at any cyanide pill!"

WHEN NIKOLAI opened the door to their apartment, Andrei was standing, flicking the dials of the television set. The radio was also on.

"Any news?"

"Nothing. No mention. It's after six; he must have finished with the Politburo meeting."

"It's always possible, Andrei, that he won't return to his desk. Perhaps not even until tomorrow morning. The way the

wiring is rigged, no cleaning lady could set it off by merely dust-
ing his desk, no matter how vigorously. Somebody would have
to actually sit down and yank the drawer open. Only then."

Andrei said, "I *know.*"

He paced up and down the little room. But he had made up
his mind. "Nikolai, I don't think we should take any chances. I
think we should go ahead with our escape plans. If they decide
to track you down, the accommodating electrical engineer,
they'd find this address in—minutes."

Andrei acted without further talk, and brought down from
the closet the carefully prepared small traveling bag, the special
papers tied together by an elastic band, and the crutch. He
went into the bathroom and emerged in fifteen minutes without
a hair on his head. He wore an old uniform, including a faded
decoration awarded to disabled soldiers. Nikolai signaled to
wait, then put a hat on his friend to hide the newly nude scalp.
Andrei extended his arm to Nikolai, who took it, and there was
a tight embrace.

"Goodbye, Nikolai. You don't know where I am going. I don't
know where you are going. But I think you should go quickly."

Yes, go quickly. Go to the large and anonymous city he
knew so well. If it worked out, he would arrive in time to meet
Tatyana's train, scheduled to arrive two days later, permitting
her to compete in a university-sponsored English composition
tournament for intermediate teachers. Nikolai had surprised her
with the news of the competition, which he had entirely impro-
vised, and surprised her with the round-trip ticket; she could
comfortably stay the few days of the competition at his Aunt
Titka's. He did not doubt that if he survived the trip to Kiev, he
could persuade Tatyana to go with him to the Crimea, and
thence to Turkey. If he did not show up, Aunt Titka had been instructed to meet the train, take Tatyana home, and wait for
Nikolai. . . . What if he never showed up? It mattered only that
neither Tatyana or Titka knew anything of the Narodniki.

Twenty minutes later an elderly man left Nikolai's apartment carrying a modest-sized bag. He took the room key from

his pocket, stared at it for a moment, then walked to the hollow elevator shaft and dropped it down. He heard a tinny scratch a few seconds later. He went down the stairs and across the crowded yard to the entrance of 2 Kutuzovsky Prospekt. He had walked only a step or two when he heard the sirens behind him. He turned. Three cars stopped and what seemed like eight men, some of them conspicuously armed, poured out. Four of them went racing into the courtyard. Four others moved to surround the building. One of them brushed by him. "Move along, old man. There is likely to be action here."

The old man obligingly crossed the street, and walked slowly toward his destination, even as he wondered whether fate would permit him to go much farther, and whether he would ever be an old man.

CHAPTER 35

P RESIDENT REAGAN SAT ALONE in the Oval Office. Soon he would climb up the staircase for a private dinner with his wife. He thought about the certain-to-be-hectic events of the next few days.

There would be opposition to ratifying the INF treaty he'd be signing tomorrow with Gorbachev. *I love my conservative friends and they've been good and faithful to me, but dammit sometimes they don't see the important things, and some of the important things I can't very well remind them of, at least not publicly. It isn't going to help to pull Gorbachev in the direction we're trying to pull him to say, Look, gang! What that fool is giving up is five times as many missiles as . . .*

Five?

Four.

Or is it three times? Doesn't matter. But more missiles than we're giving up. Well it would be just great for him in the Kremlin if I were to say, "Look what a bad bargainer this guy is."

As far as I'm concerned, the direction he's heading is the direction we want him to head, and if he reverses? So he reverses, and so do we. National Review *said we'd never succeed in get-*

222

ting the Pershings and cruise missiles back into Europe once we pulled them out. Well, we got 'em in in 1982 and 1983. And anyway, we have plenty of submarines in case Gorbachev or some successor goes crazy and starts to threaten Europe. It ain't going to happen.

And anyway, Gorbachev isn't giving away anything he isn't prepared to give away. He doesn't know how much I know about how much he's hurting. Wasteland, the Soviet economy. He'll give his usual eighteen speeches about how I should give up Star Wars, and I'll simply say No. And maybe have one more shot at reminding him that if we make progress in an anti-missile system, we'll share that progress with him, then both of us would be safe against Qaddafi types. I wonder if I should tell him Ken Adelman's crack, that the Soviet Union is the only country in the world entirely surrounded by hostile communist states? I love that one. But no, probably not. Not unless he gets into a joke-telling mood, like he did for an hour or so at Reykjavik.

First time a Soviet chief of state has come to Washington since Brezhnev in, when the hell was it? Nixon was President. I remember, he gave Brezhnev a Cadillac or something. Wonder what I could give Gorbachev, apart from the usual things? Maybe a prototype of a Brilliant Pebbles missile! For fun I'll suggest that. Maybe. I might check with Nancy. George would say No.

It was probably a good idea that we pulled away from the idea of having him address both houses of Congress. Hell, what would people like Bob Dornan do? Probably not show up, but if they did, they'd look for an opportunity to boo or—well, no, they'd behave. But it would be a pretty cold greeting, and you can't be all that surprised—the son of a bitch still heads up the biggest tyranny in the world. Well, I suppose China's is bigger. But in terms of a threat, the Soviet Union has been number one and still is.

And yes, I keep promising myself, no matter what, absolutely no matter what, I'm going to give him a list of those political prisoners we want to try to get some relief for, and once again the petition on the Russian Jews. Gorbachev—Mikhail, I got to remember to call him—sort of lets you know, at least I think I know, whether he's listening just to go through the motions of listening, or whether he's actually taking it in. I think I can tell the difference at this point.

Well, tomorrow we sign the treaty, and the day after that is the state dinner. And then before he goes off to New York we have a scheduled meeting here, and a farewell lunch. Oh God, I hope he brings another interpreter. If it's that same guy with five syllables to his name, he'll shout at me every time Gorbachev raises his voice. Maybe I can just ask him this time please not to feel he's got to interpret what Mikhail says in hi-fi.

—The house buzzer. He picked up the phone. "Yes, dear. Be right up."

The President turned off the desk light, and then the overhead light. He thought for a moment about what he was doing. *Probably most of my predecessors—except for Lyndon—left it to somebody else to put out the lights in the Oval Office. Well, that wasn't the way Ronald Reagan was raised.*

EVERYTHING HAD gone off as scheduled. The people who were against the Intermediate Nuclear Force treaty simply said that they would fight against its ratification, and that didn't surprise the President. He was confident it would be ratified, and told Gorbachev it would be. Now for the farewell session, then lunch, and off he goes to New York, first stop.

The President looked at his watch. He pushed a button on his desk. "What time was Gorbachev supposed to be here?"

"Twelve, Mr. President," the voice came in through the little amplifier.

"Well, it's twelve-fifteen."

"He's pressing the flesh on Pennsylvania Avenue. Do you want me to put on the television for you, Mr. President?"

"Yeah. Sure."

In thirty seconds he was viewing Gorbachev. He wore his fur-lined coat and hat and was smiling broadly and shaking hands at the rate of one every two or three seconds. The President enjoyed the paradoxical sight, the leader of the most powerful tyranny on earth exchanging affectionate greetings with the men and women who stoked the defensive machine designed to frustrate his designs, but got progressively irritated. "Hal, I'm not going to upset the whole schedule on account of this. Lunch was called for one o'clock. At exactly one o'clock you open that door and announce that it's ready. I don't care if we've just been together for five minutes. A schedule is a schedule."

"Yes, sir."

At that moment the television showed Gorbachev reentering his car. His caravan proceeded at a quick pace up Pennsylvania Avenue toward the White House. Reagan's schedule called for him to greet Gorbachev at the entrance to the White House. Reagan decided he would skip that—let the aide bring him right into the office. He picked up the telephone and gave instructions.

Five minutes later, Mikhail Gorbachev walked into the Oval Office. The President rose and shook hands warmly. The two interpreters filed in, and the door was closed. Reagan gestured Gorbachev to the couch opposite his own, and the interpreters took their places.

Gorbachev was flushed by his democratic exchange with the people of Washington. He told the President that he very much appreciated "the friendliness of your people."

"Well, Mikhail, they obviously like you. I'm glad you're not a Democratic candidate for President! I assume you saw the polls this morning. You have a favorable rating of fifty-nine percent. I am only four points ahead of you. I hope the Russian crowds treat me half as enthusiastically as the Americans have treated you!"

Gorbachev smiled. The smile that communicates That's-enough-of-that-kind-of-thing. "Ronald, I wish to ask you a very direct question. And I wish to pledge to you my word that your answer to that question will never be given to any other human being alive, not even to Raisa."

What on earth could Gorbachev have in mind?

"Why of course, Mikhail. If I can answer your question, I most certainly will. Just don't ask me how many spies we have in Moscow."

Gorbachev did not smile. "My question isn't that, but it is not entirely unrelated to that. Ronald, you are aware, even though we have not given it publicity, that two attempts have recently been made on my life."

Reagan was cautious. "Yes," he said. "We were told about it. We were all very pleased that they weren't successful. But things like that are hardly surprising, Mikhail. I nearly died a few years ago from an assassin's bullet, and President Ford was shot at two times, and of course there was Kennedy."

"Yes, Ronald. I know there are always risks in being a chief of state. But what I want to hear from you is one thing: that you were not personally involved in either of those two attempts on my life."

Ronald Reagan paused. He would give himself the few seconds' time he desperately needed. He leaned over and touched a buzzer on the coffee table between them. Instantly the door opened and an aide said, "Mr. President?"

"Er, bring us a little tea. I think that would be nice, Mikhail, no?"

Gorbachev nodded.

Well, this is it, Reagan thought.

He did not know what evidence the Kremlin had got together on Cyclops. He decided he dared not risk saying to Gorbachev anything that Gorbachev could establish to be false. So he said, "Mikhail. Let me give you, in turn, my personal and most solemn word that no American official was in any way involved in the attempts on your life."

"Did any American official know there would be attempts on my life?"

The killer question. But he could handle it by just the slightest shift in perspective. "I can tell you this, Mikhail. That when at one point I got wind of what was being planned I sent our top man to Moscow with instructions to take any measure necessary—including the betrayal of our Soviet contact—to abort the operation. That he did not arrive in time I deeply regret. There now, you have my word, and I know that you will never uncover a scintilla of evidence that contradicts anything I have told you. I would therefore appreciate it if we could call it quits on this discussion."

The tea materialized at this moment, and Gorbachev was now making routine comments to his interpreter, or so Reagan judged, because they were not relayed to him by his own interpreter. A steward served the tea.

Reagan said, "Mikhail, let me show you something Frank Sinatra showed me. Here"—Reagan advanced his freshly poured tea to within reach of Gorbachev. "Stick your finger in my tea. Yes, your finger, your index finger. Go ahead! Don't hesitate." Gorbachev did so, and quickly withdrew his finger.

"Now look," Reagan said, lifting the teacup to his lips. "Watch me. I can drink from the teacup"—he took a few sips. "It's quite incredible. The tissues in the mouth are stronger, more resistant to heat than even the finger of somebody like you and me . . . both of us men who, in our youths, toughened our hands with hard work. Quite amazing, no?"

Gorbachev nodded. "Yes. It is quite amazing." He looked directly at Ronald Reagan. "I shall try it on Raisa."

CHAPTER 36

Ronald Reagan dictated most letters, but often he liked to compose letters he particularly cared about by hand—on yellow legal pads, to be typed later by his secretary. This sunny California morning, after reading the reports on Senator Blanton's speech in the Senate, on reaching his office in Los Angeles he pulled out a pad from his drawer. "Dear Mikhail," he began.

Ten days later he was handed a letter—unopened, because the sender's name was among the dozen his staff knew were privileged. These letters went to the former President's desk.

Reagan took the ornate, jeweled mini-sword, a gift from King Hassan, and slit open the envelope, on the back of which was engraved in English, THE GORBACHEV FOUNDATION * MOSCOW.

He read first the covering letter, then the second letter. The first letter read, "Dear Ronald: I quite understand, and indeed I agree with your analysis. Accordingly, I am enclosing a second letter. Do with it as you like. Raisa joins me in warmest regards to you and Nancy."

228

Reagan called in his secretary, indicating that he wished to dictate. She turned on his dictaphone.

"Dear Senator Blanton: I have read the newspaper accounts of your speech on the matter of the Blanton bill and your arguments to forbid covert operations. In that speech you said that although you had no concrete evidence to back you up, you were morally certain that a covert operation undertaken during my Administration 'shook the Kremlin to the point that President Gorbachev actually contemplated a demonstration nuclear strike in protest.'

"I thought these to be matters of common concern, not only to Americans but also to Russians, and others who were once a part of the Soviet Union. Accordingly, I wrote to Mr. Gorbachev, forwarding the account of your remarks.

"I have today a reply from him touching on the matters you raise. Since the vote on your bill is scheduled for sometime in the next few days, I am faxing you a copy of the letter from Mr. Gorbachev. A copy is also going to the editor of the *Washington Times*.

"With all good wishes,

"I am sincerely,

"Ronald Reagan"

THE NEXT day's headline in the *Washington Times* ran across the entire front page. Directly under it the text appeared of the letter from Mikhail Gorbachev to Ronald Reagan dated June 10, 1995. The letter read:

President Ronald Reagan
11000 Wilshire Boulevard
Los Angeles 90024

Dear Ronald:

Thank you for sending me the notice of the speech by Senator Hugh Blanton. What the Congress does about the bill is, needless to say, entirely the business of Congress. But since you solicit my own views on the question, they are that covert activity is a very useful weapon of defense in a world in which there are both terrible tensions, and terrible weapons. I have previously acknowledged that your covert U-2's discovery of the nuclear missiles Mr. Khrushchev dispatched to Cuba was a fine example of useful covert action. Both of us, when we occupied high offices, were objects of attempted assassination. I am sure that you wished, as I certainly did, that covert action had protected us against these attempts by disorderly men. If our agents in America had learned that an attempted assassination was in prospect, we would certainly have advised you even as, I am certain, as much would be true in reversed circumstances.

On one point I must speak out, and do so with unique authority. Senator Blanton has evidently charged that I was so greatly angered by one CIA operation during my tenure that I contemplated ordering a demonstration nuclear strike in protest. Please feel free to communicate to Congress, and to the American people, that no such wild irresponsible impulse ever so much as entered my mind. Both your country and mine have engaged in covert actions, and I do not doubt that you retroactively regret some things that were authorized, even as I do. But it is not my judgment that the defensive advantages of covert action, given the variety of threats to world peace, should be eliminated.

With all good wishes to you and Nancy, from both of us.

Mikhail Gorbachev

The news story in the *Washington Times* said that Senator Blanton was not commenting on the letter. "The consensus among congressional leaders," the story ended, "is that the Blanton bill is dead.

Blackford Oakes took the entire front page of the paper, stuffed it into an envelope, and addressed it to Professor and Mrs. Nikolai Trimov, Department of English, University of Toronto, Canada.

Acknowledgments •

HISTORICAL EPISODES involving Ronald Reagan and Mikhail Gorbachev are drawn from the biography of Ronald Reagan by Lou Cannon, *President Reagan: The Role of a Lifetime,* from Mr. Reagan's autobiography, *An American Life,* and from other current accounts. Chronological and other liberties have been taken. The technical detail dealing with the attempted assassination was provided by my old friend and consultant, Alfred Aya, Jr., whose ingenuity in matters scientific reminds us how fortunate we are that he is loyal to the United States.

This is the first book by me published by William Morrow [Editor's note: 1994 hardcover edition], though I have worked before under the benevolent auspices of Howard Kaminsky and am happy to be once again in his company. Adrian Zackheim, the editorial director of Morrow, made important suggestions for which I am grateful. Dorothy McCartney did a resourceful job of research, and is considering a new career as a guide to Moscow. Tony Savage did his usual excellent job of handling the manuscript as it came in; Chaucy Bennetts once again came out of retirement to discipline my prose in her inimitable and authoritative way; Joe Isola read the galleys and advises that this is his twenty-eighth outing with my books; and Frances Bronson, as always, brought everything together and, as with so many enterprises, made it all possible.

Friends and family read the manuscript and made valuable suggestions. In particular I am grateful to Sophie Wilkins,

Professors Thomas Wendel and Chester Wolford, Charles Wallen, my agent, Lois Wallace, my brother Reid, my sister Priscilla, and my wife, Pat, for their careful and instructive readings.

It is discouraging to seek fresh ways to record my indebtedness to my editor, Sam Vaughan. But I suppose if Mr. Clinton can reinvent government, I can say that every time I come out of the experience with the sense of a book reinvented, so extraordinary are his contributions. This time around he even made a trip to Switzerland to check the book's progress and to encourage its author. He is unique.

W.F.B.

Stamford, Connecticut
October 1993